Forty & Out

C. L. Pauwels

ISBN 978-1-63789-002-8
Gordian Knot is an imprint of Crossroad Press Publishing

For information address Crossroad Press at 141 Brayden Dr., Hertford, NC 27944
www.crossroadpress.com

First Crossroad Press Edition

Chapter 1

A Tiffany lamp cast a muted kaleidoscope of color across the barren walls of the efficiency, broken only by the dim shadow of a man stooped from the burden he was carrying. It took only six steps to cross the apartment, but he was panting when he eased the unconscious woman onto the narrow bed. He bent down and slipped off her sandals before straightening her legs onto the flowered sheets. He folded her arms across her chest and tucked the comforter up around her chin. The man stood over her until his breathing returned to normal. After placing a rose on the nightstand, he double-checked all the window locks, closed the bathroom door, and replaced the CD in the stereo with one from his jacket pocket, careful to handle the disk by the edges. A final circuit of the room to wipe down any surfaces he had touched earlier. In the kitchenette, he opened the oven door and turned the gas on high, blowing out the pilot light when the electronic ignition kicked in. One more glance at the unconscious figure on the bed and the man was gone, leaving only the jarring opening notes of the Beatles' "Birthday" in his place.

Detective Sergeant Veronica Jadzinski threaded her way through the crowd milling outside the Campus View Apartments. Flashing emergency lights glared over the grumbling residents forced out of bed in the middle of a sultry August night. Jadz tossed the remnants of her gas station coffee into a trash can by the door and climbed the stairs two at a time to a second-floor unit. The small room was crowded with the coroner, five uniformed officers, a three-man Forensics team, and her boss, Toledo Police Homicide's division leader Lieutenant Adam Forester. He ignored her.

"Same cause of death as the first two?" Forester asked the shift sergeant.

"Apparently. The gas odor alerted the neighbor who called us. Lucky the whole place didn't go up. We found a rose on the nightstand, same as before."

"Estimate on time of death?"

"About midnight, but we'll know better after the coroner gets through." Patrol Sergeant Theodore Baxter answered the routine questions with no hint of impatience, even though his shift was long over. Jadz joined them near the victim's bed.

"Glad you could make it," Theo said. It had taken Dispatch almost an hour to reach her, and another thirty minutes for her to arrive. "Hot date last night?"

"Hardly." She frowned, glad the shadows hid the flush his words caused.

"This isn't a social gathering," Forester said. "Give her the rundown while I talk to the coroner." He moved away, still ignoring Jadz.

"He's always grumpy when he's dragged out of bed." Theo flipped through his pad. "At 1:37 a.m., Dispatch sent a crew to check a report from an upstairs neighbor who smelled gas. The responding officers," he pointed to the two uniforms at the door, "rousted the manager in the basement apartment to let them in.

They found the victim, Marianne Summers, white female, age forty, on the bed, the gas stove turned on high with the oven door standing open. Air conditioning was off. Windows closed. The officers shut off the gas and found an exhaust fan, then opened the windows. They called for the paramedics even though they knew it was too late. Life squad was dispatched at 1:54. Dispatch radioed me at 1:56, and called you at 02:12, 02:17, 02:22—"

"All right, Theo, you made your point," Jadz broke in. "Any prints?"

"Nothing we can use. A few smudges on the oven door, but not enough to trace."

"Okay with you if we take the body now, Detective?" Dr. Hanley, the Assistant County Coroner moved toward the officers. "I've done all I can here and Forensics is about finished. Lieutenant Forester said you'd want the autopsy first thing. Blood work will take a few days, with the weekend."

"That's fine, Doc. Can you give us the cause of death?" Jadz managed a smile. "Gas is a factor, of course, but are there any signs of trauma?"

"Nothing obvious. The coffee cup on the nightstand was half full, so I'm taking that in for tests. I'll let you know when I have anything definite." He motioned to the paramedics and they shifted the body off the bed and onto the gurney. "When will you be at the station?"

Jadz checked her watch. "Give me about two hours. If I'm not there, Dispatch will know where to find me." She continued her review of the room. Lace curtains in the kitchenette, neatly filled bookshelves, ladder-back chairs, nothing out of place. "No sign of a struggle."

"Nope." Theo returned to his notes. "According to the neighbors, Summers was single, worked as a librarian at the university. Only lived here about six months. She didn't have many visitors. A Mrs. Anna Parsons lives in the unit above this one. She called in the report. Parsons seems to know everything that goes on in the building. She stated Miss … excuse me … Ms.," he exaggerated the "Z" sound, "Summers usually watched the late news and the *Letterman* monologue before bed. Parsons can hear the television from upstairs."

"Any change in that routine last night?"

"At 10:12 p.m., and Parsons noted the time particularly because it was the first commercial break in *Survivor*. She heard the door buzzer, followed by voices in Summers' apartment. The conversation continued for some time, but she couldn't hear what was said." Theo grinned. "And I bet she tried."

When Jadz didn't respond to his jest, Theo continued. "When the *Letterman* monologue started, about 11:35, the visitor left. Parsons didn't see anyone, but she says she looked out the front window when she heard the door. The awning probably blocked her view if the subject was on foot and didn't cross the street. Parsons said the smell woke her up about two hours later. It's such a small room, the gas built up pretty fast. "

"Okay. Finish your report and have it on my desk as soon as you can. I'll talk to the manager about securing the apartment for a few days." Jadz saw Forester waiting by the door, looking even more disheveled and annoyed than usual. She took a deep breath and moved to meet him.

"Crime scenes get cold fast." Forester glared at her. "Still operating on narc time?"

"I was unavoidably detained," Jadz said, trying not to sound defensive. "I'm here now, and everything's under control."

He grunted. "It's your case until I decide otherwise." They stepped aside to make room for the gurney bearing the shrouded victim to squeeze through. "Number three, it seems. What are you going to do about it?" Forester followed the medics out the door, not waiting for a response.

Jadz grimaced, forced to admit at least to herself, *I have no idea.*

Jadz and Theo spent another hour and a half on a second, more thorough, sweep of the apartment for evidence trampled by EMTs or overlooked by Forensics. When she was satisfied, Jadz led the uniformed crew out of the apartment and locked the door behind them. The group split at the lobby, with Jadz heading for the manager's apartment. A reporter waiting by the door waylaid the men, but Theo fended him off.

"Talk to the lady in charge, not me," he said, cocking a thumb towards Jadz.

"Aw, come on, Baxter! You know she won't talk until all the reports are in. It won't be news anymore by that time." Jim Dixon was a regular on the police beat. He'd tangled with Jadz during her days with the drug task force. He usually lost.

Theo kept walking.

Thanks, Theo. The road crews accepted her authority even if Forester treated her like an interloper in Homicide. Four years with the drug task force and two commendations for service above-and-beyond didn't seem to impress him.

The clang of the elevator broke into Jadz's thoughts. Her self-imposed routine of using the stairs for exercise did not extend to the basement of strange apartment buildings at five in the morning. She stepped in and pressed the down button.

The resident manager had nothing to add to what he'd told the patrol officers. He dug out a name and number for an aunt in Connecticut as the victim's next-of-kin and complained about the loss of revenue from an empty apartment. "Owners expect me to keep these units filled, ya know. Pays my salary," he said before ushering Jadz into the dim hallway and slamming the door.

Back at Toledo Police headquarters downtown, Jadz pulled the files on the first two cases and spread them across her desk. The first death was originally tagged a suicide. Single female, depressed on her fortieth birthday, turns on the gas and never has to face another year alone. Jadz knew if Forester really thought it had been a murder, he would have given the case to a veteran Homicide detective instead. After the second death, he tried to reassign both cases. Jadz appealed to the captain for a chance to prove herself, winning a reprieve and more resentment from Forester. A third victim added fuel to his argument.

Theo flopped into the chair next to the desk and brought Jadz out of her studies. "Guess this makes three. So much for copycats." He dropped a manila folder in front of her. "Why would anyone want to kill harmless middle-aged women on their birthday?"

"Forty is hardly middle aged," she said. "It's the new thirty, haven't you heard?" Jadz scanned his report for details. "A better question is how did that someone know it was her birthday?"

"I dunno. Picked a name out of WSPD's morning birthday parade?"

"Possible, but think about it. How do you celebrate a friend's birthday? Did a florist deliver the rose that was on the nightstand? Co-workers sometimes throw a party. What about the free birthday dinner at some restaurant? Maybe they stiffed the server and he followed them home." Jadz drummed her fingers on the desk as she thought. "Ever go to one of those carnival booths where they guess your age and weight? I saw one at the Strawberry Festival in Springfield last weekend. Maybe it's a rogue carny."

"That's why you're the detective," Theo said. "I'm just a dumb beat cop. What's next?"

"Back to square one on the first victim. Talk to her family and friends again. See if she did anything special the day she died, anything out of her usual routine. Do the same thing on number two. But first I start with Summers, before Dixon hits the newsstand with his version." Jadz smothered a yawn.

"Sleep is in there somewhere, I hope." Theo straightened as Forester approached with a petite, dark-skinned woman in tow. "Uh-oh, it's the boss, and Miser."

"If your business is done, get lost," Forester said to him. "We have work to do."

Theo raised an eyebrow at Jadz as she stood to meet them. He left without another word.

"Castillo's your new partner on the birthday murders," Forester said. "Unlike you, she has more than three months' homicide experience." He returned to his office and slammed the door.

Like I need a keeper. Jadz swallowed her protest, unnerved by the appraising look from the woman left behind.

"Rena Castillo," the woman said, hand extended.

"Veronica Jadzinski, Jadz." The handshake was perfunctory. Forester's words must have carried to the farthest corner, and Jadz fumed at the amused looks their exchange received from fellow detectives scattered around the cramped bureau.

"You are a recent transfer from Narcotics, correct?" Castillo pulled out a chair next to the desk and sat down.

Her precise manner of speaking and faintly accented voice grated on Jadz's tired nerves.

"Three months, as Forester so kindly noted." She sat as well to avoid towering over Castillo even more than she did when they stood. *How did she pass the height requirement?*

"The task force speaks highly of you, as does Lieutenant Forester."

The task force maybe, but Forester? I doubt that. "How long have you been in Homicide?" Jadz shifted her chair to allow more elbow room and scooped her papers closer, protectively.

"Four years. It was accidental. I was in Property Crimes for two years after I left street patrol and one of our regular burglars took a violent turn. When I was able to help Homicide convict him of second-degree murder, Lieutenant Forester asked me to stay." Castillo set her briefcase on the few inches of the desk Jadz had cleared and pulled out a legal pad. "Shall we get started?"

Relieved to be done with the niceties, Jadz sorted through the files and shoved the reports toward her new partner. "Have you read the cases?"

"Just the patrol alerts." Castillo skimmed the pages. "I would suggest returning to the family and friends of the first two victims and finding out what may have occurred on the day they died that was out of the ordinary. And since you were at the scene this morning, you should handle those interviews. You will be better able to answer any questions."

Jadz clenched one fist in her lap at Castillo's apparent assumption of lead status. "What a novel idea."

Her sarcasm passed apparently unnoticed.

Castillo slid the Summers file across the desk and sorted through the remaining papers. "I will make follow-up calls on the other two from here. If personal visits are needed, we can do that together later."

Jadz swallowed another rude comment and gathered her things. "There's no family in town, and I left a voice mail for Summers' next-of-kin, an aunt. I'm going to the university to talk to her co-workers before they see it on the news." She didn't wait for a response. During her years with Narcotics, Jadz had become a loner, cultivating connections and informants on her own and often drawing the ire of her supervisor for the dangers of going solo.

"The task force is a group effort," Lieutenant Welch had often reminded her. "You're not the Lone Ranger. We can't watch your back if we don't know where it is."

Jadz preferred it that way. Even when her renegade activities and long hours on stakeouts led her estranged husband and fellow officer Nathan Solomon to find other companionship, Jadz walked out rather than figure out how to make the marriage work.

"I don't know what you're trying to prove," Nathan had told her more than once. "Everyone knows you're a good cop. You don't have to get yourself killed like your old man did to convince them."

Now, Jadz clung to her routine and headed out alone. She tossed her briefcase onto the front seat of her red Miata and slid behind the wheel. Boxy, unmarked sedans provided by the department were only good for stakeouts and prisoner transport. She paused, hand on the ignition, and yawned again. *Yes, sleep would be good.* She pulled away from the curb, reviewing the events of the last twelve hours that had made rest impossible.

Nathan was the reason she missed the early morning call from Dispatch. Chemistry still sparked between them, even after six months of separation. Whenever he had too much to drink, Nathan would appear at Jadz's apartment and beg her to come home. Last night's version shifted from argument to a calm discussion of the future, to fond reminiscences, and they ended up in bed. Nathan buried Jadz's cell phone in the sofa while she was making coffee, muffling the repeated calls. When she realized she had to face an angry Forester, Nathan just laughed. "Make sure you tell him why you're late."

This isn't good for either of us. The memories made her miss the turn onto West Bancroft from Monroe Street. She took the next left at North Detroit across from Swayne Field and wound her way back to Bancroft. Jadz circled the block in front of the University of Toledo library searching for an empty parking spot on the overcrowded campus. Police prerogative won out. She pulled into a loading zone, tossed her department placard on the dashboard and went inside.

Jadz's stop at Carlson Library took most of the morning. Summers had been a popular employee and Jadz had to wait for emotions to subside before she could ask questions.

"But why Marianne? She didn't have any enemies, and she never picked up strangers." Tabitha, a desk mate, sobbed into a lacy handkerchief. She replaced the soggy linen square with a box of tissues and mopped up the tears.

"Was she seeing anyone?" Jadz asked.

"No, Marianne doesn't ... didn't date much since her fiancé broke off their engagement last Christmas." Tabitha stopped to blow her nose. "Kind of down on men, you know? But she was always nice to the students and everybody. Even when she had a bad day, she didn't take it out on other people."

"The apartment manager said she moved in six months ago."

"That's when David left. Marianne said she couldn't stay in their place, made her too depressed, and she wanted to buy a house forever. She rented that dinky apartment while she hunted for the right place." Fresh tears erupted. "I wanted her to stay with me. This never would have happened!"

Jadz tried to plow through the outburst. "Can you give me his number? We'll need to talk to him."

Tabitha peeked out from her wad of tissues, eyes red and puffy but narrowed with indignation. "David would never hurt her. They just grew apart. He's out of state now anyway. New Orleans, I think. He always wanted to travel, and Marianne was pretty much a homebody. I think that's probably what split them up, in the end."

"I'll need to contact him."

With a shrug, Tabitha dug through a voluminous handbag for a tattered address book. She thumbed through it and found the information. "It's an old cell number they gave me when they went on vacation last year," she said as she scribbled on a notepad. "I think he still uses it."

"If you think of anything else, please give me a call," Jadz said. She handed Tabitha a business card, and after a stop in Human Resources for a copy of Summers' personnel file, she left the campus.

Her cell phone buzzed as she pulled back onto Bancroft Avenue. "Hi, Mom." Jadz stifled a sigh. "No, I got your message. I've been busy. I'm sorry Betty's car broke down again. I've told her if she insists on driving a classic she has to take better care of it. Yes, I know she needs it for her new job." She slowed for the light at Central Avenue, fighting a recurring wish to be an only child. Her older sister never grew up. Even at thirty-five, she depended on others to bail her out, sometimes literally, and their mother was quick to oblige. "Mom, there's a new TARTA stop up the street. She can ride the bus." Her mother's voice crackled through the receiver, defending Betty, as usual. "I'll see what I can do later. I have to go now. Yes, I'll call you tonight." Jadz dropped the phone into her jacket pocket. *I do not need Betty's problems today.*

Jadz stopped at Summers' apartment on her way downtown, skirting the yellow evidence tape draped across the door to let herself in. The chalky disruption left by Forensics outlined another ordinary, orderly life torn apart by tragedy. Jadz ran her finger across the volumes on bookshelves that flanked a picture window. Titles ranged from current best sellers to literary classics, all alphabetized and grouped by genre. A VHS tape of *The Music Man,* signed and dedicated by Ron Howard to "Madame Librarian," stood on display at the end of one shelf. Jadz chuckled at the memory of the old musical, comparing it to her own media-inspired name. *She obviously took the association better than I do.* Ever since she'd had been old enough to understand her mother's juvenile fascination with *Archie* comic books, Jadz had insisted on using her father's nickname—shortening Jadzinski to one manageable syllable—rather than the character's name of Veronica she'd been saddled with. Mom and Betty giggled together over the gaudy newsprint cartoons while Jadz and her father, the red-headed Archibald, had found more athletic pursuits to share.

The roar of a mower outside the building brought Jadz's attention back to the windows. Simple mauve drapes hung floor to ceiling. She pushed them back to find a view of Wildwood MetroPark over the privacy fence that hemmed the parking lot. Darkness had shrouded the area on her first visit. Jadz admired the nature scene in the midst of the bustling city, and imagined Summers enjoying the sight for the last time. *Why a lonely librarian?* Her thoughts echoed the recent interview with Tabitha. *And why on her birthday?*

A knock at the door interrupted her thoughts. She opened it to find a short, stocky white-haired woman in the hall who glared at her.

"What're you doing in there? Don't you see this is a crime scene?" she asked Jadz, waving the loose end of the yellow tape. "The police asked me to keep an eye on it."

"I am the police." Jadz flipped back her jacket to reveal the gold badge on her belt. "Detective Jadzinski, ma'am. You must be Mrs. Parsons. I was just on my way to see you."

"I told that good-looking officer last night everything I know," Parsons said.

"Sergeant Baxter said you were very helpful. I wanted to make sure you didn't remember something else after a good night's sleep."

Her words seemed to mollify the elderly woman. "I should hope I helped. Us gals have to look out for each other. Marianne and I weren't friends, exactly, bein' she was so much younger and all, but she'd bring my mail upstairs so I didn't have to make the trek to the box." Parsons tried to peek around the door into the apartment, but Jadz blocked her view. "Was she, you know...?"

"I can't discuss an open investigation, Mrs. Parsons. I'm sure you understand."

She looked disappointed, but backed up a step. "I don't remember anything 'cept what I told 'em last night. Didn't sleep a wink after the fire department finally let us back in. Bought a new lock for my door over at Ace Hardware this morning, though. Real good one. Manager wouldn't listen when I told him they need to protect us better. I'll take it off next month's rent, you watch."

The cell phone in her pocket buzzed again, allowing Jadz to excuse herself. "Please call me if you think of anything," she said, handing Parsons a card and closing the door before taking Castillo's call.

"The coroner's preliminary report is ready. He is confident the victim ingested some kind of sedative before the gas took effect," Castillo said. "Toxicology will take a few days."

"If you haven't spoken to next of kin for the first two victims, we'll need to get an okay for toxicology on them, too. We didn't run those the first time around, but I'm sure he kept samples. I'll meet you at the coroner's office." Jadz checked the apartment again for an empty prescription bottle. A conglomeration of vitamins and herbal supplements filled a kitchen shelf, but no sleep aids. She found a laptop computer in a briefcase next to a small corner desk and, taking it to examine at the office, she locked the door. Jadz replaced the yellow tape Parsons apparently took as a souvenir and headed across town.

During the short drive to the Medical College offices, Jadz considered what she knew about her new partner. Rena "Miser"

Castillo earned the dubious nickname during her days as a patrol officer by never picking up the tab for coffee or lunch, or sharing time with the crews in after-hours drinks. Rumor had it she wore the same two uniforms issued by the academy for the entire eight years she spent as a street cop. When Castillo made detective, her reputation followed her, and the nickname stuck. Quiet and reserved, she kept her distance from co-workers, including Jadz. *She's probably not any happier being shoved together than I am,* Jadz realized. Maybe they could teach Forester a lesson. She hit the recall button on her phone. Castillo answered on the first ring.

"I'm just pulling into Medical College," Jadz said." Can you meet me in the cafeteria before we see the doc? I think there's time, if you leave now."

"Give me fifteen minutes," Castillo said.

Jadz bought a large coffee and found a table away from the other patrons. The cafeteria buzzed with anxious hospital conversations. Tension in the air twanged on Jadz's frayed nerves. *Maybe this wasn't such a good idea.* She looked away from a family huddled in a corner booth wiping away tears, and settled on a beaming young man passing through with a bouquet of balloons proclaiming, "It's a boy." After he herded the Mylar bundle through the doors and into the hallway, Jadz turned her back to the room, losing herself in the splashes of color dotting the patio outside. Newly planted pansies spilled orange and violet blooms out of flower boxes at each end of the concrete slab, and bursting peony bushes offered hues from white through deep burgundy. A patch of irises between sapling rosebud trees added blue, gold and purple to the mix. Jadz sipped her coffee and let the warmth of the midday sun streaming through the windows seep into her tired body. She tried to blame her earlier rudeness to Castillo on lack of sleep, but she knew her dark mood had grown over the past few months of turmoil with Forester—and with Nathan. "Shape up, girl," her father's voice echoed. "You control how you react to life, nobody else does."

I miss you, Dad.

"Beautiful garden," Castillo said.

Jadz started. "How long …" She collected herself. "Excuse me, I need more coffee. You?"

"Iced tea," Castillo said, gesturing with a cold beverage cup. "Two coffees a day is enough for me, and none after lunch. Any more than that and I am awake all night."

When Jadz returned to the table, she said, "I thought we needed a few minutes to get to know each other maybe. Is your accent Cuban or something? I can't place it."

"Dominican Spanish, actually, and Japanese."

"Not a combination you hear every day," Jadz said.

"My father was from San Cristóbal and Mother was born in Kyoto. They met when she was studying at Medical College."

"What does your mom do?"

"She is an invalid."

Oops. "I'm sorry." Jadz picked at her paper cup. *This was such a bad idea.* She scrambled to balance the personal revelations scale. "My dad was a cop, followed him into the family business, I guess. You might remember when he … My older sister Betty lives with Mom since her divorce. Betty's, not Mom's. No kids or grandkids or anything. Mom was a chef before we were born—pretty good one, too. She just cooks for us now, just the three of us. And Betty, well, she's … Betty." Jadz trailed off, embarrassed again at her outburst.

After another lengthy silence, broken only by the surrounding bustle, Castillo said, "I do remember your father's death. I am sorry for your loss." She finished the tea, folded her used napkin, and placed it inside the empty cup. "We have to meet Dr. Hanley in ten minutes. I imagine you wanted to discuss more than personal history."

Jadz met her questioning gaze. "I wanted to apologize for this morning. I don't need to take my frustrations with Forester out on you. I'll quit being a jerk and we'll concentrate on solving this case together, okay?"

"I never expected otherwise." A hint of a smile broke on Castillo's face. "Solving the case that is, not the jerk part."

"Yeah, I'll have to work on that." Jadz laughed. "Let's go hear what the doc has to say. We can go over the rest of our notes at lunch. I'm starving."

They left the cafeteria and crossed the parking lot to the annex building housing the temporary coroner's offices.

"Do you know Dr. Hanley?" Jadz asked. "I've only met him a few times."

"He is a retired pathology instructor from Medical College. I found him very easy to work with on the mall shooting last year," Castillo said.

Dr. Hanley met them at the door to his workroom. He cleared a stack of files off the side chairs to make room for them to sit.

"Excuse the mess. We're finally moving to the new offices, but I have to sort all these old cases for archiving. Most of them are before my time." He added the papers to a teetering stack on top of the credenza. "So." Hanley stood, arms folded, and stared intently at the officers. "Detective Castillo I worked with on the mall shootings. Detective Jadzinski … I knew your father. Good man."

"Thank you, sir." Jadz swallowed hard, caught off guard at this second mention of her father in such a short time. "I didn't know you were acquainted."

"Did some DNA consulting work for the U.S. Attorney during the Hell's Angels case in 1990. He was lead investigator, I believe."

"From ATF, yes sir. He retired from federal service after that trial."

"Convictions on all counts." Hanley pulled his chair from behind the desk and swiveled to face them. "I was sorry to hear of his death."

"Thank you," Jadz repeated, wishing she could find other words. She caught Castillo's sympathetic gaze and looked away. "About the Summers case."

"Yes." Hanley grabbed the topmost folder in the stack at his elbow. "White female, age forty, five foot seven, one hundred thirty-five pounds, dark brown hair, green eyes, no identifiable marks other than an appendix scar, apparently several years old. Never bore children. All teeth intact. Victim presents signs of carboxyhemoglobin including severely lowered blood oxygen levels—"

"Dr. Hanley?" Castillo interrupted.

He cleared his throat. "Sorry, had visions of being in front of a class of interns again. To the important matter: no signs of physical trauma. Death was due to asphyxiation caused by inhalation of natural gas. Time of death was somewhere between nine and midnight."

"A neighbor heard her let someone in about ten," Jadz informed him.

"Fine," he said, making a note. "Time of death between ten and midnight." He adjusted his glasses and continued. "Now the good stuff. The victim had a faint discoloration on her cheek, appeared to be the outline of lips."

"Lipstick?" Castillo asked.

"More like red wine or fruit juice. I took a swab to check for DNA. That'll take about a week." Hanley pulled out another lab report. "Finally, there were traces of a barbiturate in her saliva, as I told Detective Castillo on the phone, but nothing in the coffee cup from the nightstand. No prescription bottles in the apartment?" He looked at the detectives.

"Nothing I could find," Jadz said.

He scribbled again. "So she ingested the drug in an unknown manner. I won't know what or how much is actually in her system until the blood work comes back."

"So you're saying … what? She was drugged, tucked into bed and kissed goodnight, then left to asphyxiate?" Jadz slapped the arm of her chair. "Now I've heard everything."

"I'm not saying anything of the kind." He peered over his glasses. "It's your job to put the pieces together, not mine. I just provide the information."

"Of course, Doctor," Castillo said. "Is there anything else?"

"Based on the releases signed on the earlier deaths, I've already ordered toxicology on those victims since we know what to look for now. First time around we just checked for oxygen depletion." Hanley handed Castillo the file and scooted back behind the desk. "That's your copy. I'll let you know when I have more."

Jadz and Castillo were silent on the walk back to the parking lot.

"Damn," Jadz said as they separated at their cars. "Do you think it's possible? What kind of nut puts his victim to bed before he kills her?"

"I do not begin to understand the mind of a murderer." Castillo said. "But then, I do not understand most minds."

By the time Jadz worked her way through traffic to downtown, George's Coney Island Restaurant was packed with the usual lunchtime crowd. She scooted between the tables to where Castillo waited at a booth in the corner and slid into the bench across from her.

"Have you ordered?" Jadz asked.

"Not yet. The server is bringing coffee for you," Castillo said.

A young man appeared with a thermal carafe of coffee. He took their sandwich order and rushed back to the kitchen, picking up empty plates on his way.

"Short-handed again, looks like." Jadz took a tentative sip from her mug to gauge the heat. "Sometimes I think I should just mainline caffeine, as much coffee as I drink."

"Why the tension between you and Lieutenant Forester? Does that not make it difficult to do your job?" Castillo fished an ice cube out of her water glass and crunched on it.

Jadz toyed with a spoon as she considered a diplomatic response. "Forester doesn't think I can do the work, for one. And it doesn't sound like he's a fan of the drug task force. I heard he called us grandstanders."

"Some of the officers, mostly from the smaller jurisdictions, bring a bit too much testosterone to the job, but he certainly respects the work." She chewed another ice cube. "Why did you transfer?"

"After the January drug bust, Welch said my cover was blown. They put me on a desk job for a few months during trial prep, and I hate shuffling papers. When the opening came up in Homicide, I jumped at it just to get out of the office."

"Will you return to Narcotics when your trial is over?" Castillo asked.

"I doubt it. I was with the task force for four years, and it's discouraging when the dealers we busted end up back on the street. If I can prove myself so Forester will get off my back, I'd like to stay put."

"You do not have to prove anything," she said. "You have a good reputation, and your work speaks for itself."

Jadz finished the coffee while considering Castillo's words. Lunch arrived before she had an answer. She examined her Coney dogs and squirted a layer of mustard onto the onions and sauce. After swallowing her first bite, Jadz said, "I appreciate the sentiment, but I don't think Forester agrees. Haven't you run into his chauvinism?"

Castillo picked at her BLT, adding a thin layer of mayonnaise to one half before taking a small bite. Most of the contents fell off onto the plate, barely missing her immaculate white blouse.

Jadz smothered a laugh as she passed extra napkins. "Happens every time with George's BLTs. I think he rigs them to do that."

After wiping her hands, Castillo said, "A chauvinist? In my time in Homicide, he has always been a gentleman."

"That's just it. A gentleman who thinks women belong at home, not in his department."

"I do not see that," Castillo said. "I do my job well and he treats me with respect. That is all I ask of a supervisor."

"Really? He's been a pain in my neck since day one." She munched in silence, frowning. "Something to think about, I guess." Jadz wiped the remnants of chili off her chin and poured more coffee. "So what's your story? I've been in Homicide for three months and I hardly ever see you."

"When you started, I was in trial for several weeks on the Franklin Park shootings. After that, I took a leave of absence." Castillo finished her BLT with a knife and fork while she talked. "I have been working on cold case files for the past month and a half. When this turned out to be a serial murder, Lieutenant Forester felt my time would be better served helping you resolve it quickly." Her face clouded. "Does that offend you? My joining the case?"

Jadz flushed. "It did, at first. That's why I was such an ass this morning. That and no sleep." She drained her coffee cup. "But I know any serial crime—especially murder—needs all the manpower we can throw at it. Since I don't have a partner, this only makes sense."

When the server appeared to clear the table, Jadz ordered another pot of coffee. Castillo requested more ice water, and separate checks.

"What about you? Why don't you have a partner?" Jadz asked while they waited. "Most of the guys work in pairs."

Castillo fidgeted. "I learned early on not to expect I'd work in groups if others were given a choice."

"Like being picked last in gym class or something?" Jadz said.

Castillo looked anywhere but at Jadz. "In the academy, when we were paired with our first patrol mentor, none of the senior officers wanted to deal with me. I do not blame them, really. I barely made the height requirement. They were concerned I could not protect myself, or them." She turned back to Jadz. "I have been solo as much as possible, as soon as possible, unless directed otherwise. It makes things easier."

It makes the pain easier. "Well, I'm a loner, too, Rena, but I guess we ended up together for a reason."

Rena smiled when Jadz used her first name. She pulled out her notebook. "Yes, we have a case to solve."

Jadz and Rena worked undisturbed for another hour as the restaurant's lunch crowd thinned to a few scattered tables. They compared notes from the morning interviews and searched for a pattern.

"Two had flowers delivered at work, but from different florists," Jadz said, reading through the list. "One went to lunch with the entire office the day she died. Two didn't go anywhere. One had a catered party at work. Only one of them was mentioned on the morning radio that we can find. One worked near downtown, one at Levis Park and one at the university."

"They used different hairstylists, visited different doctors," Rena added, "with no common friends or relatives that we know of. One belonged to LA Fitness, one to the Downtown Fitness Center. The other had no organized fitness routine."

"Two had semi-steady boyfriends," Jadz continued, shuffling the reports. "One dated whoever caught her fancy, of either sex. Summers recently broke off an engagement. I have a call in to the fiancé, but he works on an oil rig in the gulf."

Rena checked the time. "We should get back. Lieutenant Forester will want an update."

Jadz made a face, but gathered her things. On the walk to the station, Jadz described her conversation with Theo about the festival age-weight booths.

"I checked with CitiFest. Everybody pretty much hires their own vendors, so they couldn't provide a contractor list, but I picked up a schedule. There's a shopping center carnival at Miracle Mile tomorrow. I thought I'd check it out."

"It seems like a long shot," Rena said as they entered Toledo Police headquarters.

"Got a better idea?"

Rena punched the elevator button. "Not particularly."

Jadz waved her on. "I use the stairs. Saves me from having to take up jogging."

Jadz and Rena spent the afternoon huddled over their now-adjacent desks shuffling papers, proposing and dismissing scenarios, and scouring the reports for overlooked clues. After several hours, Forester called them to his office for an update. Rena's precise summary took several minutes, and his eyes never left her face. "Make sure an alert detailing this guy's MO gets out for area agencies, and let me know when the toxicology results are in," he said when she finished. Forester followed them out of his office, and flipped off the light. "It's late. Get some sleep, or you won't be worth a damn tomorrow."

Jadz held her astonishment in check until he was out of earshot, then asked, "Since when did he care if we slept or not?"

"He knows that for us to be at our best, we must sleep." Rena sorted the reports back to their respective folders. "He is only being a good supervisor." She stacked the files neatly on the crevice dividing their workspaces and picked up her briefcase. "Ready?"

"I don't know. Something doesn't fit."

"We have done all we can today," Rena said.

"I meant Forester. He's never treated me like a human being before."

"Stop being so sensitive. I told you. If you do your job well, he will respect you and treat you accordingly." Rena headed for the elevator, Jadz trailing behind.

"Are you sure there isn't something more we can do tonight?" Jadz said before entering the stairwell. "I don't want another late-night call."

"We can have dinner and let our minds rest." Rena said when Jadz met her at ground level. They dropped the alert at Dispatch before leaving the building.

"Where do you want to eat?" Jadz asked when they reached Rena's car.

Rena opened her mouth and closed it without speaking, shifting her briefcase to her right hand and back again. After placing the bag in the backseat, she said, "I am sorry if I misspoke. Maybe another time, when I have made arrangements for … Another time. Good night." She drove off without looking back.

Jadz shrugged and headed home. Visions of her empty refrigerator propelled her into the nearest Applebee's for take-out. Only a few stragglers were left from the Friday night date crowd, so the wait was just long enough to return the call to her mother.

"No, I can't give Betty a ride to work in the morning. I have to be in the office early. I know it's Saturday. Crime doesn't work banker's hours. Mom ... Mom, I'll call Steve. Maybe he can check out her car tomorrow. In the meantime, she can take the bus. I don't know how she'll pay for repairs, that's her problem. I am not being unsympathetic. She's an adult. She needs to start acting like one." Jadz extricated herself from her mother's demands after promising again to call her mechanic. She picked up her food and arrived home a few minutes later to find Nathan parked in front of her apartment. He followed her into the garage, opening the car door as soon as she was parked.

"Where the hell have you been?" he asked. "It's after nine. Doesn't Forester know you've been working since three this morning?"

"We are not doing this tonight. Go home."

"Wait." Nathan caught her arm as she brushed past him to the front door. "We need to talk about last night."

"No, we don't."

"Jadz—"

"Go home." She shook free and pushed him away from the door. "Don't do this. It's been a long day. I'm tired. Last night was a mistake. You know it. I know it." Her resolve softened at the look on Nathan's face. "Go home, please. We'll talk another time. Just not right now."

"Promise?"

"Maybe Sunday afternoon, if I don't work all day."

"It wasn't a mistake, you know," he called after her as she entered the building. Nathan was still standing on the sidewalk, hands in his pockets, when she looked out her third-story apartment window a few minutes later.

Jadz pulled the drapes, shutting him out. She fed her cat, Ford, and sorted through a stack of mail while eating. An hour later, Jadz gave in to exhaustion and slept.

Chapter 2

Jadz was already at her desk Saturday morning when Rena appeared bearing two tall cups of Sufficient Grounds' special blend.

"I limit my daily intake, but I still appreciate good coffee." Rena offered Jadz one of the cups. "I noticed at lunch you drink it black, correct?"

Jadz shoved her now-cold convenience store coffee aside. "You're a lifesaver. What do I owe you?"

"It is my pleasure." Jadz couldn't hide her surprise, and Rena added, "I know the nickname some have for me. It is not totally inaccurate. I am … frugal."

Jadz flushed. "Anyway, thanks."

"Where shall we begin?"

"Do we know if Olsen or Peterson were online much?" Jadz motioned toward a laptop open on the worktable next to the desks. "I found this at Summers' place yesterday afternoon, but forgot it was in my trunk. Lucky for us she wasn't big on computer security. All her passwords were saved, so I got right in. Appears she was a regular on several chat rooms, but nothing hinky."

Rena leafed through her notes. "I will make calls when it is not quite so early. Have we located her fiancé?"

"Not yet. I'll try again this afternoon. I left a message, but his office wasn't sure he could be reached on the job site before today."

Rena frowned and beat a tattoo on the desk with her pen. "We must be missing something. How are these women connected?"

"I'm going with the rogue carny until we come up with something better. I cruised the Miracle Mile strip before I came in. No age-weight booth that I could see, but I'll stop back later."

"What else do you have in mind?"

Jadz inhaled sharply at Rena's apparent dismissal of the carny idea, then let her breath out slowly. "Let's try something more visual." She brought up a spreadsheet on her laptop, set up a column for each victim with a list of identifiers and turned the screen so Rena could watch. "We know they were all forty, but start with Olsen—she's the first victim—and her date of birth."

They worked back and forth, filling in the grid, listing as many specifics on each woman as they could find from the reports, down to Olsen's tropical fish and a beagle belonging to the second victim. Jadz highlighted the rows where information was available for all three women and they searched for a pattern. Half a dozen other detectives arrived over the next hour but the commotion didn't interrupt their work. Only when someone approached the desk and stood over her shoulder did Jadz look up from her computer.

It was Nathan.

"What are you doing here?" she asked.

Rena scooted back from the desk.

"You're not answering your cell phone," he said.

"Only your calls. I'm busy." Jadz led him into the relative privacy of an empty office and closed the door. "What is it that can't wait until tomorrow?"

"What time can I pick you up in the morning? We'll drive out to Maumee Bay for lunch at the resort. I know how much you like it there."

She ignored his hopeful expression. "We're not going to Maumee Bay. I'll call you when I have some free time, after lunch maybe, and we'll have coffee. That's it."

"But—"

"No buts. Now go. This is embarrassing." Jadz stepped back from the door when she saw several co-workers watching them. "I'm sorry if I gave you the wrong impression the other night. I've told you a dozen times. It's over. The court hearing next week is just a formality."

"You don't really mean that." He tried to draw her closer and she resisted. "Give me another chance."

"We are not doing this now." Jadz was firm. "I'll call you tomorrow." She spotted Forester talking to Rena. "Damn."

Nathan followed her gaze. "Okay, tomorrow. But don't forget." He planted a kiss on her forehead and left.

Jadz ducked around the corner to the restroom and splashed cold water on her face. Legally, her six-year marriage would be over with next week's hearing. Emotionally … Jadz pushed the thought aside for a better time. She faced her reflection for a long minute, annoyed at the splotchy image. When she collected herself and returned to the office, Forester was gone.

"Where'd he go?" she asked Rena, relieved and deflated at the same time.

"Lieutenant Forester? He wanted to be sure we had his cell number in case the coroner's report comes in. He has a family gathering in Bowling Green today," Rena said. "What did Officer Solomon need?"

"Officer Solomon is my soon-to-be ex-husband."

Rena's eyebrows arched.

"I figured everybody knew. Nathan was my training officer when I graduated from the academy," Jadz said. "We didn't start dating till after I was assigned a new partner, so the brass didn't care."

"I see." Rena's brow furrowed. "There are no policies against married officers?"

"Not as long as they don't supervise each other," Jadz said. "We always made sure to work opposite shifts. I was more worried about the other guys giving me a rough time. It's hard enough for a woman in uniform to be taken seriously, you know?"

"He is a patrolman, correct?"

"He's never had ambition for anything else. Nathan's a good street cop, and he likes it that way." Jadz slouched over her desk chair and hung her head. "It's been a tough six months."

"Are you upset by the divorce?" Rena asked.

Her head snapped up. "Hell, no," she said. "He left me a long time ago."

"You are rather cavalier about it."

Jadz gripped the back of the chair, knuckles white. "Ever been married?" she asked.

"No, but—"

"Then you wouldn't understand. I can't make it work on my own." Jadz locked eyes with Rena, daring her to disagree.

"I do not have to be married to understand commitment," Rena said.

"What's that supposed to mean?"

Rena dropped her gaze. "My apology. It is none of my business."

"Damn straight." Jadz kicked her chair back under the desk and left the bureau. Three sets of stair-climbing later, she returned to find Rena staring at the rooftop next door.

"What's next?" Jadz asked.

"There is nothing more we can do today. I need to take my mother to her physical therapy session." She tucked a copy of the spreadsheet into her bag with the case file. "I will review these at home."

"Fine. I'll swing by the festival." Jadz trailed Rena to the elevator. "I hope your mother's okay?"

Rena let the doors close without answering.

The Miracle Mile carnival was billed as a fundraiser for the Boys & Girls Club, but it was as much an advertising gimmick for the local shopping center. Jadz parked at the far end of the lot between an RV and a cargo van opposite the vendor gate. She pulled a gym bag out of the trunk and detoured to the public restroom at the BP gas station on the corner. Ten minutes later, after shedding her button-down shirt and khakis in favor of biking shorts, tank top, and running shoes, she blended into the crowd at the turnstile. Her unruly red hair was caught up in a terrycloth headband which matched the oversized plastic frame sunglasses she hid behind.

Jadz steered around a young family with a wailing infant and made for the row of booths at the end of the midway. A clunky Ferris wheel towered over inflatable funhouses and carnival rides offering tinny music and spine-snapping jerks. Games of chance and food stands selling cotton candy, caramel apples, deep-fried Twinkies, and Sno-cones were crammed into the usually empty lot, exposing their wares and their patrons to the steamy afternoon heat shimmering off the asphalt.

Mounds of chopped onions and green peppers grilling next to foot-long Italian sausages distracted Jadz and set her stomach rumbling. She forced herself to keep walking, staying with the crowd's flow as she searched for familiar faces to avoid. Now was not the time to be recognized. High-strung pre-teens clashed with the deliberate nonchalance of Goth high schoolers, bouncing off each other like pinballs in an old Bally machine. Jadz dodged a toddler chased by his frantic caregiver and detoured around a young couple in a clinch. Several booths had been added since her earlier run-through. Uniformed Girl Scouts hovered over a kiddie pool with colorful plastic ducks bobbing in unnaturally blue water. The Rotary Club's Big-Six wheel clattered as it spun an enticing mantra to gamblers who were content to lose their money to charity. Tucked in between the ring-toss and the balloon-pop Jadz found what she was looking for.

A tall platform scale stood on a precarious wooden platform surrounded by hanging displays of stuffed animals and plastic trinkets. "Toledo Scales" stamped on the huge rotary dial showed the machine's age. A muscular young man in baggy cargo shorts and a bright orange polo shirt haggled with a trio of giggling women.

"I promise not to tell anyone what age I guess. You can whisper it in my ear. C'mon, take a shot." When they walked away without taking him up on the offer, he called, "How about just the month?"

Jadz squeezed into a quiet spot under the lemonade shake-up canopy to hide from the sun and watch the operation. Over the next hour, the carny convinced half a dozen couples and small groups to test his guessing skills. Four twenty-something guys who'd already hit the beer tent jostled for a turn at the scales while the women stayed with less-revealing birthday month guesses. Everyone left with a garish stuffed animal when they bested him. Losing didn't diminish his enthusiastic patter.

Not very good, is he? She shifted her location several times to avoid his notice, always keeping the booth in sight.

"Hey, Detective, thought you gave up undercover work," said a voice at her elbow.

Jadz jumped, then pulled the scruffy man aside. "Damn, Jimmy, keep it down."

"Sorry," he said, lowering his voice. "Why you watchin' the carny? He's not a local."

"How do you know?" she asked, berating herself for being tagged by one of her own informants.

"I dunno, just a guess. Thought all these guys were with the road crew."

She pointed to the Scouts and the Rotary. "Those aren't." Jadz turned back to the guessing booth as an idea struck. "Do me a favor?"

Five minutes later, they wandered past the booth. Jadz clung to Jimmy's arm and sucked on a jumbo limeade. She made eye contact with the carny to make sure he'd stop them. He did.

Jadz jiggled up and down. "Oooh! Jimmy, let's try this one. I'm psychic, ya know. I can block him guessing my mind."

As agreed, Jimmy just nodded. He handed over the five-dollar bill Jadz had given him and stepped back against the flimsy wall. While the carny was occupied with Jadz, guessing her age at twenty-three and returning her flirtations, Jimmy scanned the posted vendor's license.

"I won!" Jadz threw her arms around Jimmy's neck. "I want that purple monster-thing at the top." The carny obliged and they strolled off down the concourse.

When they were out of sight, Jadz handed the soft drink to Jimmy along with twenty dollars. "You were right. Says he's from Colorado, just joined the company last week and has never been to Ohio before," she said. "But he promised to look me up if he ever comes back." She shuddered. "Lucky me."

Jadz jotted down the name Jimmy got from the license. She found a trash bin on her way to the exit, but before she could toss the stuffed animal, an unhappy youngster in a stroller caught her attention. Jadz handed it over and the purple creature changed the toddler's tears to giggles.

At least someone can go home happy.

Back at her apartment, Jadz researched the carnival company and the guessing booth vendor online and found nothing of interest. His story matched the corporate records, and his name didn't turn up in any criminal history files. She checked her CitiFest list for any other festivals in the area. St. Patrick's of Heatherdowns carnival ran all weekend, and it was only a few blocks away. Jadz wondered if she was grasping at straws as Rena suggested. *What else have we got to go on?*

Jadz pulled her bike out of the storage room and pedaled the short distance to the church. She dismounted and walked the bike through the festival area. It was a more homegrown event than the Miracle Mile carnival. Most of the booths were run by church groups or community organizations. A quick circuit of the grounds showed no guessing booth and Jadz was on her bike again in less than twenty minutes. She rode up Eastgate, turned onto Glendale Avenue and into Swan Creek MetroPark. She followed the three-mile loop trail through the park, pushing herself physically and letting her mind sort through the tangle of the murder case. The lushness of the still park woodland couldn't penetrate her racing thoughts. Jadz slowed her pace, trying to absorb the serenity and failing. Five laps later she rode home, exhausted but no closer to answers.

After a quick shower, a jaunt to the corner grocery for coffee, cat food and toothpaste, and a detour for deli carry-out, Jadz curled up with a glass of wine, her cat, and the spreadsheet print-out Rena had provided.

Rena. Jadz considered the protocol of a partner. It had been five years since she had to share day-to-day operations, and after their earlier spat, Jadz wasn't in a sharing mood. *Should I call her about today? And tell her what? Maybe she thought of something. Then she should call me.* Jadz tossed the paperwork aside, annoyed at her indecision. The file bounced off the cat, who sank his claws into her ankle.

"Ow! Sorry, Ford, but you don't have to impale me." She scooped him up and sat stroking his ears in penance. *Is a cat the only partner I can manage, domestic or otherwise?*

The phone buzzed just after midnight. "Jadzinski. When? On my way." She stripped off her night shirt on her way to the closet and pulled out of the parking garage five minutes later.

St. Vincent Mercy Medical Center emergency room was filled with the usual Saturday night assortment of accident victims, bar fight leftovers, and sick children who waited until the weekend to spike fevers. Jadz showed her badge to the receptionist, who buzzed her into the treatment area. She followed the woman's directions to a curtain-draped treatment area halfway down the left side of the ward.

Jadz stopped just inside the curtain, appalled at the condition of the figure on the gurney. "Jimmy? What the hell happened?"

Jimmy opened the one eye that wasn't swollen shut and squinted at her. "You came," he said. "I didn't think you would, but I didn't know who else to call. The beat cops—"

"What happened?" she asked again. Jadz pulled the curtain closed behind her and perched on the stool next to the bed. While he talked, she took in the torn, bloodied shirt, and bruised face. An air splint held his left arm immobile. She only half-listened to his account of the beating until the word "carny" caught her attention.

"Wait, the guy from the guessing booth did this to you?" Jadz asked.

He tried to nod, and winced. "Yeah. I went back to the beer tent, 'bout ten o'clock I guess, and he was there. Asked me about you, said you were hittin' on him, and wanted to be sure I didn't have a claim." Jimmy squirmed and rolled his good eye toward the ceiling. "I was pretty drunk, I think. I kinda accidently told him you were a cop, and he lost it."

Jadz flinched. "What else did you tell him?"

"Not much talking, after that."

Jadz stepped out to the nurses' station and cornered an aide. "Where's the officer who took this man's report?"

"I just came on. I didn't see anybody."

"Could you find his nurse and ask?" Jadz flashed her badge again. She waited several minutes until a harried older woman in scrubs appeared from another cubicle. Jadz repeated her question.

"He was here," the nurse said, looking past Jadz to the lobby. "Maybe he finished up ... no, there he is." She pointed to a uniformed officer returning to the area, coffee in hand.

Jadz sidestepped a patient being wheeled past on a gurney and met the officer outside Jimmy's area.

"Hey, Jadz," Patrolman Diebold said. "You got here fast."

"Did you catch the guy?" she asked, motioning toward Jimmy.

"Nah, he was long gone before the EMTs found him behind Radio Shack. Night manager called it in."

"Did he see anyone?"

"Nope, tripped over Jimmy in the alley as he was locking up." Diebold handed her his clipboard.

Jadz scanned his scrawled notes. "The carnival's gone already?"

"Yeah, they tear down fast. On their way to Kalamazoo, far as we can tell. Good bet your guy didn't stay with them, though."

"Hey!" Jimmy called through the curtain, bringing them inside. "That guy, he drove a brown van, real beat-up, did I tell you that?"

Jadz looked to Diebold, who said, "No, he never mentioned it. Would have helped with an APB."

"I was kinda out of commission, ya know?" Jimmy's scolding was ruined by a hacking cough that showered blood onto his sleeve.

Diebold cringed and bolted through the curtain.

Jadz pulled back out of range. "Okay, Jimmy. Let the docs take care of you. I'll check on you later." She followed Diebold into the lobby.

"Worked him over pretty good," he said when Jadz caught up. "What were you after him for?"

"I wasn't, really." Jadz related her theory on the murders, adding, "Guess I hit a nerve."

"I'll get an updated APB on the air," Diebold said. "You need any more from me right now?"

"Just let me know if he turns up. I'll be at the station before your shift ends." Jadz left word at the desk for updates on Jimmy's status and went home.

Sleep eluded her, and Jadz was back in the office by five. She read through the finished report Diebold left on her desk with a scribbled Post-it note, "All yours!" on the front. He included a vehicle registration for a 1987 Dodge Caravan to Theodore Samuel Terwilliger of Kersey, Colorado. A quick Internet search turned up a number for the village police there, but a recording advised office hours were eight to four thirty, Monday through Saturday. After-hours callers were directed to the Weld County Communication Center or the Greeley/Weld Records

Department. Her first try to the records office also went to voice mail. Before she could try the communications center, a call came through on her cell from Dispatch. Terwilliger's van had been located at a truck stop off I-69 and SR 20 outside of Angola, Indiana. He was in custody, awaiting her instructions.

"I'll be there in ninety minutes, tops," she said, calculating the mileage as she ran out the door. Jadz signed out a marked cruiser, knowing it would make the trip faster, and in case she decided to bring Terwilliger back to Toledo.

Guilt got the best of her while she waited in line behind semis backed up to get on the Ohio Turnpike outside of Rossford. She called and left instructions with Dispatch to notify Forester and Rena of her activity if they checked in, or "after eight o'clock." *No sense getting them up early on a Sunday.* By then, she'd be in Angola.

Five hours after heading west, a subdued Jadz pulled back into the TPD garage. Terwilliger had talked willingly enough, once Jadz explained what he was up against. He'd only been in Ohio for the weekend, with out-of-state alibis for the date of each murder. During the long drive back to Toledo, Jadz called Diebold so he could take the assault charge to the prosecutor, for what little good that might do. If he was smart, Terwilliger would avoid Ohio in the future. Jadz let Forester's call skip to voice mail, preferring to face his wrath in person. Shortly before noon, she trudged up the stairs to her office, disheartened.

Rena met her at door to the stairwell. "We need to talk."

Jadz pushed aside her exhaustion and followed Rena into an interview room away from the eyes and ears of fellow detectives.

"Do you have any idea how it makes me look to hear third-hand that my *partner* has gone out of state to interview a suspect I did not even know about?" Rena leaned across the scarred wooden table, angry eyes pinning Jadz against the wall. "If you do not trust me enough to share—"

"I don't know you enough to trust you."

Rena drew in a sharp breath. "We are fellow officers. What more do you need to know?"

"I don't know." Jadz pulled out a chair and sat, head in her hands.

After a moment, Rena sat opposite her. "At lunch yesterday, I thought we made a connection, that we agreed to work together on this."

"We did." Jadz's voice was muffled.

"Then why did you not call me?"

Jadz faced her. "Old habits die hard."

Rena sniffed. "That is a cop-out."

"It's all I've got."

Rena shoved away from the table and paced around the small room. "Tell me what happened."

Jadz started with her visit to the Miracle Mile carnival, stumbled her way through the role-playing with Jimmy, and covered her stop at Saint Pat's festival. When Jadz related Jimmy's injuries, Rena turned to face Jadz, her arms crossed over her chest, hands gripping her forearms.

"You went after a suspect alone after what he did to your informant?"

"He was already in custody," Jadz said. "It's not like there was any danger."

Rena's jaw clenched. "What happened in Angola?"

"It was a wash. Terwilliger was running from a domestic violence complaint. Jimmy picked the wrong guy to confide in." Guilt over Jimmy's injuries made Jadz defensive. "You know, if you hadn't blown off my idea about the carnival booth—"

"I did not blow it off," Rena cut in. "I addressed it yesterday afternoon by calling each family, again. There are ways to handle investigations without playing dress-up and putting others in harm's way."

Jadz flushed at the deserved criticism. "You called everybody?"

"I called. Nothing definitive on Olsen or Summers, but the second victim was agoraphobic. She hated crowds of any kind, rarely went anywhere other than work and home."

"So she wouldn't have gone to a festival."

"Not likely."

Jadz brooded for several minutes as the last shred of hope for her carny theory vanished.

"If this is because of my comment about your divorce," Rena said, "I have already apologized. I was out of line."

"You were, and you did, and it's over," Jadz said. She sagged in the chair, realizing she had allowed her resentment with Forester to color her relationship with Rena. "I did exactly what Forester told me not to do, rode off on my own, trying to prove … something." Rena's assurances at lunch echoed in her over-tired brain: "Your work will speak for itself." *What does my work say to Forester now?* Jadz stood and stretched. "So I've done enough damage for today. I could use some sleep."

"Lieutenant Forester is waiting for you." Rena held the door, a smile replacing her earlier frown.

Jadz massaged her forehead as she led the way to the bureau. She took a deep breath outside Forester's door before knocking.

"I will be here when you are done," Rena said as Jadz entered the office.

Forester's dressing-down was a harsher rerun of Rena's, but not as severe as Jadz anticipated. She took it silently, knowing it was justified.

"We're on the same team here, Jadzinski, try to remember that," he said as he left.

Jadz apologized to Rena again while they walked to the elevator. She paused before entering the stairwell. "And thanks for sticking around."

During the drive home, Jadz called Nathan to beg off their meeting.

"I'm being stood up?" he asked.

"It's not like it was a date, it was just—"

"Just good ol' Nate, I know."

"Don't do this to me, okay? Not today." Jadz's voice cracked.

"Not a lot of days left," he said. "You're divorcing me next week."

Jadz coasted to a stop in the parking garage. "I'll call you tomorrow." She hung up on his protest and ignored the immediate callback. Two minutes to feed the cat and Jadz was in bed. She didn't stir for twelve hours.

Chapter 3

For the next few days, a chastised Jadz played by the rules, sharing her thoughts and findings with Rena as the investigation inched along. They spent every minute of the workday together, including lunches, but couldn't find a link between the victims. By Thursday, claustrophobia set in and Jadz took the morning off to escape. She found an early meditation session at the Toledo Zen Center.

"It's been way too long." The director greeted Jadz with a hug. "Welcome."

Jadz smiled her thanks. The *zazen* meditation was already underway. She found an empty cushion at the back of the room and settled into a Half Lotus position with her legs folded, hands cupped gently in front of her midsection. It took most of the first hour to quiet the images flooding her mind, from her father's death to the split with Nathan to the recent upheaval at the department. After her father was killed when he stumbled into the middle of drug deal, Jadz had shut down emotionally. She strong-armed her way onto the drug task force team by playing on the commander's respect for the elder Jadz and then set out to clean up the city, one dealer at a time. Her mother and sister turned to Jadz for support, and only with them did she reveal her former self. Some days their dependence was more than she could handle, and she took out her frustrations not on the job, but by arguing with Nathan. Eventually, the marriage had cracked under the strain.

Now as the buzzing in her brain receded, Jadz focused on her breathing and let the discordant thoughts wash through unhindered. The second and third hours brought a semblance of calm and eventually a renewed sense of the old self she longed to reclaim. *I need to remember this.*

When Jadz returned to the office after lunch, she found Rena engrossed in an unfamiliar file. "What's up?" she asked.

Rena held up one finger to ward off further questions as she scanned the remaining pages. After flipping the last sheet, she closed the file and handed it across the desk to Jadz.

"Swanton PD faxed over their report from an apparent suicide last night. They saw our alert and wanted to compare notes," Rena said.

"Felicia Adams, female, forty, gas," Jadz read the highlights aloud. "Sure sounds like our guy."

"Possibly. Detective Spiner will be here shortly."

Jadz opened the spreadsheet containing their victim summary and added a new row. She worked back and forth from the fax to the file, adding Swanton's data. "Not a lot here. We'll need to do some follow-up interviews."

"That will be up to Detective Spiner," Rena said. "It is his case."

"Yeah, but our three top his one."

"Possibly," Rena said again.

Swanton Detective Walter Spiner was paunchy, greying, and his face bore a sour expression that deepened when he saw the two women. "This your case?" He looked at Rena.

"Our case," Jadz said, stepping in with curt introductions.

Spiner scowled. "What've you got that I need to know?"

Rena pulled up a side chair next to her. "Have a seat and we will fill you in."

He scooted the chair two feet from the desk before sitting down. "Got any coffee?"

"Help yourself," Jadz waved toward the counter across the room. She exchanged glances with Rena and waited. He made no move to accept her offer. Jadz handed Spiner a copy of the victim summary.

"What the hell's this?" he asked with no more than a glance at the sheet.

"We have three female victims, four with Adams, all drugged and gassed on their fortieth birthday," Rena said. "By laying out the data, we are hoping to find a connection between them."

"They're all dead, what more connection do you need?" Spiner squinted at the page. "Damn small type." He pulled a pair of half-moon reading glasses from his front pocket.

Jadz drummed her fingers on the desk, torn between amusement and annoyance as she waited for him to finish.

"Am I keeping you from a date?" Spiner asked with a scornful glance that silenced her fidgeting.

"We would like more information on Adams." Rena's calm request cut off an angry retort from Jadz. She shook her head slightly at Jadz and continued. "There are several avenues we could explore with any witnesses or family members, if you do not mind our contacting them. Unless of course you would prefer to conduct follow-up yourself."

Spiner turned his back on Jadz and addressed Rena. "It's my case, my witnesses. What're you looking for that I don't already have?"

Jadz stormed out of the office, leaving Rena to work out the details with Spiner. She left the building and headed for the diner at the corner. *Get your own damn coffee.* Jadz found a stool at the counter, slowed her frustrated breathing, and focused on reclaiming the equanimity from her morning meditation. Two cups of hours-old brew helped the process. When she got back to the office, Spiner was gone.

"Detective Spiner was less than pleased with my suggestions," Rena said, not looking up from her computer keyboard. She hit print.

"What an ass," Jadz muttered under her breath.

"Excuse me?"

"Him, not you. Get anything useful?"

Rena passed Jadz an updated spreadsheet. "Not much. There are similarities, but something seems off."

"Such as?" Jadz asked as she reviewed the new data.

"For starters, Adams has, or had, a boyfriend, long-term, whom Detective Spiner suspects. And no rose was found at the scene."

"Well, we kept the rose detail out of the papers for a reason. Do we have a name on the boyfriend?" When Rena nodded, Jadz added, "Spiner can't keep us from talking to him. If he's a suspect in one, he's a suspect in all."

"Bradford Stanley. He already has an attorney."

"That was fast. She died when?"

"Early Tuesday morning, around two. Detective Spiner called Mr. Stanley in for questioning yesterday afternoon. He brought his lawyer and the interview was delayed so they could consult."

"Let's call the lawyer and set something up."

"He has retained Linda Bulger. She expects us in her office at four." Rena smiled. "Great minds."

"But why her office? If he's a suspect, Spiner should haul him in."

"Detective Spiner is accommodating Bulger's court schedule. If she has to drive to Swanton, it will be later in the week and he is not the patient type."

"Guess we have that in common," Jadz said.

The detectives reviewed Swanton's report in preparation for the meeting, but Spiner's scanty notes provided little encouragement. "Could be he's our guy and thought the earlier deaths would mask his real intention. It's not unheard of," Jadz said as they walked two blocks to Bulger's office in the Spitzer Building. "A stretch, I know, but I'm ready to believe anything at this point."

Rena punched the elevator button. "It does seem unlikely, but possible. Maybe he will confess this afternoon and Detective Spiner will have more reason to dislike us."

They exited the elevator on the seventh floor and found Spiner waiting for them, anger giving his haggard face a dangerous flush. He confronted Jadz as she stepped off.

"Bulger called me. Trying to pull an end run by horning in on my interview? I told your partner here this was my case, my witness."

"And if the cases are connected, he's our witness, too," Jadz said, meeting him head-on.

Rena stepped between them. "We all want to stop these murders. A little teamwork—"

"Don't give me that teamwork crap," Spiner said. "This is my case. You want to listen in while I question this guy, fine. I'll let you in the room. But keep your mouths shut."

Bulger opened her office door. "Detectives. A bit loud out here. Why don't you come in where it doesn't echo quite so much?"

Stanley's face paled when they entered the room. "Who are you?" he asked Jadz and Rena.

"Apparently there was a miscommunication," Bulger said. "I'm sure someone will explain why Toledo Police is interested in a Swanton suicide?" She directed her question to Rena.

Spiner interrupted, and he shifted from the belligerent tone he used in the hallway to a gruff professionalism. "They're here to observe, nothing more, just to be sure Felicia's death isn't connected to a case they're working." He sat down facing Stanley and the attorney, leaving Jadz and Rena to find seats behind him. "Mr. Stanley, why don't you tell me what happened Tuesday night?"

Stanley looked to Bulger for direction. When she nodded her consent, he said, "It was Felicia's birthday. We were supposed to have dinner on the patio at Shucker's. I called ahead and everything." His voice cracked.

"Take your time," Spiner said.

Jadz caught Rena's glance and shrugged.

Stanley cleared his throat and continued. "Just before six, I got called back to work. One of the servers went down and it started a cascade failure. Took us all night to get the network back on line."

"Computer stuff, right? Where do you work?" Spiner asked.

"I'm assistant IT manager at Owens-Illinois, out at Levis Commons," he said. OI is one of the reasons Toledo has been called the "Glass Capital of the World" since the early 1900s. The company is one of the world's largest glass producers, but they still maintained their headquarters in metro Toledo.

"You had other people working with you?

"Probably half a dozen of us at Levis, another two or three in satellite offices."

"How did you find out she was dead?" Spiner asked.

Stanley swallowed visibly. His words were strained. "Felicia's mom called, found me at work after you guys called her. I could hardly understand her she was so hysterical."

Spiner continued the questioning, drawing out more details of the relationship between Stanley and Adams. After five years together, he planned to propose at the birthday dinner. Stanley displayed a full-carat diamond ring still in the Osterman Jeweler's box. When Spiner shifted to the possibility of suicide, Stanley's voice grew defensive.

"Felicia wouldn't do that. We were happy."

"There were no signs of forced entry," Spiner said. "Who did she let in?"

"I don't know, but somebody must have. Maybe whoever killed all those women in Toledo. Can't you check fingerprints or something?" Stanley rested his elbows on his knees, turning the ring box over and over in his hands. He seemed hypnotized by the plush sheen.

"We are, and we'll need you to come to the station so we can take a set."

Stanley jerked upright. "What for?"

"It's routine," Bulger said. "So they can eliminate your prints from any we found."

"There were prints found at the scene?" Jadz spoke up, earning a glare from Spiner. He ignored her question and turned back to Stanley.

After another twenty minutes gathering contact information for family, friends, and Adams' employer, all which Rena made note of behind Spiner's back, the interview ended.

"The sooner you can provide those prints, the better," Spiner said as he shook hands with Stanley. "And I'm sorry for your loss."

Spiner was quiet until the elevator doors closed on the detectives. "I told you to be quiet in there. I don't need your interference." His anger boiled over. "It's a damn suicide, and you want to make out like you know more about crime scenes than I do. I told the chief not to bring Toledo into this."

"Why are you so sure it was a suicide?" Rena asked. Her quietness brought Spiner's temper down a notch.

Jadz stayed back controlling her own anger and let Rena handle him. *This partner thing has its benefits.*

Spiner breathed heavily and wiped a hand across his damp forehead. Weak air conditioning amplified the rising humidity. "Like I said, no forced entry, prints everywhere, nothing wiped down and it doesn't match your guy's MO. Plus his alibi checks out. I tracked it down this morning after talking to Adams' mother."

"You read our reports?" Jadz couldn't contain her surprise.

"'Course I read 'em." He scowled at Jadz. "I don't have the luxury of working only one case like you, but I do my job. This is a suicide, plain and simple. She probably read about the others, related to the whole being-a-spinster-at-forty thing, and turned on the gas. End of story."

"But she had Stanley," Jadz said.

Rena cut off Spiner's retort. "If you do not mind, please keep us informed of your progress. Lieutenant Forester will insist on our follow-up."

Mollified by her reference to appeasing their supervisor, Spiner said, "Yeah, whatever. Just keep it quiet, so maybe we don't end up in the papers like you guys. *The Blade*'s really doing a number on you two."

At the curb outside the Spitzer Building, Rena stopped Spiner as he got into his car. "When is the autopsy?"

"Tomorrow morning. I'll let you know if anything turns up."

"Gee, thanks," Jadz called after his departing vehicle.

Back at the station, Jadz read through Swanton's report one more time. Nothing from Stanley's interview conflicted with the official version. She tossed the file aside in disgust. "I really thought we had something."

"Too many inconsistencies," Rena said. "No drugs that we know of, no rose, a boyfriend with an alibi. As frustrating as it is, Detective Spiner may be right. She mimicked the other deaths for reasons we will never know."

"But she didn't leave a note."

"Few suicides do, you know that." Rena checked the time. "I think we are done for today."

Friday was another fruitless day. Rena left early to be with her mother. Jadz's edginess as she prowled the bureau drew less-than-flattering comments from her fellow detectives. She overflowed the coffee pot, jammed the copier, and yanked a stuck file drawer so hard its contents dumped onto the floor.

"Get out of here, Jadz," Forester said as she scooped up the papers. "Go find a meth dealer to bust or something. Come in tomorrow to make up for it. Maybe you'll have your head on straight by then."

Jadz stepped out of Toledo Police headquarters into the blinding afternoon sun. She brushed past a scruffy street person huddled in the entrance alcove stealing a bit of coolness from the air conditioning which burst out of the building when the heavy glass doors swung open.

"Afternoon, Detective, ma'am."

"Excuse me?" Jadz pulled back instinctively as the old woman followed her down the sidewalk, keeping an arm's length between them.

"I hear yer lookin' for a real badass, killin' lots of defenseless women in their beds," she said as she leered at Jadz. "Buy me sumtin t'eat, I might help ya snag 'em."

"How do you know about my case?" Jadz asked. She edged into the sliver of shade offered by the slanted awning to block the glare. "Do I know you?"

"Not so's you'd remember, prolly, but this here's been my corner since that bastard slum lord tore down my building six years ago." The woman drew herself up and arranged her tattered, too-large jacket on her thin shoulders. Like many homeless, she carried her entire wardrobe on her back to prevent pilfering. "I don't go to them shelter places less'n it's too cold ta spit."

"What makes you think you know anything about the murders?" Jadz was intrigued.

She grunted. "I know lots more'n most give me credit." The woman leaned closer. "And secrets? You don't know the half. 'Specially 'bout him." She nodded toward a uniformed officer pulling a cruiser out of the lot next to them.

Jadz stepped into the shadows as she recognized Nathan heading out for second shift. "His secrets I don't need."

When Nathan was gone, Jadz turned to the woman who hovered at her side. "What's your name?"

"Catherine."

"Your friends call you Cathy?"

She drew herself up as tall as her short frame could reach. "Not if they want to stay friends. Don't have much left but my name, and it's Catherine."

"Okay then, Catherine. C'mon, I could use some coffee."

The woman parked her shopping cart in the bushes outside the city building next to police headquarters and followed Jadz to the deli at Huron and Jackson. Jadz waited while Catherine polished off a burger and fries at the counter before asking any more questions. She signaled the server to top off both coffee cups and took Catherine to a now-empty booth in the corner.

"What do you know about the murders?" Jadz asked.

Catherine ducked her head and squinted at Jadz. "I hear things."

"What things?" Years on the task force grooming informants gave Jadz the patience to play the game.

"There's a guy, follows 'em home. Kiss 'n kill." Catherine slurped her coffee.

Jadz hid her surprise. The lipstick mark had been kept out of the papers for a reason. "What guy?"

Catherine slouched low and peered outside. "Don't know, just a guy. Can't say too much. Almost forty myself, ya know. I could be next."

"Catherine, you're at least sixty, come on."

She sat up and tossed her head, brushing strings of black hair out of her face. "I was forty once. Real beauty, too. He coulda' come after me."

"Nobody's coming after you." Jadz studied her companion. She probably had been attractive at one time. Behind the silver-streaked hair, Jadz caught a glimpse of sharp green eyes that seemed to fade in and out of a reality no one else could see. High cheekbones framed a narrow face now drawn and gray from hard years on the streets. Layers of mismatched clothing hid Catherine's frame, but Jadz guessed she was no more than five two, maybe a hundred pounds without all the rags. Her long fingers jittered non-stop, tapping the coffee spoon and swirling the dregs in the bottom of the cup.

"Tell me about the kiss," Jadz said.

Catherine froze. "I ain't been kissed, not in a long time."

"Not you, Catherine. Those women. Tell me about the kiss."

She fidgeted for another minute, dumping cream into the remnants of her coffee and gulping the murky results. "I was at Saint V's, outside the ER, when they brought her in. She was already dead."

"Who was dead?"

"The library lady. I read it in the paper. She worked at the library."

"Marianne Summers? Yeah, she was a librarian." Jadz flagged down the server for more coffee and forced herself to wait for Catherine.

"Madam Librarian …" Catherine whispered under her breath. "*Music Man*'s always been my favorite. My daddy took me to see it. He was handsome, my daddy, just like that Preston guy in the movie."

"Catherine." Jadz prodded gently. "What about the kiss?"

"I heard the medics when they brought the librarian to Saint V's. 'Forty years old and finally been kissed,' they said. They laughed." She snorted. "I didn't think it was funny."

So much for keeping a secret. An ambulance crew blowing off steam, a too-easily-overlooked homeless person in the shadows. "All you know is what you heard at the hospital?"

Catherine's eyes filled with tears. Her voice took on a petulant tone. "You mad at me? I didn' mean no harm. Just hungry, is all, and you—" Catherine wiped her face with the back of her sleeve.

"What about me?" Jadz asked.

"You look like my Lucy," she said. "Lucy in the sky …" Her off-key singing faded away.

Jadz sat with Catherine for another half hour, plying her with coffee and pie à la mode. She listened to disjointed stories of Catherine's home on Utah Street, torn down to make room for a bypass, of a reluctant husband who left for work one day and never came back, and of her daughter Lucy.

"She was my baby," Catherine said, brushing back tears. "She died, just like that library lady, 'cept she didn't make it to forty."

"How did Lucy die?" Jadz asked.

Catherine scowled. "Bastard took a tire iron to her, said she was running around on him. He was the one couldn't keep his fly zipped." She swept the empty coffee cup off the table in anger. It shattered, quieting the few customers and bringing the server running.

Jadz waved him off. "I'll take care of it." She stacked the pieces on the table, tossed a twenty next to the check, and led Catherine outside.

"You mad at me?" Catherine asked again. "I made a mess."

"Don't worry about it." Jadz handed Catherine a twenty. "Get yourself some dinner later, okay? And try the Sparrow's Nest. It's not bad for a shelter."

Catherine stuffed the bill into her pocket. "Lucy's husband, he was like your old man, cattin' around." She grabbed Jadz's hand. "Don't let him hurt you like Lucy was."

Jadz was caught by Catherine's unexpectedly lucid gaze. *How much does she hear when people simply ignore her existence?* "He won't, I promise." Jadz squeezed her hand before pulling free.

Catherine nodded. "Okay, then." She wrestled her shopping cart out the bushes and trudged down the street.

A cruiser was parked outside the apartment building when Jadz got home shortly after five. Nathan.

"Aren't you supposed to be in your own district?" she asked as he entered the parking garage.

"I was on an escort. Keep your shirt on."

"What do you want?"

"You promised we'd talk. Can't we go inside?"

"No. And you're on duty." Jadz leaned against her car and waited.

"So meet me after. You can't just divorce me without hearing me out." Nathan shuffled his feet and stared at the ground.

How did we get to this point? Memories of their years together ran through her mind. The initial, intense spark that brought them together after a dangerous high-speed pursuit and shooting during training. An intimate family wedding on the beach at Maumee Bay State Park eighteen months later. Three years of a passionate marriage with little else to support the relationship, followed by a slow decline into unrelenting discord. Jadz caught Nathan's woebegone expression and caved.

"Alright, after. Mulvaney's?" Jadz asked.

His eyes lit up and she regretted her impulse even before he could respond.

"Mulvaney's it is."

Jadz dodged his kiss, catching only a brush of his lips on her hair. He trotted back to his cruiser whistling.

"Nathan," Jadz called before he reached the car.

He turned back with an eager expression that tore at Jadz.

"Do you remember a domestic homicide about ten years ago?" she asked. "Guy took a tire iron to his wife."

His face fell, but he answered readily. "Yeah, just after I started on east side patrol. Yondota Street, I think. Why?"

Why indeed? "Somebody mentioned it," she said. "Did you work it?"

"Wasn't my case, but they caught the guy in the act, so there wasn't much work, either. What's up?"

"What makes a couple go from loving each other enough to get married, to—that? I mean, I've seen enough domestics in my time, but damn, a tire iron." Jadz collected herself. "Never mind, go back to work."

"You sure?" Nathan asked.

Jadz shifted from one foot to the other. She moved a few steps away. Unspoken regrets hung in the thick humid air as Jadz faced the man she'd promised to love "as long as we both shall live."

"You're not comparing them to us, are you?" Nathan's words were low.

"Not … no, not the violence, but—" She met his eyes and held them. "I still wonder what happened. To us."

Nathan's radio crackled to life. "Paul-37, take a 10-50, three vehicles, Front and Main. No injuries reported."

"Paul-37 en route," he said into his shoulder mic. "I gotta go," he told Jadz. "Sure you're okay?"

"Go. I'll see you later."

After unloading the few groceries she'd picked up on the way home, Jadz changed into her biking gear. She dodged the tail end of rush hour traffic en route to the MetroPark. Half a dozen laps of furious pedaling left her physically exhausted but still mentally wound. On the ride home, she pushed aside whirling thoughts of murder and focused on the meeting with Nathan.

How do I convince him it's over when I don't understand it myself? Through a shower, dinner, and a few household chores, an answer eluded her. Jadz left for Mulvaney's Pub at eleven with no idea what she would say when Nathan arrived.

The pub was crowded with off-duty officers trickling in at shift change. Jadz joined in with the grousing and departmental gossip, glad of the distraction. A glass of wine to relax and Jadz was ready to resolve things with Nathan.

Her cell buzzed at five to midnight.

"Jadz? Can you hear me?" Traffic noises drowned out Nathan's words.

Jadz plugged her free ear and escaped to the relative quiet of the ladies' room. "What? Try again."

"... six-cars ... one dead ... be here all night." Even with all the interference, his disappointment came through.

"Call me tomorrow," Jadz said. "And Nathan—" The line went dead before she finished, and their routine closing echoed through the empty stalls. "Be careful out there."

Chapter 4

Jadz was on the phone when Rena arrived in the office Saturday morning. Jadz mouthed, "My treat," and pointed her to the Sufficient Grounds cups waiting on the desk.

Rena nodded her thanks and doctored her coffee while she waited.

"Uh-huh, sure, I'll hold." Jadz cupped her hand over the mouthpiece. "Northwood had a suspicious death last week. Same MO. The coroner picked up on it and—Yes, I'm here. Hi, Paul. What have you got? Can we get a copy of your report? Even better. We'll fill you in when you get here. Thanks."

Jadz hung up. "That makes four, if we don't count Adams. And they're getting closer together."

"Closer in time, but further afield," Rena said. "The Northwood officer is on his way here, I take it?"

"About half an hour. He has to brief his chief first."

"Lieutenant Forester said he might be in later. I will call him." Rena reached for the phone.

"Can't that wait until we've talked to Paul?"

"I will keep it short." She paused in the middle of dialing and added, "Look at it as earning Brownie points to offset your next confrontation."

Jadz chuckled. "You win. I'll go make another set of report copies so Northwood can have it. Give Forester my love."

Detective Tomas Garcia followed Jadz into the copy room. "Looks like you're getting along with Miser pretty well." He leaned against the copier while she entered the keypad combination.

"Don't call her that," Jadz said. "Rena's okay when you get to know her. And we work together just fine." As she got the sequence of commands straight and the machine hummed into action Jadz said, "She's smart, has great insight, and given half a chance, a sense of humor."

"Wow, an admirer in only what, a week? She must be something."

"Oh, give me a break."

The wiry detective shrugged. "Whatever you say. I've never heard two words from her, and we've been in Homicide together for almost five years."

"Have you tried?"

"Like it's my fault she's anti-social." He pushed away from the copier and started back to his desk. "Women. Always stick together, don't you?"

She flipped an obscene gesture at his departing back and drew a snicker from his partner. Garcia turned to catch her in the act, returned the salute, and went back to work.

The copier jammed on one of the carbonless sheets and Jadz spent several minutes trying to rescue the page without shredding it. She freed the offending document and stacked the new copies on the desk as the Northwood detective appeared.

Jadz made the introductions. "Do you know each other? Rena Castillo, Paul Wiley from Northwood. He was at the academy with me."

"I think we met on a robbery case last year," Paul said to Rena's nod of greeting.

"May I see your file?" Rena asked.

"That copy's for you," he said.

Rena handed him their updated spreadsheet in return. "What do you make of this?"

Paul studied the comparisons, adding notes for the fourth victim when they matched a category. "I don't see a connection other than the age," he said. "Have you found anything else?"

"Nada." Jadz gave him the highlights of their work so far. "I even checked out some guess-your-birthday booths at local festivals, but that doesn't fit either." She left out the details of her ill-fated adventure with Jimmy and Rena didn't elaborate.

"The MO matches, right down to the rose on the nightstand," Paul said.

"More than we can say for Swanton." Jadz gave Paul a summary of the Adams case.

Rena returned his file along with the copies Jadz made of the TPD reports. "We are fortunate the coroner caught the similarities. Apparently we need to send our alert to more areas."

"Nah, I just got back from vacation. Your notice was buried on my desk," Paul said. "I'd have found it eventually."

Jadz flipped through the Northwood report. "Sure hate to think this guy gets around too much."

"What's next?" Paul asked. "I can take you to our crime scene, but it's been picked over pretty well by state forensics."

Jadz glanced at her watch. "How about lunch? We can talk while we eat." While they waited for the elevator, Jadz asked, "What sounds good? We had George's yesterday."

"My car's out front," Paul said. "Let's go to Frisch's."

Rena grimaced. "Could we not? I always get heartburn."

"Easy Street? Or Mano's?"

It was Paul's turn to make a face. "Not Greek. Reminds me of my last unfortunate encounter with ouzo."

"Easy Street it is," Jadz said.

Traffic lights didn't slow Paul. He made the half-a-dozen city blocks to the corner bar and grill in a white-knuckle two minutes.

"I see you still drive like the devil's on your tail, don't you?" Jadz staggered in exaggerated panic as she climbed out of the back seat.

He snorted. "I remember a prisoner transport that broke a land speed record with you at the wheel."

"That was in my younger, wild days," she said, waving him off.

The good-natured banter continued throughout lunch, but it took Rena several minutes to join in the camaraderie. After Jadz and Paul recounted yet another practical joke, Rena said, "My days at the academy were not nearly as enjoyable. All I recall were long hours and difficult instructors, and that obstacle course."

"That thing was a killer," Jadz agreed. "It took me all three tries to pass it."

"Wimps," Paul said. "Afraid of physical exertion, maybe a little sweat." He twisted away from the punch Jadz aimed at his shoulder. "Okay, sorry, just kidding." When the server approached with the lunch checks, he snatched all three of them. "You two are going to make me look good with the chief when you solve this case."

Their exuberance dimmed with his reminder of the work that brought them together and the ride back to the station was subdued.

"I have an interview on another case this afternoon," Paul said as he dropped them in front of the police department. "If you find anything new, give me a call." He pulled away from the curb with a squeal for Jadz's benefit.

Rena met Jadz at the stairwell and they crossed the hall together, stopping short at the door to the detective bureau. The room was deserted.

"Where is everybody?" Jadz asked.

Rena indicated a poster on the wall near the door. "I would imagine they have gone to Fifth Third Field for the Police Athletic League baseball outing."

"I forgot about that." Jadz shoved the files together and stowed them in her briefcase. "I'm supposed to chaperone." She was on her way out the door when she realized she was alone. "Aren't you going to the game?"

"I am not involved in PAL."

"We can always use another body, preferably an adult one. Come on, it's a great day for baseball."

"I should work on our report." Rena's excuse failed since Jadz had the case files.

"Nothing more to report till Monday, so come for the popcorn and hot dogs," Jadz said. "No beer today, because of the kids, but there'll be a get-together at Fricker's after the game."

She took Rena's continued hesitation for agreement and hustled her out the door. "We'll have a great time and forget about murder for a few hours. Trust me."

The Toledo Mud Hens Stadium at Fifth Third Field buzzed with activity when Jadz and Rena pushed through the Madison Avenue turnstile. Jadz led Rena toward PAL's lively group in the left field stands.

As Jadz had promised, for the next two hours they lost themselves in the children's contagious joy. When the youngsters learned Rena had never been to a Mud Hens game, Max, a ten-year-old in dreadlocks and an oversized baseball jersey, took charge.

"I can tell you everything you need to know about baseball," he told Rena. His elaborate explanation of balls and strikes, fielding techniques, and batter's errors, kept her occupied for several innings. "Playing small ball," he said. "That's what they call it in the big leagues." When her cell phone buzzed at the top of the fifth inning, she excused herself to take the call in the relative quiet of the concourse.

Rena returned a few minutes later and pulled Jadz aside. "I just spoke to the coroner," she said. "The DNA test on Summers is pointless. There is not enough material for a valid comparison."

"Damn," Jadz muttered. "We need to call Forester."

"I already spoke to the lieutenant. He agrees nothing can be done until Monday." Rena grinned. "He said to tell you to enjoy the rest of the game."

"Are you kidding me?" Jadz's response made Rena laugh.

"I told you he is human." Rena waved to Max, who was watching for her. "Maybe I am, too." Rena tossed Jadz a foil bag. "Here, I bought you the Cracker Jacks you wanted." She returned to her seat next to the youngster and asked, "What have I missed?" He launched in to a play-by-play to rival Bob Costas at his best.

Jadz stood for several minutes watching the pair, pondering Rena's odd comment on being human. "Heads up!" someone shouted. A fly ball ricocheted off a nearby pole and bringing Jadz's attention back to the game. She set aside thoughts of murder and lost herself in the children's enthusiasm.

After the crowd finished a rowdy, off-key chorus of "Take Me Out to the Ballgame", the off-duty police chaperones helped herd the kids onto the TARTA buses lined up on Madison Avenue. "I love you, Miss Rena!" Max shouted, waving frantically as they drove off.

She returned the wave. "I love you, too, Max."

Jadz touched her arm. "Hey, there are still two innings left in the game. My daddy always taught me to stay till the last out, no matter who's winning." They settled in to the now deserted left field stands to watch the rest of the game and shared a box of popcorn. A companionable silence stretched between them as thoughts kept at bay by the children's energy now resurfaced.

Jadz's mind wandered from Nathan, to Rena's emotional thaw, to her father's love of baseball. "Watch how the catcher frames the ball," he told her during one of their many outings. "He shifts just a little to the right after the pitch for a slider, and pulls it back center so the ump is more likely to call a strike." The mental aspects of the game fascinated him, and he took great satisfaction in sharing them with his younger daughter. *One more inning, Dad.*

Rena barely noticed the ballplayers. Her emotions churned, dredging up memories long since buried of a sunny afternoon twenty-five years earlier.

"C'mon, My-own," her father coaxed, using the pet name her mother hated. "Come to baseball with me. The sun is shining. There will be hot dogs and ice cream. It will be good for you to be outside away from your books."

"Daddy, you know Mother would not like that," she said, even then echoing the disapproval her mother so often directed at him. "School starts in a few weeks and I want to be ready. I am a college student now. There is no time for childish games." He gave up and went alone, as usual. Rena was so absorbed in her studies she didn't notice his disappointment. It was the last time he ever invited her to a game.

The Mud Hens' final out brought Jadz and Rena back from very different memories, and they fumbled for reality.

"Thanks for helping out today," Jadz said as they inched through the crowd to the gates. "The kids really like you."

"It was my pleasure."

"PAL can always use more volunteers."

"I have other commitments. Thank you for asking."

"There'll be a group at Fricker's if you'd like to come," Jadz said.

"I must get home. I can walk back to the station. Unless something else happens, I will see you Monday morning." Rena melted into the crowd streaming up Superior Street.

What just happened here? Things had gone so well all afternoon. Rena had seemed to enjoy the children, and the game. *Maybe I misread things.* Jadz walked the few blocks to Fricker's alone in a puzzled fog.

The distraction offered by the raucous gathering of officers in the sports bar brushed away the gloom. A glass of wine, good companions, and Jadz gave herself up to the moment. Nathan's arrival caused a momentary tension, but he raised a glass in her direction and kept his distance. Relieved, she sought out the bartender for a refill and perched on a stool to wait.

"So, Detective, leaving the city unprotected?"

Jadz scowled at *The Blade* reporter hovering at her elbow. "Don't you ever take a day off?"

"Not with a serial killer running around." Dixon stumbled as he set his beer mug on the counter.

"What makes you think that?" she asked. "There's been a couple of deaths, nothing for you to fret about." Jadz sipped her replenished wine and willed the reporter under the bar rather than at her side.

"That's not what I hear." He leaned in closer. "C'mon, Jadz, you can tell me. How bad is it? I hear half a dozen women, attacked in their beds. Some kind of pervert?"

Jadz nearly choked on the Riesling. "Where the hell do you get your information? The only pervert in the room is you."

"And half the guys on the force," Patrol Sergeant Theo Baxter said as he perched onto the stool next to the reporter. "Making a pest of yourself again, Dix?"

"Damn, Sarge, sneaking up behind a guy like that!" Dixon scrubbed at a damp spot on his sleeve. "Waste of good beer, too." He eyed the officers. "So you two spend a lot of time together these days?"

"Not nearly enough," Theo said. "Take a hike. The detective and I need to talk."

Theo steered Jadz toward a vacant high-top across from the bar.

"What a jerk." Jadz slid onto a tall chair in the corner. "Thanks for the rescue."

"He's just doing his job, I guess," Theo said, "but he doesn't know when to quit."

"So were you at the game? I didn't see you." They compared notes on the rookie pitcher's outstanding debut. "I think the Hens have a shot at the playoffs this year, if Leyland doesn't need the best of them in Detroit," Jadz said.

"Could be." Theo took a deep breath. "Look, Jadz—"

"What did you want to talk about?" Her words overran his. "Sorry." She pushed the wineglass away. "I need a decent meal. Popcorn and Cracker Jacks don't cut it. Go ahead, I'm listening."

He shifted on the stool. "If I'm off base, say so, but I'd like to see more of you. I mean, off-duty, as real people. Could we have dinner sometime?"

Jadz caught her breath.

"I know you were with Solomon for a while, but I hear that's pretty much over. I could be wrong. I thought maybe we could get together, see how things go." His awkward rambling faded off.

"I need food. Do you want anything?" She flagged down a server and ordered spicy garlic chicken chunks and a salad.

"Burger and fries," Theo added. When the server was gone, he said, "This is probably a bad time."

Jadz closed her eyes, searching for words. "It's not that," and opened them to find Nathan weaving his way towards their table. She reached for her wine glass, draining it.

"We're supposed to talk," Nathan said as he tripped into Jadz.

"Not now, maybe tomorrow." She shifted away from him.

"Always tomorrow." Nathan wavered around to Theo. "Puttin' the moves on my girl, Baxter?"

"I'm not your girl, Nathan." Jadz beat a gentle tattoo against the wall with her head and counted to ten.

Theo shoved a stool towards him. "Sit down before you fall down, Solomon."

Nathan climbed onto the stool. "What're you doing with my wife?"

Theo sputtered into his beer.

"I am not your wife anymore." Jadz tried to figure out what karma she attracted to bring this about. "Theo, Nathan and I were married for almost six years. It's over."

"Not yet s'not," Nathan said, slurring his words. "I have ten days to change your mind."

"Why ten days?" Theo brow furrowed with his effort to keep up with the conversation.

"We've been separated for almost a year, and the final divorce hearing is a week from Wednesday," Jadz said.

"Not if I can help it." Nathan's argument was undercut by the weaving in his posture.

She ignored him. "He thinks I'm going to back out at the last minute, but I'm not." The last words were flung at Nathan. "I've told you more times than I can count. It's over."

Theo stood up. "Maybe I should leave you two alone to work this out."

"No." Jadz caught his arm. "Don't go. Nathan was just leaving."

"I am not."

"You are, if I have to pour you into a cab myself." She reached for her cell phone.

Nathan slid off the stool. "Don't bother. I can fin' my own way home." He glared at Jadz for a long minute, and lurched against Theo as he left the table. "You have no idea what you're up against." Nathan staggered back to his buddies and collapsed into a chair.

Jadz shoved the phone back in her pocket and cradled her head in her hands. "What a nightmare." Theo sat watching her, silent. "I am so sorry," she said. "You didn't deserve that scene."

The server arrived with their meals, but Jadz could only pick at her salad.

"How were you two married for so long and I never knew?" Theo asked, his food untouched.

"We kept it quiet to avoid department problems. Seemed like a good idea at the time." Jadz was relieved to see Nathan's buddies help him to the door and into a cab. "He just won't let go."

"Why the breakup? If you don't mind my asking."

She laughed shortly. "You of all people have a right to ask, after all that." Jadz shoved the salad aside and attacked the chicken, forcing down a few bites. "He didn't like the hours I put in on the task force. He doesn't like being alone." She found herself making excuses for him. "Nathan isn't cut out for marriage. I guess I should have known. I was wife number three."

"He had a girlfriend," Theo said. "That wasn't a secret."

"Several actually, over the years, and it was news to me." Jadz gave up trying to eat. "When I found out about the last one, he thought telling me about the others would make it okay, like it was a hobby or something." She stared out at the darkening sky. "Seems the department is really good at keeping all kinds of secrets."

Awkward silence stretched as the party around them wound down. Jadz nodded absently when the server asked if she wanted her food boxed for take-out, and was surprised when the container appeared on the table.

"I guess I should be going," Theo finally spoke. "Looks like that rain might be on the way and I left my windows open." He reached for Jadz's dinner tab, pulled back, and said, "See you around, okay?"

"Sure, thanks. And—" she caught herself. "I'm sorry."

Theo sketched a wave and left.

Jadz unlocked her apartment door a little after eight. Storm clouds blocked the last rays of the evening sun, but the rumbles of thunder were still miles off. A perturbed Ford greeted her with a loud meow. "Hungry, are you?" She scooped the tabby into her arms and crooned to him softly while she filled his water and food dishes. When he began nibbling his dinner, Jadz tended to the few housekeeping chores needed to keep her tiny home livable. She ran a dust cloth over the bookshelves and desk, swept the floor, and filled the dishwasher, setting it on a delayed cycle. A hot shower removed the ballpark grime and by nine-thirty, Jadz was curled on the sofa with a cup of Irish coffee, accumulated mail, and the latest book on her self-prescribed Great Classics reading list. Ford snuggled at her feet, purring himself to sleep.

A reminder from the apartment manager that the lease expired in sixty days raised a new set of possibilities. *Really should think about buying a house now, being officially single again.* She added the letter to her to-do stack of bills and paperwork and vowed to make a decision soon. Jadz sipped the coffee, heaved *Atlas Shrugged* onto her lap, and found her bookmark. *Rand really could have used a lesson in brevity.* Just before eleven, her cell phone buzzed, jolting the silence. When Jadz saw the name on the screen, she hesitated, answering just before voice mail kicked in.

"What do you want, Nathan?"

"I want to apologize for earlier." Sincerity echoed in his voice, even through the alcohol-stoked ramble. "I was an ass. I overreacted. I embarrassed you."

"And Theo."

"And I really am sorry. Can I still see you tomorrow?"

Jadz closed her eyes, fighting the sudden return of exhaustion. "We should talk."

"About the future."

"We have no future." She tossed her book aside and sat up, startling Ford. "Only as friends, maybe, and co-workers. You need to accept that."

"Tomorrow, okay?" he asked. "We can work this out."

After another round of circular conversation, they agreed to meet at the Panera Bakery café on Talmadge at four in the afternoon. Jadz hung up first, cutting off another reconciliation attempt. She tried to return to *Atlas,* but gave up after rereading the same paragraph three times. She found a *Globetrekker* rerun on PBS and let the Australian outback distract her thoughts. When the credits rolled, she turned out the lights and went to bed, Ford curled at her side.

Chapter 5

The loneliness was suffocating him, perched on his chest like a malevolent ghoul, pressing the life out of him. It came more often these days, disrupting his thoughts more insistently as the milestone came and went. His twenty-year burden of guilt at not stopping her pain or preventing her death grew heavier each passing day. Music didn't help any longer, and all the anti-depressants and mood stabilizers were useless. His work, his only non-chemical lifeline all these years, eluded him, stamped out by the pills and alcohol. Sleep came only with more drugs. His only escape, the only way out of his anguish was to free another from pain. It created a new guilt, but it was more distant, somehow easier to bear. A part of him rebelled, but that part of his soul grew smaller and less effective with each escape. He fingered the slip of paper, studied the scrawled name, address, and date. It was time.

The doorbell jolted the woman's concentration from the evening paper. She checked her watch: ten-fifteen. A second buzz brought her to her feet.

"Who is it?" she asked through the security intercom.

"Josh McDaniel. We met last week? I hope I'm not intruding, but, well, I was on my way home from the gym and I kept thinking about what a crappy birthday it's been. I remembered meeting you, and sharing the same birthday and all, and, well, I hope I'm not intruding."

The attractive gentleman at the Bureau of Motor Vehicles had been attentive, flattering, making conversation while she waited for her new license.

"How did you find me?"

"Your address was on your license. You showed me your new picture, remember? And I'm cursed with a photographic memory. I'll leave if I'm bothering you. It's just—" A passing motorcycle drowned out his next words. "… should be something special, and I'd hate to see you spend it all alone, like me. I picked up a bottle of wine next door and thought maybe we could share a toast. That's all, honest."

The woman hesitated. He'd offered to share her misery at yet another lonely milestone. She hardly knew him, but it had been a rather disappointing fortieth birthday. One drink couldn't hurt … could it?

Chapter 6

The telephone rescued Jadz from a confusing dream involving Nathan, Theo and Forester, all chasing her through the darkened halls of the police station. Her eyes too blurry to see the ID pad, she cursed Nathan's persistence. "Do you have any idea what time … Oh, sorry, yes, this is she. Hold on, let me write that down." She fumbled in the nightstand for a pen and switched on the light. "Give it to me again. Okay, on my way. Twenty minutes tops. Have you called Detective Castillo? Thanks."

Jadz was out of bed and rummaging through her closet before the phone hit the bed where she tossed it. *Should have done laundry when I was cleaning.* She pulled out fresh slacks and a blouse, shedding her nightshirt as she entered the bathroom. A quick splash on her face, comb through the tangled red hair, and a cursory visit with the toothbrush took two minutes. Two more for dressing, one to find her keys and the phone which had burrowed into the sheets and she was out the door.

"Not bad for a three o'clock wake up," she muttered as she pulled out of the parking garage. Thick, splotchy raindrops drenched the night, and it took several seconds with the defogger on high to clear the dense haze on the windshield. She drove through the blur, checking her note for the address, and barely slowing for stop lights. Her dash bubble light cast eerie red shadows on the wet pavement as she sped through the deserted streets. Jadz slowed to check house numbers before spotting the fire department lights bouncing off the buildings around the next curve. She pulled in behind the ambulance. *At least Forester's not here.* Jadz dodged raindrops and the grumbles from bystanders as she ran into the building.

"Another happy crowd, I see," she said to the officer at the door as she shook off the rain.

"Fire chief evacuated the building again," he said. "Gas was pretty strong before we got here."

Jadz followed his directions to the second-floor apartment where the fifth victim waited. It was a repeat of the night in Summers' home. Different officers, different décor, but the rose on the table and the lingering gas odor highlighted the tragic—and deadly—similarities.

Rena arrived as the coroner was finishing up.

"Déjà vu all over again," Jadz said as the medics rolled the gurney past them.

"We could not have prevented it," Rena said.

"You sure about that?" Jadz clenched her jaw, biting back angry words.

"We did all we could."

"We could have warned them."

"Who? The entire county?" Rena frowned. "And how would you do that without causing a panic and sending our suspect underground where we will never find him?"

Jadz moved across the room, distancing herself. She raised the blinds to peer out over the rain-soaked parking lot. Residents were moving back into the building, huddled under umbrellas and holding jackets held overhead. A lone figure stood at the edge of the driveway, making no effort to shelter from the rain.

Jadz straightened. She squinted through the streaked pane trying to get a better view.

"What is it?" Rena asked over her shoulder.

"There, near the corner." Jadz dropped the blind back into place, blocking out the darkness. "He's gone. There was a guy standing alone, watching. No umbrella, just shirt sleeves. I couldn't see his face."

"Do you think the killer waited around? That would be foolish."

"I don't know what to think at this point. Arsonists like to watch, why not serial killers?"

Rena released the uniformed officers back to patrol, and after another two hours, they followed the forensics team out the door. Jadz locked the apartment, pocketed the keys, and after a short discussion with the building manager, headed downtown. Rena followed in her car, trailing Jadz through the quiet neighborhoods as sunlight broke through the morning clouds.

Jadz and Rena arrived to find Forester waiting for them in the otherwise empty detective bureau. "Morning, ladies," he said, feet propped on the worktable, coffee cup in hand. "Glad you could join me."

"How did you—" Jadz left the question unfinished.

"It's a good idea to keep everyone in the loop, don't you think?" he asked.

"Sure, whatever." Jadz busied herself emptying her briefcase and avoiding his gaze. "I thought you didn't like early morning calls."

"I don't." Forester dropped his feet to the floor. "But since I was still up, it wasn't so bad."

Jadz dropped the folder she was holding and papers scattered across the desk.

"Don't look so surprised," he said. "I do have a personal life."

"I never said you didn't."

"But you thought it." He turned to Rena. "Detective Sergeant Jadzinski thinks I'm an unfeeling, chauvinistic blow-hard who needs to be kept at arm's length." Forester waved Jadz's half-hearted protest aside and asked, "Detective Castillo, what do you think of your new partner's assessment? Am I a pig?"

"Not at all, sir," Rena said. "But in her defense, you have been rather hard on her."

"With good cause." Forester glared at them. "You two couldn't be more different, in personalities, in appearance, in how you handle a case, but you've clicked." He shook a finger at Jadz. "Know why I put you two together? So maybe Rena's sanity would rub off and you'd stop being such an ass. When you go off half-cocked, you're a menace. To the bureau, to the department, and to yourself. I hoped she'd show you it's not necessary to ride solo to get the job done. She's a loner, too, but she's not afraid to ask for help. You don't have to take stupid risks to prove yourself to me or anyone else."

"That's not fair." Jadz's voice shook with anger.

"Maybe," Forester said. "But it's true. You think I didn't have a long talk with Welch before approving your transfer?" He grunted at her reaction. "You think your little chat with the captain got you here? My twenty-three years as a cop carry a lot more weight than you realize. If I didn't want you in my division, you wouldn't be here."

Rena shifted awkwardly. "Lieutenant, maybe we could talk about the case."

"I'm not finished." Forester rolled on, standing now, and towering over Jadz. "Maybe we should have had this out six months ago. Welch keeps telling me you'll come around. Well, I'm tired of waiting. If you can't work within the rules and regulations of this department, guidelines that are there for a reason I might add, then go screw up someone else's division, not mine. And don't waste time pouting because you think I don't like you, that I'm mean and heartless or whatever other crap you use to justify your attitude. I know all about your antics in the task force and I won't stand for that here. We deal in life and death every damn day, not whether somebody wants to buy a pound of coke to shove up their nose. In Narcotics, maybe you have to create your own danger. Homicide throws it in your face, and it'll kick you in the ass if you're not careful."

"Damn, Lieutenant, breathe already," Jadz said. Her smoldering defensiveness gave way to a grudging realization that he was right.

He collapsed into the chair. "See what you do to my blood pressure?" Forester tossed his coffee cup in the trash and took a deep breath. "You're a good cop or you wouldn't be here," he said. "Stop being such pain in the ass and do your job. If I didn't think you were up to this case, I'd have reassigned you long ago. Rena's here so you have someone to bounce ideas off of, since you won't come to me." His raised hand stopped her objections. "I know, I know. We got off to a bad start. Let's try this again, okay?" He stood again and held out his hand. "Detective Jadzinski? I understand you go by Jadz, like your dad. Good man. Welcome to Homicide. I hear good things about you. I look forward to working together."

Jadz caught her breath. She rose to meet Forester's gaze and shake his outstretched hand. "Thank you, sir. The feeling is mutual."

As the specter of Forester watching over her shoulder vanished, Jadz tackled the investigation with renewed vigor. She added another column to the victim spreadsheet and Rena updated the information as initial reports on the latest homicide filtered in.

At eight o'clock, Jadz's cell phone rang.

"I hear you had another one," Paul said. "You in the office? Be there in ten."

Jadz hung up, puzzled. "Paul's on his way. He sounds awfully revved up about something."

"Good thing Sunday morning traffic is light," Rena said with a chuckle.

Paul blew through the door fifteen minutes later.

"You get lost?" Jadz asked.

He dropped a small plastic card on her desk and stood waiting while she examined it.

"A driver's license?" Jadz studied the data. "Who's Wrenn Herzog? Not another victim, I hope."

"My sister," Paul said.

"Not another victim," Rena repeated, her voice tense.

"Nope." Paul's eyes darted from Jadz to Rena as his smirk morphed to a grin.

"I don't get it," Jadz said. "Chalk it up to exhaustion, but what's your point?"

"She's thirty-six, just got her new license."

"And?"

"Check the renewal date."

"Four years." Realization hit. "Age forty." Jadz dropped the license and dug through the files. "I know we had printouts on the victims here."

Rena pulled a computer page from the folder on the first victim. "Number one, renewed eight days before her birthday."

"Here's number two, ten days before." Jadz grabbed the keyboard for the department computer system. "Let's get the driver's license record on the others."

"The first two were renewed at the same agency," Rena said, comparing the sheets. "Which registrar is 4828?"

"Paul, you're a genius. How did we miss this?" Jadz said. She hit print on the first record and started on the second.

He pulled a chair up to the desk, beaming. "Guess I owe Wrenn dinner. I was telling my brother-in-law about the case last night when she came in whining about the awful mug shot on her license, said something about having to live with it until she was forty."

"So you lifted her license?" Rena asked.

"I'll give it back."

Jadz returned from the printer with two pages of data. "They both renewed at the same place, registrar 4828 on Airport Highway. Ladies and gentlemen, we may have our link. Five victims renewed their driver's license at the same deputy registrar within two weeks of their deaths."

"What about Adams?" Rena asked.

Jadz shrugged. "She renewed two years ago for some reason. Spiner always said she was a suicide. Maybe he's right."

"So when do we hit the registrar?" Paul asked.

Jadz made a few calls, navigated through automated answering systems, and hung up annoyed. "The internal licensing system is down for maintenance until midnight."

"Can we reach the manager?" Rena asked.

"And ask him what? If he has a murderer on staff?" Jadz drummed her fingers on the desk. "If we can't get into the system, neither can he."

"She," Rena said, turning from her computer. "The registrar at Airport Highway is Jeanine Highsmith-Troyer. Home number is unlisted."

Jadz grinned. "I'm impressed. We can find a number, but like I said, ask him—I mean her—what?"

Rena kept working. "I have it." She made the call.

"There's got to be hard copies of their files somewhere," Paul said. He spun his chair around to scan the room. "Look at all the paper in this office. A state office like that has to be even worse."

"You'd be surprised," Jadz said. "So much of that stuff gets shredded once it's in the computer."

Rena hung up the phone. "The universe is not cooperating. Woodward is in the middle of an Alaskan cruise, not scheduled to return until next week. The office manager, a Kim Angelo, is at Cedar Point for the day. Her family will ask her to call us when she returns."

"She doesn't carry a cell?" Jadz asked.

"Apparently not today." Rena's face mirrored a shared frustration.

"So we wait until morning," Paul said. "Got any coffee?"

Forester stopped next to Rena's desk on his way out. "Something I need to know?"

Jadz looked to Paul. "It's your breakthrough. You tell him."

Paul handed Forester Wrenn's license and gave a rapid summary of the connection.

"Northwood's not in Lucas County," Jadz realized. "Why did number two renew her license way up on Airport Highway?"

"She worked at print shop over at Byrnegate Plaza, probably did it at lunch or something," Paul said.

"Good job, Wiley," Forester said as he returned the license. "Nice to see teamwork pay off. What's next?"

"We can't get anything from the registrar until tomorrow," Jadz said. "System's down, and the manager is out of town."

"Then get some rest. Street crews talked to all the neighbors already, so you can't do anything more until the coroner's done." Forester stretched. "It's been a long night for all of us."

"But—" Jadz bit back her objection.

"My guilt-laden partner fears we could have prevented this last death, and that there may be another," Rena said.

Forester shook his head. "Not an issue. Get rid of that thought right now before you drive yourself over the edge. We do what we can do, and I won't let you do less than your best." He ushered them out the door and into the elevator. "We'll get the bastard," he promised as they parted at the street.

After more thanks from Jadz and Rena, Paul left them standing at the curb.

"I've never seen Forester smile before today," Jadz said.

"He does, quite often actually," Rena said. "You have not noticed." She turned toward her car, adding, "Get some sleep. It was a short night."

"You, too," Jadz stood alone for a few minutes, watching the last of the thunderheads scud off to the east. The storm had passed.

The ringing phone shattered Jadz's dreamless sleep an hour later. She squinted at the clock. 1:35. The number on the caller ID turned her yawn into a groan.

"Hi, Mom." Jadz punched her pillows into a backrest and settled against the headboard. "Yes, I know what time it is. I had a late call. Channel eleven has a story on it? Wonderful. No, we don't know who's responsible. No, I really would not be happier as a teacher. What? Oh, damn—I mean, darn. I forgot. I'll call Steve now and get back to you." Jadz disconnected in the middle of her mother's scolding. She leaned her head back, eyes closed, and tried to focus. After a few minutes, when the prospect of facing the day didn't seem quite so insurmountable, she slipped out of bed, nearly tripping over Ford, and went in search of coffee. Her auto-start Bunn offered an almost fresh cup. Jadz gulped it down as she fed the annoyed cat and called her mechanic. Betty insisted on driving their Dad's beloved 1976 Jeep

CJ7 hardtop, but she had no clue how to care for it. That responsibility, like so many others, always fell to Jadz.

"I know it's Sunday, so if you can't get to it until tomorrow, she'll survive. You will? Thanks, you're a doll." Jadz hesitated. "And send me the bill."

She fortified herself with another cup of coffee before calling her mother back. "He'll be there around three. I don't care if it's convenient for her work-out schedule. He's doing us a favor by even looking at the car on a Sunday. I'm sure she appreciates the effort. I'll talk to you later. I have to get ready to meet Nathan."

Damn. Why did I say that?

"No, we're not getting back together. We're just clearing up details for Wednesday's hearing. I will not change my mind." She rolled her eyes at her mother's usual litany of Nathan's sterling character. "Then you marry him. Gotta go." She hung up, drained.

"And I've been out of bed a whole twenty minutes," she told Ford. He ignored her now that he had been fed, and curled up in a sunlit spot on the rug for a nap. Jadz did a quick mental calculation and decided she had time to fit in an over-due meditation session. She set the timer and stepped onto the tiny balcony overlooking what passed for a backyard off the parking lot. Ford meowed a protest when she slid the screen closed, locking him inside.

The early afternoon sun was warm on her upturned face. She folded her legs into the Half Lotus position, breathed deeply, and focused on emptying her mind. *Om.* As Jadz relaxed into her mediation, waves of contentment chased away the frustration of the past few weeks. For twenty minutes, nothing existed but the moment—not Nathan, not the department, not deranged serial killers. A helicopter buzzing overhead distracted her for a moment, but she brought her mind back into focus until the small Tibetan clock behind her on the desk chimed softly.

Half an hour and another cup of coffee later, Jadz was showered and dressed and on her way to Panera to meet her almost-ex. *I hope he at least plans to buy food.*

"It's a beautiful day," Jadz said when she arrived, turning her cheek to Nathan's proffered kiss. They made polite conversation about the weather, the baseball game, and work while they waited in line to order a late lunch. Jadz deliberately sat across the table even though he scooted over to make room next to him in the booth.

Nathan wasted no time. "I know I've hurt you, but I'm really sorry. I promise to do better." He reached for her hand, which she parked in her lap. "Give me a chance here."

"I have given you a chance. To apologize and to move on." Jadz gathered the calm courage she had recovered in her mediation.

"I went back to AA this morning," he said.

She measured her response. "Good for you."

"I realized when I saw you with Baxter, I had to. I screwed up. You were the best thing that ever happened to me." He swallowed hard. "And when you brought up that domestic homicide the other night … I can't stand thinking you're afraid of me."

"I'm not, but that whole thing got me thinking, too," Jadz said. "It's just over. We had a good run, some great times and some not so great. I learned a lot from you, about police work, about life, and about myself. Now we need to get on with our lives. Separately."

Nathan stared at her. "You really mean it, don't you? I thought you were just punishing me for Amy."

"And Fran, and Suzie, and Carol—" Jadz broke off he hung his head. "Sorry, I was trying to be cute. I'm not punishing you. We loved each other, once upon a time. And in some ways, probably always will." Their number squawked over the loudspeaker. She waited while he collected the order from the counter.

Nathan returned with the trays. "I need to tell you something, should have told you a long time ago. It's not an excuse, just an explanation."

She waited while he sorted out the food. He set a plate and bowl in front of her, added a napkin, centered the silver on top of it. His plate and silver were next, just as carefully placed. He made a second trip to the counter for more condiments.

"I know you like water with your meal," he said. "Is a fountain cup okay or should I get a bottle from the counter?"

"Nathan, sit down. What is it you want to say?"

Nathan sat. He fidgeted with his spoon for a long minute before speaking. "When I was eleven, I went to Jamboree in Valley Forge with the Boy Scouts. I'd never been away from home before, cried my eyes out the first night after lights-out, but after that it was amazing."

Jadz listened, bewildered, as Nathan talked. He stared past her.

"We got to shoot a bow and arrow, learned to use a compass, went canoeing. All the usual Boy Scout stuff, but it was fantastic. I'd never been out of the city before. The only mountain I'd ever seen was on *Death Valley Days*. I was the littlest kid from Toledo and the guys never let me forget it. When I won the knot-tying competition, one guy, Billy Walters, was pissed." Nathan took a gulp of coffee.

"The last day was a test of all the outdoor skills we'd learned. They gave us a map and a compass and turned us loose in the woods to find our way back to camp. I found out later Billy swapped the trail signs as a joke. I followed a side spur up the mountain, away from the pack." His hands shook with the retelling even thirty-five years later. "For two days I wandered around by myself until rescue teams found me over ten miles from camp. Billy apologized, sort of. Guess he was almost as scared as I was when I didn't show up. Almost."

Silence stretched between them as Jadz tried to make sense of his story.

"It was a month before I could sleep in my own room again," Nathan said. "I got really good at finding ways to not be alone." He ripped open the bag of chips on his tray, spilling the contents all over the table. "Amy, and all the rest, even the drinking, it kept me from facing the old fears."

Compassion struggled with anger at his secrecy for so many years. *Would it have mattered if I knew?*

"I said it's not an excuse." Nathan broke into her thoughts. "It's just … I don't want you to hate me."

"What an awful thing for a kid to deal with." Jadz mentally kicked herself for the lame response. "I guess I wish you had told me before now. Maybe it would have made a difference."

"Or not."

"And I don't hate you. I just can't live with you, not anymore."

"What about Thursday night?"

"That was a mistake. I was tired, and depressed. Forester was making my life miserable, Betty started drinking again and Mom expected me to rescue her. I needed a friend."

"So I'm still your friend." Nathan pounced on her words.

Jadz sighed. "Of course we're friends. Just not married, and no more nights like that."

"I'd like to make it up to you. I'd like to fix things."

"Why? Am I part of your Twelve Step now?" Nathan's expression stilled her rude humor. "That didn't come out right," Jadz said. "Let's eat, before I say something even more idiotic."

"I guess I deserved it."

"No, you didn't." She stirred her tepid soup. "I'm glad you're back in AA. You get stupid when you drink."

They finished the meal in silence, but more companionable and less tension-filled than they'd shared recently. Nathan handed her an extra napkin when she spilled her soup. She refilled their coffee and dumped the trays when the food was gone. They faced each other over the mugs and shared an awkward smile.

"So now what?" Nathan asked. "Is Baxter waiting in the wings?"

Theo. "You know we were at the academy together. We're friends." Theo's offer from Saturday evening didn't bear considering—yet.

"You're going to live alone with your goofy cat in that dinky little apartment?"

"Actually, I've been thinking about buying a house," she surprised herself by answering.

Nathan toyed with his mug. "You can have mine."

Jadz's eyes widened. "You don't mean that. That house has been in your family for sixty years. You love it."

"If I thought it would change things."

"It won't," she said. At his crestfallen expression, she softened. "But thanks for the offer. I'll find something when the time's right. In the meantime, Ford and I are happy where we are."

"Okay, then. I'd still like to fix things, but I guess that's it. I know when to quit." As Jadz smothered a smile, he laughed. "Eventually."

Nathan took his turn at coffee refills. When he returned, he said, "Dixon did a number on you in *The Blade* this morning. He quoted Forester defending you, though. Thought that was interesting, considering your run-ins."

"I realized this morning he might be human after all," Jadz said. "I've been so wrapped up in my problems I never gave him a chance. And Dixon's an ass."

"He's a good guy. Forester, not Dixon. He had a hard time when his wife died, rode the guys pretty hard for a while, but he's settled down."

"Wonder how I missed that."

"You were still a rookie, and he was in Internal Affairs. You know they don't mix with the rest of us much. Not too long after she died, maybe six, eight months later, he transferred to Homicide."

"Interesting." Jadz pushed her mug away. "Sometimes there's no privacy at all in the department, then other times, you find out there are all sorts of secrets."

Nathan scowled. "If you're talking about Amy—"

"I wasn't bringing that up again. I meant in general, things I've picked up on recently. Maybe secrets isn't the right word. More like hidden personalities." They carried the empty cups to the bus bins on the way to the door.

"Thanks for lunch," Jadz said when they were outside. She stood with a hand on her car door. "You don't have to come to court Wednesday, you know. Since there's no joint property or anything, the lawyers can handle it. My being there is only a formality."

"If I do come, I won't make a scene, promise. I guess I believe you now, but it'll take a while to sink in. Hearing a judge confirm it might help." He waited until she started the car and rolled down the window. "When you go after your killer tomorrow, be careful out there, okay?"

She smiled. "I will. And take care of yourself. I'll see you around." With a final wave, she left without a backward glance.

Chapter 7

After a full night's sleep with no disturbances for a change, Jadz was downtown by six Monday morning. Catherine unfolded herself from a bench across the street from the station and met her at the entryway.

"Had 'nother one, huh?" Catherine asked.

"Thought I told you to check out Sparrow's Nest." Jadz tucked her briefcase under one arm. She shifted her coffee cup to the other hand so she could help Catherine pull her shopping cart over the curb.

Catherine grimaced. "Wanted me to take a bath every night. Not healthy, all that scrubbing."

"I don't have time to visit this morning," Jadz said. "When did you eat last?"

"Yesterday noon maybe, Salvation Army. Or was it Good Sam's?" Her voice trailed off.

Jadz dug into her pocket and handed Catherine a ten. "Get some food. I'll talk to you later."

"She get kissed, too?" Catherine hollered at Jadz as she walked away.

"Hey." Jadz came back. "That's our secret, remember?"

Catherine clapped a hand over her mouth. "Sorry," she whispered. She trundled her cart north up Jackson Street to the soup kitchen on Bancroft, still muttering, "Sshh, our secret. Sshh!"

Jadz finished a review of BMV records as Rena arrived, followed by Forester and Paul. She printed out a list of personnel for the Airport Highway office and started preliminary background checks on the names.

"None of the registrar employees has a record in the local or federal databases," Jadz told them a few minutes later.

"Not surprised," Paul said as he handed out the coffee cups he'd brought in. "Probably couldn't get hired if they did."

"How do you want to approach the registrar?" Rena asked.

"You two go inside and talk to the manager. Rena and I will cover the entrances in case we flush out a suspect." Forester pulled back. "If that works for you, Jadz. It's your case."

She nodded, swallowing a grin.

They drove across town to Airport Highway in unmarked cars. Jadz fidgeted at being Rena's passenger and jumped out as soon as they pulled up to the registrar's office.

"Does my driving make you nervous?" Rena asked.

"Of course not," Jadz said. "Okay, maybe a little. But it's better than Paul's."

"That is not much of a compliment."

The license bureau occupied the end storefront of a strip mall. Rena and Forester positioned their cars with both exits visible but facing opposite directions for quick pursuit. Rena sat with her back to the building, adjusted the rearview and side mirrors for a better view of the doors, and waited.

There were only two customers in the lobby when Jadz and Paul entered. Three clerks—one male, two female—were busy with paperwork or talking to the few customers. One woman was on the phone. Paul watched the employees for signs of nervousness while Jadz approached the nearest unoccupied agent, displayed her badge, and asked for the manager. None of the staff gave them a second look. A forty-ish woman in a bright sundress appeared from the back, and showed them into her office.

"Kim Angelo," she said by way of introduction. "Did you leave that message yesterday? We didn't get home until after midnight, so I figured it could wait. Is this about that hit-and-run last week?"

"Not today." Jadz declined her offer of coffee. "Do you work the counter issuing licenses and such?"

"No. Since I handle the books and financials, it keeps the audit trail clear if I stay out of that. Why do you ask?"

"Can you tell which agent handled which license?"

"Of course." Kim reached for a notebook on her desk. "Everyone has a log-in code that follows each transaction." She handed a page to Paul, who was closest. "What's this about?"

Mentally checking the manager off as a suspect, for now, Jadz sketched the outlines of the case, ending with, "We have five victims, all who renewed their driver's license in this office within two weeks of their deaths."

Kim's face paled under her tan. "Oh, my God! You think one of my agents is involved? But that's ridiculous." She swiveled around to face the lobby, scrutinizing each employee as if looking for a sign of who had betrayed her.

Jadz took the agent code list Paul passed to her. She compared it to the employee roster from BMV to make sure it matched, and asked, "Can you check the victims' names and tell us who handled the renewals?"

"Sure." Kim forced her attention back to the victim list and pulled up a computer file. "Let's see. The first one ... that would be Greg Logan. He's been here since he graduated high school. Next ... Dolly Kitchner. She's next in line for Saturday manager. Number three ... Greg." Her voice broke. She cleared her throat and continued. "Four ... Greg again. And this last one ... Dolly." Kim pushed away from the desk. "Of course, we only have eight agents, counting part-timers. So the odds of any one—"

"Is Mr. Logan working today?" Jadz interrupted.

"He's off Mondays because he always works the Saturday shift with Dolly." As the names coincided again, she pursed her lips and hurried on. "I've known Greg for fifteen years. He's a sweet guy. Always gives that little extra attention that keeps the customers happy."

"Likes to talk to people, does he?" Paul asked.

"Greg is very personable. The women ... all the customers love him." Kim stumbled over her words. "I think I need to call my supervisor."

"You can do that when we're done here," Jadz said. "We'll need a copy of the agent transactions, and a current home address for Mr. Logan."

"Don't you need a warrant or something?" Kim asked.

"We can get one, but so far this is all public record," Paul said.

She hesitated briefly and pursed her lips, but she produced the information.

"Do you have a picture of Logan?" Jadz asked.

Kim's eyes strayed toward a group photo on the wall. "Not readily available."

Paul followed her gaze. "Is he in that picture?"

She looked distressed. "It was taken a few years ago on my birthday. Greg … all the agents threw a big surprise party for me because they knew how much I hated getting older."

"Could you point him out, please?" Paul asked.

Kim paused for a long minute. "The tall man on my left, in the navy blue."

"There's a Kinko's next door," Paul told Jadz. "I'll get copies made while you finish up here." He took the picture from the wall and left, closing the door on Kim's protest.

"Is he always that pushy?" she asked Jadz.

"He's just doing his job, ma'am. We have a murderer to find before another woman dies."

Jadz's pointed words drained the color from Kim's face. "You don't really think it's Greg, do you?"

"We have to check every possibility." Jadz leafed through her notes. "You said Logan has been here since high school. When did he start, exactly?" She spent the next few minutes overcoming Kim's continued reluctance as to provide background information. After all the questions, Jadz studied the agents in the lobby. "Is Ms. Kitchner off Mondays, too?"

"She takes Wednesdays. That's her in the red." Kim identified a chubby young woman taking ID pictures at the far end of the counter.

"I'd like to talk to her for a few minutes, please."

Kim's mouth twisted. "Wait here." She sent another agent to relieve Dolly at the camera and led her to the office.

"Dolly, this is Detective Jaz—" Kim garbled the name.

"Jadzinski. How do you do." Jadz noted Dolly's sharp inhale at the introduction. "Why don't we sit down? I'd like to ask you a few questions."

Dolly barely perched on the edge of a chair before she asked, "Is this about my leaving early? I only did it a couple times."

Kim's eyes widened. "What are you talking about?"

Dolly wrung her hands, eyes downcast. "On Saturday, when I left early 'cause my sitter couldn't stay. I know it's against the rules, but I didn't think it was breaking the law or anything. Greg always closed up for me." She peeked at Kim. "He won't get in trouble, too, will he? He was just doing me a favor."

"How often did you leave the office unsupervised?" Kim's anger found an outlet.

Jadz cut in. "When Mr. Logan was helping you, did he have your log-in codes?"

Tears welled in Dolly's eyes. "I always left my account logged in. That way he could use it for a transaction or two, like I was still here, and no one would find out. I'm really sorry."

A tap at the door announced Paul's return with a large Kinko's envelope. "Excuse me, ladies." He replaced the picture on the wall and stood near Jadz in the crowded office.

"I can get another chair," Kim said, rising.

"Not necessary, thanks."

"When you left your log-in for Logan to use on Saturday mornings, did you ever go back to check what he did with it?" Jadz asked, recapping the discovery for Paul's benefit.

Dolly shook her head, still avoiding Kim's angry gaze. "He's my friend. I trust him."

After making note of the dates Dolly left Greg unattended, Jadz said, "Okay, that's all for now. We may have more questions later." She stood and gave Kim a business card. "Have your supervisor call me if there are any questions. I'm sure I don't have to tell you not to discuss this with anyone else."

Kim flushed. "I won't call Greg, but what do I say when he comes in tomorrow?"

"If he comes in, he'll already know," Jadz said.

As Jadz and Paul made their way to the exit, another clerk asked, "Is Dolly in trouble?"

"Not with us," Jadz said. The slamming of the door and snap of the blinds over the office window suggested a different possibility as they left the building.

Outside with Rena and Forester, Jadz detailed the visit while Paul spread the photocopied pictures on the hood of his car so everyone could see the images. "Logan is our guy, I'm sure of it," she said when she finished.

"Slow down," Rena said. "None of this is hard evidence."

Forester shooed them away. "Bring him in for questioning, but do it quietly," he said. "I'll meet you at the station. I have to give Chief an update for his press conference. Dixon's pushing pretty hard on this."

Jadz radioed Dispatch to arrange for a patrol unit to watch Logan's residence until they arrived. "Suspect drives a 2004 Grand Prix coupe, dark blue. Run his name for plates and put out an APB, surveillance only, just in case. We're on our way." With Paul close behind, Rena pulled out of the lot and headed north on Reynolds Road. Three slow city traffic miles later, she turned into the residential neighborhoods along Holland-Sylvania Road. Logan's house was just off the busy thoroughfare in an older residential district.

"Nice view of the Botanical Garden," Jadz said as they cruised by, taking stock of the area. Paul parked on a side street within view of the house to stand guard. Rena pulled in behind the patrol car waiting in front of the residence.

"Grand Prix's in the drive just behind the house," the patrolman told Jadz when she approached the passenger side of the cruiser. He indicated a small clapboard cottage nestled in a grove of elms. "No sign of life."

"Thanks. Wait here for a few minutes in case we need back-up."

"Do you want us to transport?"

Jadz considered the offer. "That's not a bad idea. Too many unknowns at this point."

"That would be wise," Rena agreed. As they crossed the quiet street and walked towards the door she added, "I am glad you are showing more caution than has been your practice."

Jadz bristled. "I don't intentionally put anyone else in danger." She waved off Rena's apology. "We have work to do."

They took up positions on either side of the stoop, exchanged glances and a nod. Jadz rang the bell. A musical chime sounded. "*In-A-Gadda-Da-Vida*," she said, recognizing the opening notes from the legendary sixties rock song. "Interesting choice."

A slender man wearing cut-off jeans and a Grateful Dead T-shirt opened the interior door. Jadz guessed him to be in his early forties, even with artfully streaked blond spikes and a discreet diamond stud earring. An unnaturally early tan couldn't hide the wrinkles at the edge of his pale blue eyes. "Whatever you're selling, ladies, we're not interested," he said through the screen.

He didn't match the photo from the registrar.

"Is this the Logan residence?" Jadz asked.

"Proust and Logan, yes. What can I do for you?"

Jadz displayed her badge and ID. "Detective Jadzinski, and Detective Castillo. Is Mr. Logan home?"

He straightened and moved back half a step. "No, but he should be back any minute. He's at a class at the Garden. What's this about?"

"We'd like to talk to him about a matter relating to his office," Jadz hedged. "We'll wait in the car." She nodded to Rena and they turned to leave.

Proust unlocked the door and pushed it open. "It's getting awfully warm. You may as well wait inside." His polite smile didn't extend to his eyes.

Inside, the home was an eclectic mix of ultra-modern glass and chrome and '70s kitsch. A large stuffed parrot perched on a wooden rail in a corner of the living room. Floor-to-ceiling bookshelves lined a small den off to the left. They passed through a snug eat-in kitchen and onto a screened porch that overlooked Toledo Botanical Garden at the back. Sitting on edge of nearly sixty acres of lush landscapes and old-growth forest, the small home offered an oasis from the bustle of the city which intruded just down the block.

"Have a seat. I just brewed a pot of iced tea." Proust stopped at the kitchen door. "Unless you'd prefer coffee? I understand that's the drink of choice for men, and women, in blue."

"Iced tea is fine," Rena said. "Thank you."

Proust left the room and Jadz scowled. "I don't want tea." She took a wicker armchair facing the yard, her back against the wall. The garage at the side shielded the neighbor's house from view, and with the park adjacent, it gave the area an isolated feel that added to her growing anxiety.

Rena sat on a wrought iron bench near the edge of the room where she could watch the back door. "Relax. It will pass the time and give us a chance to make small talk without making Proust defensive."

"Small talk is not my strong suit."

Proust returned bearing a tray and four tall glasses of tea.

"Nice place," Jadz said, making a face at Rena when Proust's back was turned.

"Surprising so close to Reynolds, isn't it? It's one of the reasons Greg bought it. I prefer the city, but, well, home is where the heart is," he said with a studied nonchalance.

Jadz and Rena exchanged looks.

"I'm sorry, Mr. Proust. I missed your first name." Rena asked.

"Marc, with a 'C', not a 'K'. Actually, my legal name is Louis Georges Marcel Proust, but friends call me Marc. Oops, coaster, please, Greg would have my head if you leave watermarks," he said as Jadz looked for a place to set her glass. He passed her a brightly colored sandstone disk. He leaned back and crossed his legs. "As I was saying, my mother was a devoted Proust fan. She liked to claim we were related, but could never prove it. Somehow having the same name was enough for her. When I was growing up, she read *Remembrance of Things Past* repeatedly. As soon as she finished volume six of the English translation, right back to volume one. It always annoyed her that she couldn't read the original French." His nasal laugh echoed in the small room. "She tried grooming me to write like Proust and was terribly disappointed when I settled on science fiction."

Amazing how much people ramble when they're nervous. Jadz watched his dangling foot jiggle and twitch in the stream of sunlight.

"You are a writer?" Rena asked.

"I've had some success," he said. Proust's nervous chatter ranged from his novels, to a screenplay, to an off-Broadway production.

Jadz sat silent, only half-listening while Rena probed for information. She kept an eye on the sidewalk from the Botanical Garden for Logan's approach and grew more impatient with the passing minutes.

"So how did two such attractive ladies end up in the gritty world of law enforcement?"

Proust's question went unanswered as Logan entered through the kitchen door, catching them off guard. Jadz and Rena rose to meet him.

"Greg, these detectives have been waiting for you." Proust handed him the fourth glass of tea. "They want to talk to you about the registrar's office."

"And it couldn't wait until tomorrow?" Logan settled into the glider across from Jadz. "What can I help you with?"

Jadz wasted no time. "Mr. Logan, where were you Saturday between nine in the evening and say, one in the morning?"

His eyebrows rose. "I certainly wasn't at work." Logan set his glass aside and leaned forward. "Why don't you tell me what this is really about?"

Rena took over. "A woman who renewed her driver's license in your office last week, a Vicki Lingler, was murdered. Did you know her?"

"I see a lot of renewals in the course of a day, much less an entire week."

Jadz and Rena waited.

"No, I don't recall the name." Logan's voice lost its pleasant tone.

"He was here with me Saturday," Proust said. "He finished a class at the Garden late, maybe nine-thirty-ish. We had a quiet evening and went to bed early."

"I saw something in the paper about this." Logan squinted in thought. "Over near Maumee. Fourth woman found dead at home recently."

"Five, actually, maybe more," Jadz said. "Mr. Logan, we'd like you to come downtown with us for more questions."

"I'm a suspect?" He rose to meet Jadz, now back on her feet. They stood nose-to-nose, eyes locked.

"You can't be serious." Proust seemed more upset than Logan. "I told you, he was with me all night."

"Aren't you supposed to read me my rights or something?" Logan asked.

"When it is time." Rena directed him toward the front door and followed close behind.

Proust tried to step between them. "You're not actually going with them."

Logan took his arm and steered him out of Rena's way. "Call Luke Madigan for me, will you?"

"Luke's a family attorney," Proust said. "I doubt he's qualified for this."

"He can recommend somebody later, if necessary. Tell him to meet us—where will we be going?" Logan looked to Jadz at the rear of the short procession.

"Toledo Police Homicide. He'll know."

Rena stopped Logan at the front door. "I will need to check for weapons before you get in the patrol car. I am sure you would rather do that here than outside."

He stood silently, eyes fixed on the parrot across the room, while she performed a quick but efficient pat-down. When he offered his wrists for handcuffs she said, "That will not be necessary right now."

"A patrol car?" Proust faced Jadz, his color heightened even through the tan. "Have you any idea what the neighbors will think? Why can't we meet you there?"

"You're not coming, Marc." Logan was firm. "It's better if I go alone for now." His face softened at his partner's distress. "Call Luke for me. I can't imagine this will take long."

Jadz called Paul while Rena followed the patrol car downtown. "I don't know what to think," she said. "He's pretty calm for being accused of five murders. And with an attorney coming in, it'll be a very short interview."

"I'll head back to fill in the chief. See you downtown later," Paul said. When Rena took the Erie Street exit off I-75, he continued past them to cross the Maumee River into Northwood.

When Jadz and Rena got off the elevator, Logan between them, Forester was waiting. "Interview room two is open," he said, leading them down the hall. He opened the door to a dingy windowless room. "Mr. Logan, if you'd have a seat across the table, please. Detective Jadzinski will be right with you." Forester closed the door and joined Jadz and Rena in the hall. "The press conference didn't go well," he said, his face grim. "Somehow Dixon made the connection to the registrar."

Jadz swore under her breath. "He probably followed us this morning," she said. "That's his style."

"He doesn't know we suspect an employee. He's implied that Lucas County or the state could be held liable for improper release of personal information. The mayor's pushing for an arrest." Forester took a deep breath. "Don't let the media rush you. I'd rather you get the facts straight and make the right arrest."

"Of course," Rena said. She turned to Jadz. "Would you like the first round, or shall I?"

Jadz handed Rena her briefcase. "I'll start. Dump that on my desk, and give me about ten minutes." She entered the interview room.

"Mr. Logan's partner called an attorney as we left the house," Rena told Forester. She detoured past her desk to unload before following him to his office. "He will probably arrive very shortly."

"Then talk fast." Forester paced half-circles around his desk while Rena summarized the visit on Elmer Drive. When she was finished, he sat down and leaned back in his chair, fingers tapping the desk in a steady beat. After a few minutes of silence, he said,

"Depending on what Logan says, we'll need to talk to Proust again. Decide if you want that to be here or there, since he's not a suspect, and set it up as soon as you can."

The phone buzzed. "Forester. Okay, send him up." He ran a hand through his thinning hair. "This is why I'm going bald. His attorney's here. Go relieve Jadz and I'll run interference as long as I can."

They returned to the lobby just as the elevator doors slid open revealing Proust and the attorney. Rena slipped down the hall and into the interview room before they spotted her.

Jadz met Rena at the door and said, "I'm not sure Mr. Logan appreciates the gravity of the situation." She made no effort to keep Logan from hearing her frustration.

"But I do understand," he said. "Five women are dead. By some bizarre circumstance they all renewed their license in my office. That in no way indicates I'm involved in their deaths. I deal with hundreds of people every week." He leaned back, crossed his arms and waited.

Rena skimmed the list on the legal pad Jadz handed her. For the date of each murder, he'd provided an alibi. "How are you so certain of your activities six months ago?"

Logan ticked off the days on his fingers. "I teach a regular class at the Botanical Garden every Tuesday and Thursday, plus occasional workshops, like today. I've been doing that for the past three years. Wednesday I have book club. Marc and I have season tickets to the Valentine Theater, so I'm there almost every weekend." He sat back. "I lead a very routine—some would say boring—life."

"Can anyone other than Mr. Proust verify these activities?" Rena asked. A knock on the door prevented his response.

Forester followed the attorney into the increasingly crowded room.

"Tsk, tsk, ladies, you started the party without me," the attorney said, moving to Logan's side of the table. "Mr. Logan, I'm Alan Keyser. Your attorney asked me to be with you for this."

"Thank you for coming," Logan said.

Keyser glanced from Rena across the table to Jadz hovering in the corner avoiding his gaze. "Have these detectives been annoying you?"

"No annoyance," Logan said. "Detective Jadzinski very efficiently recited the Miranda warnings to me and I agreed to answer preliminary questions until you arrived."

"Preliminary questions are over." Keyser took control. "Unless you're charging Mr. Logan with a crime, I assume he's free to go."

"We're investigating the deaths of five women," Jadz said. "Seems you might be civic-minded enough to want to help."

"Oh, I am," he said. "And when I've had sufficient time to confer with my client, we'll be happy to attend any further question-and-answer sessions. Until then, if you are not filing charges?" When Forester shook his head, Keyser motioned to Logan. "We'll be leaving. Enjoy the beautiful weather. I understand it's supposed to rain tomorrow." He ushered his client out and closed the door firmly behind them.

Jadz shoved her wooden chair across the room. "Damn!"

"We knew that would happen," Rena said.

"Rena's right," Forester nudged Jadz. "Focus that anger on finding solid evidence to link him to the murders."

Jadz and Rena spent the next several hours trying to puncture Logan's alibis. The Garden confirmed his employment, and the

Valentine faxed over a copy of his membership records and ticket usage. Calls to the few book club members Logan could name only cemented his claims.

Jadz's frustration grew with each confirmation. She sifted through the growing stack of paperwork searching for any overlooked detail. Rena called the families of each victim again to ask if they recognized Logan's name. Nothing.

Paul returned shortly after one-thirty with pizza and words of encouragement from his department. "I figured you wouldn't stop to eat," he said as they passed the box across the desks. They ate while they dissected the morning and filled Paul in on the aborted interview.

"When can we talk to him again?" he asked when the food was gone.

"I have a call in to Keyser's office," Rena said. "He is in court."

Jadz tossed the empty pizza box in the trash and prowled around the desks. "So we can't talk to Logan, or Proust, more than likely. We can't get a search warrant for the residence yet. But we can talk to neighbors, family, co-workers, teachers—anyone who might show us a side of Logan we haven't nailed down."

"That is reasonable," Rena said.

"Chief says I'm yours for the duration," Paul said. "How do you want to start?"

"We need to talk to all the registrar employees, past and present." Jadz paced while Rena took notes.

"Where did he go to school?" Rena asked.

Paul shuffled through the file. "Start High School and Owens Community College."

Rena added the locations to the list. "The rest of the book club members, Botanical Garden staff."

"I doubt if any of his family members will talk to us," Jadz said. "Let's hit his neighborhood, see if anyone there will. Logan said he bought the house about ten years ago."

"We could take a photo spread to the other victims' neighborhoods, in case anyone saw him," Paul said.

Jadz considered his suggestion. "No, not yet. From the initial interviews, none of the residents saw anyone out of place. We're going to be pretty busy with these other people for a while."

"How about this," Rena said. "Give the photos to district patrols and ask them to check when they can."

She relented. "I suppose that makes sense. I just don't like to make other people do my work."

"Our work, and we only have so many hours in a day." Rena scribbled for another minute. "I have separated our tasks by general areas of the city, one for each of us. Which do you prefer?"

"I'll take downtown and south. Owens, the book club lady, the Valentine," Paul offered, reading off the list. "I'm more familiar with that end of town."

"I will go back to the registrar, stop at the high school on the way. That should be a short visit since he graduated fifteen years ago." Rena set her list aside.

"That leaves me the Botanical Garden and his neighborhood," Jadz said. "Sounds like a plan." A wiry black man entered the bureau. "Lieutenant Welch?"

"Missed you this morning, Jadz." The task force supervisor eased into Jadz's vacant chair. "Forget about your old friends, did you?"

"This morning?" She searched her memory and her desk calendar. "Today starts trial prep, doesn't it?" Jadz's flush rose to meet her red hair.

He chuckled. "Don't get to see you rattled very often. This is a treat."

"I can't believe I forgot about the meeting," she said.

"No problem," Welch said, still laughing. "The Assistant U.S. Attorney blocked out this afternoon to meet with you one-on-one." He sobered. "I saw the press conference this morning. I know what you're up against. Timing couldn't be worse for this trial to finally get on the docket, but that's how things usually happen."

"This afternoon." Jadz perched on the edge of the desk. "Damn. We need to get started on these interviews."

"It cannot be helped," Rena said. "Paul and I can begin. If we have time later, we will start with Mr. Logan's neighborhood. If not, we can team up on it first thing tomorrow."

"Look at it this way," Paul added. "We've put Logan on guard. He won't try anything else. I'd bet on it."

Jadz threw up her hands. "Okay, guess I'm yours, Lieutenant. What time?"

"Ten minutes ago." Welch grinned as she blushed again. "C'mon, I'll walk you over."

During the short walk, Jadz and Welch replayed the high points of the eighteen-month drug investigation that was headed for court. Breaking the close-knit family ring using Toledo as a distribution hub had been impossible until Jadz wormed her way into the confidence of a peripheral player. Dogged persistence finally produced the evidence the task force needed, but it cost Jadz her ability to work undercover. Now Jadz had to set aside her new Homicide duties and focus on what had become ancient history in just a few short months. When they arrived at the hulking federal building along the riverfront, Assistant U.S. Attorney Roger Giappoli was waiting in his office. Welch left them to their work.

"Looks like my desk," Jadz said as he shuffled aside case files to make room.

"I heard you've got another big job on your hands," Roger said. "Sorry to pull you away, but the defense attorneys finally agree we're ready for trial."

"Attorneys are not my favorite people today. Present company excluded, of course." She sketched the morning encounter with Keyser, adding, "We can't talk to the suspect until he's ready. It's aggravating."

"Keyser's a good guy, but he'll make you earn a conviction." Roger handed her the case notes she had submitted after the drug arrests. "Let's get started."

They discussed the testimony needed, going over each detail so Roger wouldn't elicit anything surprising while questioning Jadz in front of the jury.

"Answer the question asked, don't volunteer anything extra," he said.

Jadz nodded, engrossed in her notes. "Can't read my own writing half the time," she said. "Good thing most of these were transcribed."

"Nope," Roger said. "Don't use those on the stand. Use your handwritten notes if you need to, but make sure you can read them. Transcriptionists make mistakes. It can cost your credibility."

A tap on the door and his secretary entered. "Sorry, Roger, but the boss needs to see you," she said.

"Keep reading," he said as he hurried out.

Jadz squirmed into a comfortable position in the chrome office chair. She forced herself to focus on details of the drug bust instead of wandering off to the interviews Rena and Paul were conducting. Scenes from the drug investigation ran through her mind, filling in the blanks of her clinical report with graphic images right up to the arrests seven months ago.

Warren DeMarco, the ringleader. Smart, driven, loyal to his friends and ruthless to his enemies.

Freddie DeMarco, Warren's younger brother. Not so bright, but strong and obedient.

Gerald Bernanske, a cousin who acted as courier for Warren, shuttling kilos of cocaine between suppliers in Detroit and outlets in Toledo and Lima, Ohio, further south.

Assorted minor distributors and relatives who helped with money laundering, all with "plausible deniability," according to their savvy defense attorneys.

And Jadz's hard-won informant, Gerald's girlfriend, who was now dead. The nineteen-year-old woman had tried to warn Gerald of the impending raid and was killed by one of the gang members during the arrests. Jadz shook herself. *I did what I could to protect her.*

Roger burst through the door in high spirits. "Freddie cracked. He'll plead to one count of possession with intent to distribute the stash we found in his car in exchange for testifying against the rest of them. With his record, he's facing seventy to eighty-five months instead of twenty years. When the others hear about it, they'll fall all over themselves to be next in line."

"No trial then?" Jadz asked.

"Not likely, at least not now. The plea hearing's set for tomorrow morning. After that, we'll see who else folds."

"Then you'll excuse me." She stood and tossed the file on the desk. "I have a murderer to catch."

"Pachecki's courtroom, ten o'clock, if you want to be there," Roger said. "Or I can just let you know what happens."

"We'll see how the interviews go this afternoon. I'm sure Freddie misses me."

Roger laughed. "Let's say he thinks of you often."

Jadz called Rena on the short walk back to TPD from the federal building. "They got a plea. Roger said I'm off the hook for at least a week." Rena filled her in on their progress as Jadz located her car. She had thirty minutes to reach the Botanical Garden before closing.

Shadows filled the parking lot as Jadz pulled into the Garden with ten minutes to spare. She allowed herself a moment to drink in the beauty of the park before entering the small octagonal building which housed the classrooms and conference center. The manager's office was right off the lobby, and when she knocked, a pleasant voice invited her in.

After brief introductions, Jadz said, "It's late, Ms. Lytle, and I don't want to keep you. But I need to ask about Greg Logan."

"He's been an instructor here since before I took over five years ago," Lytle said. "He's a wonderful asset, so good with the students and staff."

"Do you have records of when Mr. Logan taught for the past three months or so?"

"I do." She pulled out a ledger and laid it on her desk. "May I ask what this is about?"

"We need to verify some information Mr. Logan has given us." Jadz said.

"If you've already talked to Greg, I suppose it's all right." She gave Jadz a copy of the schedule.

"Are there any other staff members who would know Mr. Logan, maybe outside of classes, who I could talk to?" Jadz asked.

Lytle frowned. "Are you sure you can't tell me what this is about? I'd hate to think Greg was in some kind of trouble."

"I really can't say anymore. I'm sure you want to protect Mr. Logan's privacy."

Lytle bit her lip and riffled the pages of the ledger. "Greg and Suzanne taught together a few times. I think …" She craned her neck to look into the lot. "No, her car is gone. She'll be in tomorrow by eight-thirty."

"Suzanne's last name?" Jadz's pen was poised, waiting for a response.

"I really don't like this." When Jadz didn't respond, Lytle said. "Suzanne Armstrong. And that's all I'm going to say until I talk to Greg."

"If there's no discrepancy in your information, talking to me shouldn't be a problem. I'm sorry if you feel otherwise." Jadz kept her voice level, even though the woman's implacable demeanor annoyed her. "I'd hate to bother a judge for a warrant to get the information we need. That's so hard to keep quiet." She left with a promise to return in the morning, the frown on Lytle's face showing the words made an impact.

Jadz made the short drive to Damon's Restaurant to meet Rena and Paul. No matter which way she sorted what little information they had on Logan, it wasn't enough, and she was exasperated at the continued stalemate with people who seemed intent on protecting him. She found Paul alone in a booth opposite one of the big-screen televisions. The second game of an afternoon double-header between the Detroit Tigers and the New York Yankees was deep in the eighth inning, score tied.

"Where's Rena?" Jadz asked, sliding into the seat. She ordered a glass of wine from the hovering server. She waited until a double-play ended the inning and then repeated the question to pull Paul away from the game.

"She said she had to get home." He opened the menu. "What sounds good to you? I can't decide between the ribs and the wings."

"She always goes home early when she can. I wonder if there's more she's not telling me about her mother."

"What about her?"

"Never mind. It's none of my business, I guess." Jadz sipped her wine and flipped through the menu. "Ribs tonight, I think. That pizza didn't stay with me long."

They ordered dinner and compared notes from the day's interviews while they waited for the food.

"Rena said there wasn't much to report," Paul said. "Everybody remembers Logan as a great guy, quiet, hard working, no skeletons in his closet that she could find, his co-workers all love him. Blah, blah." He drained his beer mug and looked for the server. "Never here for a refill when you need it."

"What about your people?"

"Pretty much the same. Nobody at Owens remembers him. It's been too long. Even the counselors are different. The book club lady …" he paused to consult his notes, "Glenda Rivers, had the same opinion. Nice guy, charming, intelligent, good cook. Couldn't get her to shut up about his Dutch apple pie. No discrepancies I could find."

Jadz drained her glass. "Something doesn't add up. How does a charming, hard-working intellectual murder a bunch of women and lie so convincingly?"

"Maybe he didn't." At her protest, he said, "I'm just saying! Somebody would have to know something, and nobody's talking. You think he's psycho?"

"Of course he's psycho. He killed five people."

"I mean schizo, split personality or something. You got a better idea?"

Frustration from the day combined with exhaustion spilled over. "Contrary to popular belief, schizophrenics do not have a split personality. They're no more likely to be criminals than the rest of us, they're just ill," Jadz said. "And no, I don't think he's schizophrenic."

"Damn, didn't mean to set you off."

Jadz took a deep breath and held it a moment before exhaling slowly. "Not your fault." She propped her elbows on the table and cradled her head, shutting out Paul and the noise around them. When the server returned with dinner, she sat back and forced a smile at Paul's concerned expression. After the server left, she tried to explain. "My best friend from grade school was diagnosed with schizophrenia in junior high. She was a sweet, bubbly person, and most of the time she had it under control. When her meds were off, she was—" Jadz swallowed hard. "She OD'd our junior year in college."

Cheers erupting around them at the Tigers' walk-off home run in the bottom of the ninth drowned out Paul's apology.

"Don't. It's okay. I just get defensive when people say things like that about a disorder they don't understand." Jadz unrolled her silverware from the napkin bundle. "Let's eat."

Chapter 8

Rena pulled her Toyota Camry into the garage, waiting until the overhead door closed before entering the house. It was just after six. She knew her mother's companion would be gone for the day. Rena surveyed the quiet rooms as she passed through, satisfied that the Spartan surroundings were in order.

"Mother?" She tapped on a closed bedroom door.

"I am awake." The quiet response was barely audible.

Rena slipped into the room. The drapes were drawn against the evening sun slanting through the trees at the west side of the house. A small ginger jar lamp on the side table next to her mother's wheelchair shed a confining circle of light, leaving the rest of the spacious room in shadows. An incense burner flickered on the *Butsudan* family shrine shelved in a raised alcove near the door. Rena didn't need the dim glow reflecting off the *ihai*—gilt mortuary tablets which served as monuments to dead ancestors—to pick out the items displayed on her mother's altar. A darker tablet slightly apart from the others stirred a customary pang of loss. It represented her father.

Rena's mother didn't look up from her book as Rena entered. "You are late." Keiko Ishikawa's voice carried no emotion.

"*Kanji,* I am sorry," Rena said. "This case—"

"I do not care to hear about such violent matters." Keiko continued reading.

Rena flushed. "Of course, *kanji*. Would you like dinner now?"

"I have already eaten. Emi left a tray."

"Then I will leave you to your book," Rena said. "I will be here all evening if you need anything."

"Unless your department calls, no? Then you will leave me." Keiko turned a page, still not looking up.

Rena stood in the doorway staring at her mother, wondering again at the immense bitterness contained in her tiny frame. It had been many years since Keiko let down her guard and sang Japanese folk tunes with a young Rena as they prepared meals together or worked in the garden. They had been inseparable, making the annual pilgrimage to Kyoto for the *Bon* ceremony to honor their ancestors each July. Keiko took her familial obligations seriously, and as the only child of now-dead parents, the task fell to her. As a teenager, Rena adopted her father's casual indifference to the rituals, and the emotional rift began. Since the accident which killed him and sentenced Keiko to the wheelchair, her mother rarely smiled, and never at Rena. She never spoke of her grief, never gave voice to blame for the loss of her husband. In her culture, Rena's dedication to her mother's comfort was an expected duty, with no consideration of personal sacrifice.

But it was never enough.

"Good night, Mother," Rena spoke quietly, her voice an emotionless echo of her mother's. She closed the door on Keiko's silence.

In the kitchen, Rena sautéed chicken and chopped vegetables mechanically while her mind circled around Keiko's words.

Then you will leave me.

As she did every night before falling asleep, or when faced with her mother's displeasure, Rena saw again the flash of headlights as the oncoming SUV had veered into her lane.

Nineteen-year-old Rena swung the wheel hard to the left, trying to escape collision. The passenger side of the car where her parents were seated took the full impact. Rena's father died at the scene, Keiko sobbing his name. Everyone said Rena was the lucky one. A concussion left her unconscious for several days. Shards of glass lacerated her face and arms, but she had no other injuries. An uncle from San Cristóbal claimed her father's body and returned him home for burial before Rena regained consciousness or Keiko was out of surgery long enough to object.

Injuries from the accident left Keiko an invalid, dependent on Rena. Recruitment announcements for a new police class triggered memories of her father's longing to reclaim the badge he'd worn at home in the Dominican Republic. It gave Rena a focus as she struggled with misplaced guilt over his death and the need to support her mother. She left her studies in classical literature for the more practical field of law enforcement. With Keiko immersed in eight long months of hospitalization and rehab, Rena passed the civil service test and was sworn in at the academy before her mother came home, confined to a wheelchair. Despite Keiko's protests, Rena remained firm in her commitment, finding strength in her role as head of the family. She arranged for the best home care for her mother, juggled the demands of her new career and denied herself a personal life in order to be home as much as possible. Keiko never wanted for physical comforts. Her thanks came in the form of a passive emotional bullying Rena had learned to ignore. Most days.

Tonight the added stress of knowing she and Jadz were all that stood between a serial killer and his next victim cracked Rena's composure. When she scorched her fingertips on a hot skillet, Rena dropped the pan, and her dinner, into the sink, letting the tears come. The clatter would earn a rebuke from Keiko, but Rena was past caring for the moment.

It was never enough.

Chapter 9

When Jadz arrived at the detective bureau the next morning, Rena was already at her desk.

"Missed you last night," Jadz said as she sorted through the incoming mail stacked on her desk. She skimmed a department memo, added an HR form to her briefcase to review later at home and tossed a munitions catalog into the recycle bin. Jadz stopped puttering when she realized Rena didn't answer. "Everything okay?"

"I am fine," Rena said, too carefully even for her.

Jadz noted the puffy eyes and lines of tension on Rena's normally serene face. She sat down. "You want to talk about it?"

Rena avoided Jadz's gaze. "Not really. It should not concern you."

"But it does concern me." Jadz tried again. "We haven't worked together very long, but I think we hit it off pretty well after a rough start. I don't know about you, but I could use a friend. It's a lonely world out there for us single gals in uniform." Jadz was startled by the tears welling up in Rena's eyes. "What did I say?"

"Nothing, and everything," Rena answered. She glanced around the now bustling office and collected herself. "I will be fine. And I would be happy to talk about this another time, if you like."

"Looks like you're busy most evenings. What works best?"

"Actually, Wednesdays are my own."

"Tomorrow night it is." Jadz remembered what else tomorrow held. "I'll probably need a friend myself, after the divorce hearing."

Rena cleared her throat and tapped a file of papers into a precisely aligned stack. "What do you plan for this morning?"

Jadz repeated the conflict with the manager of the Botanical Garden. "I need to go back out there today, but I'm not sure she'll talk to me. And I'd really like to be at DeMarco's plea hearing at ten."

"I could talk to the Garden employees while you are in court," Rena said. "A different face may ease things. We can do the neighborhood together after your hearing."

"Good idea, thanks. Paul had one more book club member to track down before tackling the neighborhood, too. With all of us on it, we should be able to finish up today."

"I also need to call Mr. Keyser. He is meeting with Mr. Logan at eleven-thirty and said we could schedule an interview for tomorrow afternoon."

"Not in too big a hurry, is he?" Jadz finished updating her calendar, determined not to miss another appointment. "Afternoon's probably better anyway. My hearing's at nine-thirty."

"We should inform Lieutenant Forester of our plans," Rena said as they saw him enter his office.

"I'll do that before the plea hearing, if you want to head for the Garden." Jadz was puzzled by the disappointment which flashed across Rena's face, but hesitated to stir up more emotions. "I'll call you when I'm on my way to Elmer Drive." She gathered her notebook.

"Morning, Lieutenant," Jadz greeted Forester. "Got a minute?"

"Sure." He turned to watch Rena leaving the bureau. "Where's your cohort off to?"

"Botanical Garden." Jadz gave him a rundown of the previous day's events and their plans for further interviews. "Keyser will bring Logan in for questioning tomorrow afternoon. Until then, we'll keep gathering all the background on him we can."

"Just be careful," Forester said. "Don't create a PR nightmare by tarring the wrong guy with bad publicity."

"I know. Rena said the same thing. But, damn it, look at the registrar data. No one else has that kind of connection to all the victims. It's too much to be coincidence."

"No one we know of." He slouched forward to rest on his crossed arms on the desk. "I understand your frustration. But I've been in this business long enough to know things are rarely as simple as they seem. And so have you."

"You're right," she said. "But if he's not guilty, I'll—"

"Whoa, watch it!" Forester shoved back off the desk and held up both hands. "The universe has a way of making you eat your words."

Jadz grinned. "Too true. Okay, we'll see how this plays out." She rose. "I'm off to a plea hearing that may keep me out of trial next week, so keep your fingers crossed."

He dismissed her with a wave of crossed fingers on one hand while the other dialed the phone he propped under his chin. "Sally? Adam. I need a few minutes with Captain Stanford and the Chief when they're both available."

The guard at the federal court building security station met Jadz as she pushed through the heavy glass doors. "It's been too long, girl." The retired deputy was her father's former partner and he'd known Jadz since her birth. He pulled the cordon aside, allowing her to bypass the metal detectors as was standard for fellow officers. She followed him to the security office to check her firearm and once out of public view, wrapped him in a hug.

"So good to see you, Bob."

"You're a busy girl these days, high-profile investigator now like your daddy was." His smile faded. "Still can't believe he's gone."

"I miss him, too," she said.

Bob gave a short cough and drew himself up. "So what brings you to visit? The DeMarco plea, right?"

"I'm hoping his buddies all fall in line so we don't have to go to trial."

"Good luck with that." He returned to his post. "Pachecki's in rare form today."

Jadz jogged up the wide marble steps to the second-floor courtroom. She found Roger, Welch, and the federal case agent huddled at the prosecutor's table.

"How's it going, guys?" She nodded toward the empty benches behind the bar. "Where's the crowd? I thought the family would be out in force."

"Most of them are pretty unhappy with Fred right now," Roger said.

"That'll change," Welch said. "When his buddies hear what he has to say today, the dominoes will start falling."

U.S. Marshals entered the side door of the courtroom with the shackled defendant between them. Defense attorneys huddled with Fred at counsel table as the handcuffs were removed. The Marshals took up their posts at the big swinging doors, one on each side of the short aisle.

The court clerk readied the case file on the bench. "Are you ready?" she asked counsel. At their nods, she tapped on the door to chambers to alert the judge. As the black-robed figured moved to the bench, the clerk gaveled everyone to their feet and recited, "All rise! The Honorable Barbara Pachecki, Judge of the United States District Court. Hear ye! Hear ye! Hear ye! All who have business before this honorable court draw nigh, give attention, and ye shall be heard. God save the United States of America and this honorable court."

The archaic court opening never failed to amaze Jadz. *So much for separation of church and state.*

As the judge sat down, a commotion at the entry disrupted the momentary silence. The unindicted members of the DeMarco clan shuffled in, defiantly late, and crowded into the first row behind the defense team.

Pachecki frowned at the latecomers and gaveled them into silence before addressing the lead defense counsel. "Mr. Glendower, your client has requested to change his plea." An angry buzz rose from the family members and Pachecki gaveled again. "I warn you all, for the first and last time, any further disruption and you will be removed from this courtroom."

The group remained quiet but sat, arms crossed, eyes focused on Freddie's back, during the hearing. When he made the required statement of admission of guilt detailing his illegal activities, one of the younger family members stormed out. The head Marshal spoke quietly into his two-way radio, alerting security, and the hearing continued without further interruption.

Pachecki formally accepted Freddie's guilty plea and instructed him to cooperate with the pre-sentence investigation. Freddie nodded, head down, and the hearing was over.

As soon as the judge was off the bench, the Marshals hustled the defendant out the side door. Bob and a third deputy appeared at the main entry and hovered near the unhappy family. "Damn liar!" one of them called after the defendant. The officers circled the group and escorted them out.

"Was that Ricky who left early?" Jadz asked at the prosecutor's table.

"Yeah, he's a punk," the case agent said.

"He's a hothead," Welch corrected. "We need to keep an eye on him."

"I'll leave that to you guys," Jadz said. "I have a murderer to catch." She retrieved her firearm from security before hurrying to her car. By the time she merged into westbound traffic on the Anthony Wayne Trail, the courtroom scene faded from her mind. She focused on the interviews ahead, considering how best to approach Logan's questioning in light of the sterling character references. Jadz slowed her Miata for the light at South Avenue, then sped up and slipped into the left lane to pass slower traffic as the signal changed.

As she returned to the center lane and cruising speed, a grey sedan zigzagged through traffic behind her. It came at her from the left and forced her into moving traffic in the next lane. The sedan clipped her front bumper, sending her careening onto the berm and scattering other motorists as they fought to avoid collisions. Jadz struggled to control the Miata. It spun one hundred eighty degrees before the passenger door slammed into a light pole, jarring the car to a stop. She sat holding her head, stunned. Blood trickled down through her hand as she fingered a gash on her forehead.

Before Jadz could make sense of what happened, a man appeared at the driver's window. "Are you okay? Don't move. I called 911."

She unlocked the door so he could pull it open. "I hit my head," Jadz said. "I think that's it."

He laid a hand on her shoulder when Jadz tried to sit up. "A rescue squad's on the way, and here's the police now. Quick response for a change."

"They do what they can," she said, automatically coming to the defense of her fellow officers. "Did you see who hit me?"

The first figure disappeared and a dark blue uniform swam into view. "Jadz? What the hell happened?"

"Theo?" She squinted, trying to focus on his face. "This isn't your shift."

"I'm covering for vacations. What happened?" He squatted down next to the car. "Anything hurt besides your head?"

"I don't think so," she said, wincing at the sharp pain any movement caused. "Talk to that guy, will you? I think he might have seen who hit me."

"Stay put. You could have a concussion. The squad's on the way." He stepped away to question the caller and another driver who stopped to assist.

Jadz sat still as the world pitched and reeled around her. She closed her eyes to block out the confusing images. *I was supposed to call Rena.*

"Miss? Can you hear me?"

She opened her eyes to find a paramedic at her side. Jadz started to nod and flinched again as the pain exploded. "I hear you."

He pulled her hand away to check the gash. "You hit your head, but it looks like the bleeding's stopped. Don't fade out on me again. You have to stay awake." After a quick check for other visible injuries, the medics got Jadz on a gurney and into the ambulance, ignoring her protests.

"I'm fine. It's just a little cut. I don't need to go to the hospital."

"Yes, you do." Theo reappeared next to her horizontal figure in the back of the rescue vehicle. "I'll let Forester know where to find you."

The paramedics chased him out, slammed the doors and took off, lights and siren, for Saint Vincent's Mercy Medical Center.

One of the crew started an IV on one arm and attached a blood pressure cuff to the other while the second medic made notes.

"Where does it hurt?" he asked.

Jadz closed her eyes and took inventory. "My left foot?"

"At least you can make jokes. Not very good ones, but I'll take it." He scanned her police ID emergency card. "Do you want someone to call your husband?"

"No!" Jadz winced again. "He's not my husband anymore, well, sort of I guess, until tomorrow when we go to court. Can I go home, please? I have work to do." Her head whirled in a fog she struggled to clear.

"You live alone? Then you probably won't be going home tonight." At her protest, the medic added, "Accident victims usually need to be monitored for 24-48 hours. Can't do that if you're home alone."

"Forty-eight hours? But I'm getting divorced in the morning, and there's a killer on the loose."

"I'm not sure how that fits together, but I'll tell the docs." He scribbled on the chart. "Is there someone else we should call? Maybe a parent?"

"Oh, jeez, don't call Mom," Jadz said. "You'll need to find a bed for her if you do." She closed her eyes against the flash of shadows and light across the ceiling. *This can't be happening.*

"Okay, fine. I'll let the hospital sort this out." He stowed the documents in the back of the gurney and braced himself against the door as they turned into the ER driveway.

The hour after the accident passed in a blur of questions, x-rays, blood work, poking and prodding. Jadz wanted to sleep, but medical personnel kept rousing her with dire warnings of possible consequences from a head injury. A dozen hairline stitches closed the gash and eventually she was left alone in a curtained cubicle, waiting for the doctor.

Twenty minutes later, a duty nurse parted the curtain to admit a uniformed officer. "Five minutes, no more," she said.

"I'm here to finish the crash report," he told Jadz. "Can you answer a few questions?"

"You're new, aren't you? Where's Theo? I need to make sure he called Forester."

"Sergeant Baxter said he'd stop by later, and I was to tell you to stop worrying about work," he said. He opened his clipboard. "I found your registration in the glove box. Still live on Bancroft?"

"Yes." Jadz resigned herself to the formalities. At least it helped keep her awake.

When the personal data was complete, the officer took notes for the statement. "What do you remember about the accident?"

"Very little." She tried to picture the vehicle that pushed her off the road. "All I saw was a dark green, maybe grey, side panel, pretty sure it was a four door, maybe a Mercedes? It had tinted windows," Jadz said, relieved to recall any minor detail. "But I never saw the plates. It happened too fast."

"Two witnesses gave a similar description, but again, no plates. We put out an APB. The vehicle will have substantial damage and lots of red paint on the right rear quarter panel where he clipped you. Should be easy to find."

"Substantial damage?" Jadz clutched the sheets in hard fists. "My car? I don't remember."

"Sorry, I thought you knew. Your car's pretty banged up. Both front quarter panels, passenger door, and hood all have to be replaced, probably the bumper. And the driver's headlight is gone."

"Damn." Hit-and-run, her beautiful car ruined. "Any more good news?"

The officer looked through his notes. "Paramedics gave your service weapon to Sergeant Baxter. He's got your briefcase, too." He cast a sideways glance around the clipboard. "You two old friends?"

"We went to the academy together."

"Seemed pretty protective, Sarge did."

Jadz shuddered as much from the creeping shock of the accident as from his words. "Don't go there, okay? I'm not even divorced yet."

A bustling nurse interrupted him before he could comment. "Your five minutes were up long ago," she said. "Let the poor thing rest." She shooed the officer out of the ER and returned to check on Jadz. "The doctor will be with you in another minute. He's getting your test results now."

Jadz licked her dry lips. "Could I have some water, please?"

"A little crushed ice, that's all, until the doctor's been in." She slipped around the curtain and reappeared a minute later with a small paper cup and a plastic spoon. "Do you need help with it? I can only raise the head of the bed a few inches for now."

"I can manage, thanks." Jadz chewed on the ice chips, feeling her parched throat relax. Exhausted by the minimal effort, she handed the cup to the nurse and fell back. "Damn. You'd think I'd been run over by a truck."

"Head injuries can do that." She tucked the sheet around Jadz's shoulders and left her alone. "Don't go to sleep," she said again.

The doctor arrived fifteen minutes later. He ran through the test results, hardly looking at Jadz. "Blood work is fine, nothing broken. No damage to the neck or spine. CT scan shows a mild concussion. You'll be fine in a few days." He checked her personal data. "You live alone? Then you'll be our guest for the next twenty-four hours. If all is well at noon tomorrow, you can go home."

"But I have to be in court at nine-thirty." Jadz tried to sit up, only to set the room spinning again.

"Not tomorrow, you won't. Reschedule. Now get some sleep." He patted her shoulder and left to give the nurse final instructions.

"Can I get some water now?" she called after him. "Hello?"

Another hour passed. Jadz dozed. When the nurse reappeared to check her vitals, Jadz kept her eyes closed to avoid conversation. Eventually an orderly came to take her to the short-stay ward. Down one hall, then another, through a wide doorway. Lights flickered through her eyelids, barely registering.

"Veronica, my baby! I thought they'd lost you!"

Jadz forced her eyes open to find a petite woman with a mass of bright crimson hair hovering over her bed. "Hi, Mom." A dry throat left her voice harsh and low. "What are you doing here?"

"What do you mean? I'm here to take care of you, of course. You know how hospitals are. If you don't have someone to keep them in line, you'll be dead before you go home." Mavis Jadzinski bustled around straightening the sheets and plumping the pillow Jadz had been given when she left ER. "Now where is the cord for these blinds?" Mavis found the controls and swooshed the window covering open. Glaring sunlight streamed into the room, making Jadz squint. "There, isn't that better?"

"Not really."

Mavis grabbed the call button. "The nurse should be here by now. I won't have them neglecting you." She punched the bright red button repeatedly. "Why won't she answer?"

"Mom, don't." Jadz struggled to sit upright. "Give me that, please. I don't need the nurse."

"Did you want something?" A voice squawked over the speaker.

"No, I'm fine, sorry." Jadz tucked the control under the sheets, out of her mother's reach. "Why don't you sit down and keep me company for a while?"

Mavis dragged the high-back recliner closer to the bed and perched on the edge. "My poor baby. I always told your father you had no business being a police officer. You could have been killed."

"It was a car accident. I wasn't shot."

"But you could have been. Then where would I be? First your father, then you. I'd be lost!"

"I'm not going anywhere. Get a grip." At her mother's hurt look, Jadz rushed to make amends. "I'm okay, really, and you have Betty."

Mavis brushed aside the suggestion. "Betty couldn't find her way out of paper bag. Her drinking has just destroyed her, you know that. Who do you think has been taking care of her all these years?"

I have. "How did you know I was here?"

"Your new partner, lovely girl by the way, you should bring her to dinner sometime, but such an odd name—Rhino?"

"Rena."

"I didn't answer the phone when she called, sleeping off a nasty sick headache. She came to the house to tell me what happened. I should have been here sooner." Hysterics threatened again. "My poor baby!"

"Mom, stop it. I'm fine. It's just a concussion. I can go home tomorrow."

A knock at the door quieted Mavis. Theo poked his head around the corner. "There you are."

"Theo, come in, please." Relieved at the distraction, Jadz raised the bed to a sitting position. "There's a stool over on this side. Doesn't look very comfortable."

He slid it out of the corner and sat down. "It's fine."

Mavis cleared her throat loudly.

"Sorry, Mom. This is Sergeant Theo Baxter. Theo, my mother, Mavis."

"How do you do, ma'am? It's a pleasure." He rose to shake her hand, and settled back onto the stool.

"Do you work with my Veronica?" Mavis beamed. "What a silly question, of course you do. Have you known each other long?"

"Mom."

"I brought your things from the car," Theo said. "Your weapon's with Forester, but here's your briefcase. Cell phone's inside. I didn't see a purse."

"Thanks. I don't carry one." Jadz tapped the nightstand. "You can put that stuff over here for now."

"Forester—" He stopped, glancing at Mavis. "He'll stop by this evening. Rena, too."

Jadz caught the intention in Theo's eyes. "Mom, would you see if you can find a nurse for me? I'm really thirsty. It would be quicker than using the call button. You know how they are."

"Oh, of course, sweetie, I'll take care of everything." Mavis scurried out, a woman on a mission.

"Sorry about all that," Jadz waved after her. "She means well."

He shrugged. "She's being a mom. Anyway, Forester talked to Welch after I called him. Guess there was some excitement at the plea hearing?"

She recounted Ricky's angry departure.

"Makes sense now. Welch thinks Ricky might be the guy who ran you off the road."

Jadz's eyes widened. "Why would he think it was intentional?"

"One of the witnesses said the guy looked like he was following you before the crash, had been for several blocks."

"If that's the case, my observations skills are worthless," she said with disgust. "I never saw him until he hit me."

"No reason to think you'd be tailed," he said.

Unconvinced, she continued, "Why didn't the accident investigator tell me about this?"

"I asked him not to until I'd talked to Forester."

"Has anyone talked to Ricky?"

"Who's Ricky?" Mavis bustled in bearing a water pitcher and a plastic cup. "Best I could do for now, dear. Dinner trays are on the way. I told them you don't like liver." She filled the cup, added a bent straw, and held it toward Jadz. "Drink up, sweetie."

"I can do it myself," Jadz took the cup, irritated at the helplessness she felt. She pushed the straw aside and downed the water in one long gulp. "Much better, thanks."

"So who's Ricky? Another handsome friend of yours?" Mavis eyed Theo. "Always did love a man in uniform."

"Ricky is someone we know from work," Jadz said. "Leave Theo alone, okay? You're making him nervous."

"I'm sorry, sweetie. I didn't know he was spoken for."

Jadz flushed. "He's not … never mind. Do you know where my car is?" she asked Theo.

"The wrecker took it to Brown Mazda, on Central," he said, avoiding Mavis' appraising stare. "They'll get an estimate for you in a couple days."

"You really should drive a bigger car," Mavis said. "This wouldn't have happened if you were in a Hummer."

"I wouldn't be caught dead in one of those gas-guzzling monstrosities," Jadz shuddered. She saw Theo shake his head. "I suppose you agree with her."

"Not an H2, maybe," he said, "but the Miata is awfully small."

The promised dinner arrived to cut short the debate, and Theo rose to leave.

"I need to stop by security before I go back downtown. You'll call me if you need anything?"

"Sure, and thanks again." Jadz caught his hand in a grateful squeeze as he crossed to the door. "I should be out of here by noon tomorrow. We'll talk then."

"Security? What for?" Mavis was on alert.

"A different case," Jadz lied. "Relax."

"I should be going, too, I suppose." Mavis fussed with the bedclothes again. "Betty will be expecting dinner, but I hate to leave you."

"I'll be fine, and Betty needs you," Jadz said, welcoming the thought of time alone.

"If you're sure." Mavis eyed Theo. "Walk me to my car?"

"I'd be happy to. Why don't you meet me at the front desk in five minutes?"

Jadz nodded her thanks. He smiled and left.

"Such a nice young man," Mavis started in as soon as the door closed behind him. "Is he why you don't miss Nathan so much?"

"No, he's not." Jadz laid her head back and closed her eyes, stifling a moan. *Nathan, tomorrow's hearing, the murders.* Events caught up with her in a rush.

"Poor thing, I'll let you sleep," Jadz heard Mavis whisper. A rattle of the dinner tray followed by, "Ooh, oatmeal cookies. You don't like those, sweetie." Plastic wrap rustled, Jadz felt an air-kiss over her cheek, and Mavis hurried off to meet Theo.

Dinner cooled untouched while Jadz slept. She woke three hours later to find the blinds drawn against the setting sun. It took her a minute to orient herself to the unfamiliar room. Memory flooded in and she groped for the control to raise the bed.

"You are awake."

Jadz dropped the remote with a clatter. "Damn, you scared the life out of me."

"I am sorry," Rena said as she slid her chair out of the shadows and closer to the bed. "I did not intend to disturb you."

Jadz shoved the pillows behind her back and scooted into an almost comfortable position. "What time is it? I think I missed dinner."

"Just after eight. The nurse said she would bring you something if you are hungry."

The speaker crackled in response to Jadz's summons. "Yes? Do you need something?"

"Could I get something to eat, please?"

"Someone will be right in." The red light blinked out.

"I need to pee. Is that the door?" Jadz threw back the sheet and eased herself to the edge of the bed. "Lovely gown, isn't it?"

"I am not sure you should be up on your own," Rena said.

"Then give me a hand, will you? I can't wait for a nurse." Jadz steadied herself on Rena's arm and maneuvered cautiously to the bathroom. She jostled the IV past the side chair, supporting herself with the pole connected to her needle-impaled arm. Jadz was only on her feet a few minutes, but when she edged her way back around the door, the room spun. She settled into bed with a grimace. "That took more out of me than I expected. My whole body aches."

"Do you remember what happened?" Rena asked.

"Most of it. My head is killing me. Where's the nurse?"

As if on cue, a candy striper appeared. "Hi, I'm Jennifer. Glad to see you're awake. You slept like forever. Are you hungry? I can get you soup or some Jell-O, and maybe a few cookies." She adjusted the pillows and refilled the water pitcher while she chattered.

"Soup would be fine. And maybe something for my headache?"

"I'll ask your nurse if the doctor prescribed anything. Tomato, chicken noodle, or split pea?"

"I'm sorry?" Jadz rubbed a hand across her forehead, wincing when she brushed over the stitches.

"What-kind-of-soup-would-you-like?" the aide enunciated.

"Oh, tomato I guess, thanks."

"Be right back."

"Would some water help?" Rena filled the plastic cup and pushed the bed tray within reach.

"Thanks." Jadz sipped the cold liquid. "I bumped my head. Why do I feel like death warmed over?"

"It takes time to recover from the trauma inflicted by even a relatively minor accident."

"I don't have time. I have to be in court in the morning and we have a case to solve."

"And you're not going anywhere until the doctor says otherwise." Forester's voice boomed from the doorway, his face hidden by a huge spray of sunflowers that looked like it had sprouted legs. "Where do you want these?"

"Where did those come from?" Jadz shifted the blankets to make sure she wasn't too exposed.

"The front desk sent them up since I was headed this way."

Rena took the vase to the windowsill and handed Jadz the card. "They are beautiful."

"Must be from Mom," Jadz said, not opening the envelope. "Thanks for coming, Lieutenant. Anything from Welch?"

"Not yet." Forester perched on the stool Theo used earlier. "There's an APB out for the car, and for Ricky. They'll find him."

"I heard the APB, but did not relate it to your accident," Rena said. "Who is Ricky?" After Forester explained, she asked, "Should there be a guard posted here?"

"Theo said he was alerting security this afternoon," Jadz said. "At least, I think that's what he meant. It's still a bit fuzzy."

The night nurse arrived with a syringe on a gauze pad and a tablet in a white paper cup. "Which will it be?" she asked, waving the options in front of Jadz. "The shot has to go in the hip. How severe is the pain, on a scale of one to ten?"

Jadz cringed at the needle. "Let's try the pills for now. It's not *that* bad."

"Vitals first." She checked Jadz's temperature, and applied the blood pressure cuff. "Hold still, please." She inflated the cuff and simultaneously checked the pulse. "130 over 85, a bit high yet, but it's coming down." The nurse entered the numbers in the chart while Jadz downed the pill. "You can have something for sleep later, if you need it." She collected the unused syringe and left the pills behind, passing the aide on her way back in.

"Soup's on." The girl arranged a steaming mug, a pack of crackers and two oatmeal cookies on the bed tray. "Can you manage?"

"I'm good." Jadz sipped the hot soup. "Ummm, food." She spotted Rena and Forester with their heads together in the corner. "What's up, you two?"

"We, ah, I was just telling him about the day's interviews," Rena stammered.

"Any progress?" Jadz spotted the cookies. "Oatmeal raisin, my favorite!"

"Nothing to speak of. We are scheduled to meet with Mr. Logan and his attorney tomorrow at two," Rena said.

Jadz choked on the crumbs. "I have to be there. Lieutenant, help me out here."

Forester shook his head. "Sorry, it's out of my hands."

"We do not have much to go on anyway," Rena said. "No hard evidence ties Mr. Logan to the murders and his alibis all check out."

"Damn." Jadz pushed the bed tray aside, sloshing the water jug. "And I'm stuck in this bed because a punk doesn't want his big brother to go to jail?"

"We're done talking about the case," Forester ordered. "You're getting worked up."

"You haven't seen me worked up."

"If you do not cooperate, you will not be discharged tomorrow," Rena said.

"Let them try to keep me here." Jadz folded her arms over her chest like a petulant two-year-old, spoiling the defiant gesture by getting tangled in the IV line and call-button cord.

"The doctor has to clear you for duty before I can let you set foot in the office, you know that," Forester said. "Don't argue with him."

The nurse hurried in. "What's all the noise? This is a hospital, remember?"

"Your patient was expressing her joy at being your guest," Forester said.

Jadz resisted the urge to stick out her tongue at his lame humor.

"Let's keep the celebration to a minimum, shall we? You'll make the other guests jealous." The nurse checked the IV drip. "Doctor says this can come out when the bag's empty, probably another twenty minutes or so. I'll be back." She pulled the door shut behind her as she left.

"You are making progress," Rena said.

"Progress is going home," she muttered.

"Come on, Detective Castillo, let's leave your partner to pout on her own. Apparently our presence only adds to her discomfort." Forester pushed the stool out of the way and opened the door.

Rena hesitated. "Are you sure you would not like us to stay? Visiting hours are not over for half an hour."

"Don't you have somewhere you need to be?" Jadz's anger found a handy target. "You don't like being out after dark."

Rena flushed. "Good night." She left.

"Well, aren't you the charming one." It was Forester's turn to be angry.

Jadz had the grace to look ashamed. "That was stupid. I'm sorry."

"Tell your *partner*, not me." He followed Rena.

Alone with thoughts she preferred not to face, Jadz dropped her head back and closed her eyes. *What an idiotic thing to say, especially after our talk this morning.* A high-speed rerun of the day troubled her mind for several minutes, slowing as the pain medicine took effect. She didn't stir when the nurse returned to disconnect the IV and turn down the lights.

The night jolted by in a jumble of temperature checks and blood pressure readings that interrupted Jadz's sleep. After the midnight staff visit, she realized she wasn't alone in the room.

She squinted at the dark figure in the corner. "Nathan?"

He scooted closer. "I didn't want to wake you."

"How long have you been here?" Jadz fumbled for the overhead light, blinking at the brightness.

"Maybe half hour, after I finished my shift. We're still married, so they let me in."

She raised the head of the bed and punched the pillows into a wad behind her. Nathan sat just outside the pool of light, bathed in shadows.

"I see my flowers made it," he said.

Jadz caught her breath. "You didn't sign the card."

Nathan shrugged. "I didn't want you to toss them."

"I wouldn't—" She floundered. "They're beautiful. Thanks." Jadz closed her eyes against his intent gaze.

After several minutes of silence, Nathan stood up. "Guess I'll head out then, since you're okay."

"Thanks for stopping by." She didn't object when he caressed the bandage on her forehead.

"G'night."

The door swished shut behind him leaving Jadz alone.

Chapter 10

Jadz slept fitfully after Nathan left, disturbed by confusing dreams as much as physical aches. When she awoke, the sun was just peeking through the blinds. The aroma of eggs and coffee from the breakfast trays stacked in tall carts in the hallway reminded her she'd had nothing but soup and a cookie in nearly twenty-four hours.

"Good morning. Just enough time for a bathroom break before breakfast, if you like." The day nurse ran one more round of vitals. "Do you want a hand?"

"No, I'm fine, thanks." Jadz swiveled to the edge of the bed.

"Let your feet dangle for a minute before you try to get up."

She nodded carefully, relieved to find the headache was nearly gone. She found her footing and stood still for a minute to make sure the room no longer spun. It didn't. Encouraged, Jadz made it to the bathroom without assistance. She took time to brush her teeth and wash her face with the hospital-supplied toiletries. Dark purple splotches spread out from under the bandage and another bruise covered her left cheek. Jadz shuffled back to the armchair. *Coffee*. Even the institutional scrambled eggs tasted good.

An aide came in to change the sheets while the bed was empty. "I think you're on the morning news, if you're interested," she said.

"No kidding." Jadz flipped on the television. She surfed through the half-dozen available channels and settled on the local NBC affiliate as the anchors began a news segment. A reporter stood next to the battered red Miata as the camera recorded the rescue squad leaving the scene.

My poor car.

"... Detective Sergeant Veronica Jadzinski, an eight-year veteran of the force, was taken by LifeSquad to Saint Vincent's Mercy Medical Center with unspecified injuries. Police are searching for this man," a mug shot appeared on the screen, "Ricky DeMarco. Witnesses say it appeared the officer was run off the road intentionally, and several members of the DeMarco family face serious drug charges in part because of Detective Jadzinski's investigative work. If you have any information on his whereabouts, please contact Toledo Police immediately. This is Alexis Means, 13 Action News."

Jadz muted the television, breakfast forgotten. *Would Ricky really be that stupid?*

Mavis burst in to the room. "There you are. You look terrible, sweetie." She was followed by a younger mirror image. Betty.

"That makes me feel so much better." Jadz used a napkin to scrub off the bright red goo caking her cheek from her mother's lipstick kiss. Catherine's words echoed in her head. *Kiss 'n kill.* She forced her attention back to her mother and sister.

"We saw you on the news last night," Betty said. "Your car's totaled, I bet." She flopped on the side of the bed and sat bouncing her foot off Jadz's chair, apparently insensitive to the annoyance it caused.

"I just saw the report." Jadz tried to slide the chair away from Betty, but it was jammed against the wall already. "Could you not do that, please?" The headache was making a fast comeback.

"Don't start, you two," Mavis said. She dragged the stool out of the opposite corner and shoved it next to Jadz's chair. "How was your night? I'll bet you didn't sleep a wink."

"Not too bad, actually," Jadz pushed the now-cold breakfast tray aside. "I wonder if I can get another cup of coffee."

Betty remained absorbed in examining her new manicure.

Mavis jumped up. "I'll find one for you. Darn nurses are never available when you need one." She scurried out.

"Excuse me." Jadz scooted back into bed, nudging Betty aside.

Betty promptly took over the armchair.

"How's the new job?" Jadz asked as she arranged the blankets.

"It sucks."

"So the trend continues."

"Why can't you get me a job at the police department? You make good money, and you're surrounded by gorgeous men."

Jadz gritted her teeth. "I make good money because I finished college, plus I busted my butt at the academy for eighteen months. Not to mention getting shot at from time to time."

Betty waved a green-taloned hand. "You always got the breaks. Everybody knows Dad got you that job."

Mavis returned with a cup of steaming coffee, cutting off Jadz's angry retort. "Are you two having a nice visit? It's so good to see my girls back together." She pulled the bed tray closer and sat the coffee within reach. "Like pulling teeth to get this out of the hospital staff, but it was worth the effort for you, sweetie." Mavis puttered about the room straightening the blinds, fluffing pillows, and adjusting the volume on the television no one was watching. Her chatter hid the simmering tension between Jadz and Betty. "There! Isn't that better? Much homier, well, as homey as a horrid hospital room can be. Who are the flowers from? That young man who was here yesterday was nice. Walked me all the way to my car when we left. He even waited to make sure I made it out of the garage safely. So courteous, too. Just like your father." She finally stopped to breathe, then turned to Betty. "Tell your sister about your new beau."

"She doesn't care about my love life," Betty said. "Makes her realize how pitiful hers is."

"Now, Betty," Mavis scolded. "She isn't up to your teasing today." She patted Jadz on the knee. "Hasn't the doctor been in, sweetie? I have a lunch meeting I don't want to miss, but I need to make sure you're settled at home before I toddle off."

"The nurse said he'd be in before ten." Jadz ignored Betty's insults for the moment. "You don't need to wait. I can call Rena."

"Nonsense. We take care of our own, don't we, Betty?"

"Whatever. Is there a smoking lounge on this floor?" Betty left the room without waiting for an answer.

"I thought she quit smoking," Jadz said.

Mavis' hands fluttered. "She's having a rough time. Those AA meetings her probation officer makes her attend every day aren't helping one bit. That's why she started smoking again. It's all they do there, that and talk about drinking." She cracked the door to peer down the hall after Betty. "I wish she could find a nice husband to take care of her so she didn't have to work so hard."

Jadz choked on her coffee. "Betty? She hasn't held a job for more than six months in the last three years."

"I never had a job after your father and I got married. Some of us aren't as strong as you are. We're better off at home without a pushy boss looking over our shoulder all day."

"She's a salesclerk at Target. That's hardly a demanding job."

"The customers are so mean to her. She came home yesterday in tears." Mavis plucked at an invisible speck on her jacket. "I wish you'd try to understand her better."

"Oh, I understand her. I'm just not sure you do." Jadz finished the coffee and eased out of bed. "I'll be right back." She slipped into the bathroom and closed the door, leaning against it briefly to gather her thoughts before taking care of business.

When she returned, Mavis was seated in the armchair chatting with Theo, who stood at the end of the bed.

"There you are," he said. "Feeling better?"

"Yes, thanks." Jadz climbed back into bed, clutching the edges of the short hospital gown to avoid flashing. "I didn't expect to see you this morning."

"I wasn't sure if you had a ride home."

"Her sister and I came in early to take care of that," Mavis said. "But I can see where Jadz might prefer your company."

"You have a sister?"

Betty's return from her prolonged smoke break answered his question. "Couldn't resist talking about me as soon as my back was turned, huh?" She spotted Theo and her demeanor changed. "Why, hello." Betty extended her hand. "I don't believe we've met."

"Theo, this is my older sister. Betty, Sergeant Theo Baxter." Jadz caught herself. *Did I really say older?*

While Mavis and Betty jockeyed for a seat closer to Theo, he whispered to Jadz. "Betty and Veronica, like in the comics?"

"Don't start with me," she said as Betty claimed his attention. Jadz was annoyed at her sister's antics and embarrassed for Theo, but she was willing to let him suffer a bit in exchange for teasing her. When Betty cornered him near the closet, she rolled her eyes and shrugged an apology. The doctor's arrival rescued him.

"Vitals are good. Slept okay." The doctor leafed through Jadz's chart, peered in her eyes with a penlight, and checked her reflexes. On his way out the door, he said, "Take it easy for a few days. You can go back to work tomorrow, nothing strenuous. Follow up with your family doctor next week to have those sutures removed."

Jadz exploded as the door closed behind him. "That's it? I spent twenty-four hours here for a two-minute exam? I could have called that in for all the good this damn confinement has done."

"Sweetie, don't be like that," Mavis said. "Doctors are very busy, with all the people they have to tend to. I'm sure if you were really sick, he would stay longer."

"I'm getting out of here." Jadz threw back the sheet and scrambled out of bed, oblivious to the flash of skin she revealed. "Where are my clothes?" She rummaged through the closet, most of her backside exposed, and tossed her rumpled clothing onto the bed before she caught Theo's sudden interest in the brick wall outside the window. "Oh!"

"I'll just wait outside," he said. "Unless you don't need me to take you home?"

"We'll make sure my little sister gets home."

"We could use your help to get my baby to the car," Mavis said.

"Don't go!"

The women spoke in unison, all eyes on Theo.

Jadz smothered a laugh at the panic on his face. "Mom and Betty can take me home. Give me a minute to change and I'll walk you out. I could use the exercise."

By the time Jadz was dressed, Theo looked like he needed rescuing from the dual threat of Mavis and Betty. He offered Jadz his arm but she shook it off. "Thanks anyway, but I need to get back on my feet."

"I'll go with you to make sure you get back okay," Mavis said, hovering behind her.

"No, stay here with Betty. We're going to talk shop." Jadz led Theo out the door, walking carefully to stretch out her sore muscles as they strolled to the lobby.

"We're talking shop?" Theo asked.

"Okay, lame excuse, but it worked. Mom doesn't like to hear much about the department since Dad died. Unless there's something new?"

"Not that I've heard, still looking for Ricky or the car."

The front desk was empty when they reached the lobby. Sunlight streamed through the glass paneled walls and reflected off the glistening floors as a custodian swirled a wet mop in lazy circles. Jadz dodged the yellow Caution sandwich board propped near the door. They loitered for a minute watching him work and enjoying a quiet moment together.

After the custodian gathered his bucket and moved on, Theo said, "Guess I should go. Call you later?"

"Sure. Thanks again for checking on me." Jadz soaked in the warmth of the sun as she watched him cross the parking lot. When he was gone, she made her way back to her room, still unsteady but determined to make it without resorting to the handrails lining the hall. Halfway back, she passed a deserted family waiting room and sat down to catch her breath.

"Mornin', Detective. Glad to see you're alive."

Jadz squinted at the woman who stood between her and the hall window, backlit by a glare that hid her features. The voice was familiar. "I'm sorry, do I know you?"

She stepped in front of Jadz, out of the sunlight. Jadz gasped.

"Catherine?"

The ragged layers and too-large jacket were gone, replaced by a shapeless but clean sundress. Her hair was pulled back in an untidy bun with a few strands framing her face. She wore the same unlaced work boots, but now with bright red tights on her thin legs. Catherine rubbed her hands over the cotton skirt, smoothing the material and fidgeting at the same time. "Went to that shelter for a bath. Figured I need to look presentable to get inta' the hospital, make sure you was okay. They took my clothes, gave me this thing to wear."

"You did that for me?" Jadz pulled Catherine down on the seat next to her.

"Saw it on TV, guy ran you off the road. Thought you might be dead and they just wouldn't say." Catherine ducked her head. "Glad you're not."

"Me, too."

"Was it 'cause I told about the kiss?"

Jadz had to strain to hear the question. "The accident? No, why would you think that?"

Her voice quavered. "I didn't mean to cause trouble."

"This isn't your fault," Jadz said. She took Catherine's hand. "You look good. I'm glad you went to the shelter. Did you eat?"

"When he asked me 'bout you—"

Jadz froze. "When who asked?" She knelt in front of Catherine to see her face, staggering a bit as her aching legs protested. "Catherine, when who asked?"

"He came out of the police station, figured he was okay. He was with that attorney, Keyser. 'Bout the only lawyer guy who's nice to me." Catherine pulled back, sat up straight. "Didn't think they heard me laugh at 'em, people usually don't."

"Why did you laugh?"

"'Cause they didn't know nothin'. Said you had it all wrong." Catherine looked smug. "So I laughed, told 'em you was smarter than that."

"What did you tell them?"

"That you wouldn't let the bastard kiss no more women to death." Catherine hesitated. "You won't, will you?"

"Not if I can help it. Tell me what you heard them talking about."

She wrung her hands in her lap and shuffled her feet. "You sound mad."

"Tell me what you heard, Catherine."

Catherine slipped into her own reality. "Everybody plays the fool," she sang under her breath.

"Catherine." Jadz touched her bare arm and shook her slightly. "Talk to me. What did you hear? Who's the fool?"

The PA system binged twice and paged the on-call plastic surgeon to the ER. A patient transport team wheeled past, followed by a clutch of tearful family members. The flurry of activity shifted Catherine back. When she looked at Jadz again, she said, "I stuck up for you. He said you were a fool, chasing the wrong guy. I laughed."

It took several minutes of gentle prodding before Jadz had what she hoped was the full story. Logan and Keyser had passed Catherine outside the station when they left after the interview. She heard them discussing the murders, and Jadz, although Catherine couldn't remember who used the term "fool," and jumped in to defend her.

Jadz slipped back onto the chair. "Did he say anything else?"

"The little guy wanted to, but Keyser wouldn't let him. Gave me a buck for coffee though, like he usually does." Catherine fumbled in her pocket. "Guess I spent it."

"You can't talk to people about me like that, about my work." She dropped her head back and stared at the mottled ceiling tiles.

"I screwed up, huh?"

"No, just don't—" Jadz pulled back a scolding. "Like I told you before, keep our secrets between us, okay? Or we can't be friends anymore."

"I'm sorry."

Jadz patted her knee. "I have to go."

"You gonna be alright?" Catherine faced her, eyes still downcast.

"I'm fine." Jadz took a deep breath and resumed her walk. Before turning the corner for the hallway to her room, she looked back. Catherine was watching her. "You look good, Catherine. Thanks for coming."

Catherine gave an awkward wave and shuffled away.

The nurse followed Jadz back into her room, scanning a sheaf of stapled papers. "I see you're all dressed to go. It'll take a few minutes to process all this before you can leave." He disappeared down the hall.

Jadz perched on the edge of the bed, drumming her fingers on the railing as she thought about Catherine.

"Your friend is cute," Betty said. "Is he why you left Nathan?"

Nathan. I was supposed to be in court two hours ago. She scowled at Betty. "Theo's a co-worker and friend. He has nothing to do with my divorce."

"Whatever. But if you're not interested, I'll take him."

"He's a human being, not a puppy. You can't just take him."

"Sweetie, don't be so defensive," Mavis said. "All Betty means is she doesn't want to interfere. She's being thoughtful."

"Sure she is." Jadz pulled her briefcase out of the nightstand and checked to make sure nothing was left behind.

Betty grabbed the leather satchel. "What are you doing with Dad's briefcase?"

Jadz jerked it away from her. "You took the car, I took the briefcase. I've been using it for two years. Where've you been?"

She glared at Jadz for a long minute, caught in a stare-down. Betty lost. She tossed her head, reverting back to nonchalance. "Whatever. Just an old bag."

An aide appeared with a wheelchair, followed by the nurse.

"It's time." The nurse recited the doctor's instructions, handed Jadz the release forms to sign, and gave her a prescription for pain medication. "Fill this right away, but don't use it unless you really need to. Ibuprofen will probably be enough for the muscle aches." He jiggled the wheelchair. "Have a seat."

Jadz frowned. "Do I have to? I just walked to the lobby and back."

"Only if you want to leave on my shift." He stood waiting, the release forms tucked under his arm.

"C'mon, sweetie, enjoy the ride." Mavis hovered at her side.

Jadz flopped into the chair. "Can I go now, please?"

Betty stacked the briefcase and sunflowers on Jadz's lap and headed out the door, leaving Mavis to maneuver the chair.

"It's been a joy for us, too," the nurse said as they paraded down the hall. He handed over the release when they parted ways at the elevator. Jadz sulked in the wheelchair during the short walk to the parking garage. As soon as they cleared the building, Jadz pulled out her cell phone to call her lawyer.

"Phillip? I missed my divorce. Rena called?" She listened for a few seconds. "Okay, Friday morning, ten o'clock. I'll be there." She called Rena next, but got her voice mail, so Jadz searched her call log for Paul's cell number.

Mavis took the phone from Jadz and dropped it into her shoulder bag. "The doctor said you're not supposed to work until tomorrow. They can live without you for one more day." Mavis' unaccustomed sternness startled Jadz into compliance.

Betty climbed into the front seat of Mavis' Concorde and left her mother to help Jadz from the wheelchair into the back seat. She started to light a cigarette, but blew out the match when Jadz forced an exaggerated cough. Betty snorted and tucked the pack back into her purse. "Fine. I'll wait."

Mavis chattered non-stop during the ten-minute drive, bouncing from the unseasonably warm weather, to complaining about the rising gas prices, to tittering over the latest gossip from her Euchre club. Her comments needed nothing more than an occasional "Uh-huh" response to keep the words flowing. Jadz clambered out of the car as soon as they parked in front of the apartment. She steadied herself on the door when the exertion made her head spin. Mavis took her arm and together they unloaded the car and entered the building, Betty trailing behind them empty-handed.

Ford greeted them at the apartment door with a chorus of indignant meows.

"I am so sorry, old man." Jadz cuddled him and crooned softly while filling his food and water dish and scooping out the litter box. "Poor thing."

"It's just a damn cat," Betty said, prowling around the room. "You act like he knows what you're saying."

"He understands me better than you do," Jadz said.

Mavis flitted about opening the patio door, checking the contents of the fridge, and shaking her head at its barrenness. "Don't you ever buy groceries?"

"I'm not hungry." Jadz stretched out on the couch. Her body ached. The headache was back. She couldn't work for another twenty-four hours and food was the last thing on her mind. "I'll order something later." Betty's scrutiny of her desk irritated Jadz further. "Can I help you find something?"

"Chill already," she said. "I'm just looking."

"Don't you have a lunch date?" Jadz asked her mother.

Mavis started, then checked her watch. "What time is it? I have to go. Are you sure you'll be okay? Betty could stay."

"No!" Jadz and Betty answered in chorus.

"I'll be fine," Jadz continued. "Thanks for taking care of me this morning. Go enjoy your lunch."

After they left, with promises from Mavis to call later, Jadz lounged with her feet propped on the coffee table and considered her options. She needed to check in with Rena, but the phone still went directly to voice mail. Jadz left a message at Dispatch and dug through her briefcase for Paul's number.

"Hey, it's me. Yeah, I'm fine. Doctors and lieutenants overreact. It sounds like my car got the worst of it." She listened to Paul for a moment. "No, doesn't sound like they found Ricky yet. I've been trying Rena all morning, but no one is answering." Her unwarranted rudeness to Rena in the hospital added a layer of guilt to Jadz's discomfort. "What time's the interview with Logan? Damn, and Forester won't let me come back until tomorrow morning. Have Rena call me before you start, okay? Thanks."

Jadz hung up and pulled a legal pad out of her bag. She jotted names and locations from the case, linking people and actions with arrows and lines, alternately searching for a connection other than the driver's license and trying to break Logan's alibi. Nothing else fit. It was nearly three o'clock when she noticed the time. She tried Rena's cell phone again. No answer. Jadz braved Forester's wrath and called the detective bureau directly, leaving another message when the secretary told her Rena had been and gone. She tossed the phone across the couch and brooded.

Ford curled into her lap, meowing for attention. Jadz obliged by rubbing his stomach while she wondered about Rena's absence. When Ford jumped down in search of food, Jadz stretched. She eased through a few yoga poses to loosen her aching muscles. Focused breathing calmed her racing thoughts, and she found a semblance of calm. *Maybe a shower will help.* Hot water soothed the lingering pains. Fresh clothes, a passing swipe with a comb, and she emerged from the bathroom in a better frame of mind.

Jadz tackled overdue household chores, moving slowly as she dusted, vacuumed, tossed in a load of laundry and sorted through the paperwork on her desk. She ignored the dull pain that circled her head. Her phone remained silent.

A check of the pantry and refrigerator at five-thirty confirmed Mavis' assessment of the food situation. Jadz reached for her keys before remembering she didn't have a car to go with them. She dug out a stack of delivery menus to review her limited options when the doorbell rang. Jadz peeked through the door's security viewer. Rena stood in the hall, her arms loaded with carry-out food containers. Paul was with her.

"I was considering ways to avoid starvation," Jadz said as she opened the door. "And deciding how best to throttle you two for ignoring me."

"I am sorry," Rena said as she unloaded her packages onto the counter, "but the lieutenant was very explicit. No work for you until tomorrow."

"So we're not working," Paul said with a wink. "This is a mercy call for an injured comrade."

The doorbell rang again.

"That should be Theo with the beer," Paul said.

While he answered the door, Jadz pulled Rena aside to apologize. "Guess I haven't conquered being a jerk yet. Last night was uncalled for."

"I learned long ago never to take seriously anything said in a hospital room." Rena smiled. "Now sit, so I can tell Lieutenant Forester I was here to take care of you."

Jadz sat.

Rena took over the kitchen with Jadz pointing her to plates and silverware while Paul and Theo pulled chairs closer to the coffee table.

"You guys should take up catering," Jadz said as they passed around the take-out cartons. "This is just what I needed."

"Pass the General Tso's, will you?" Theo took the white box from Paul and emptied the spicy chicken entrée onto his plate. "Hope nobody else wanted any."

Genial conversation mingled with the enticing aromas of Chinese food and they avoided discussing the case until dinner was over. Jadz obeyed further orders and curled up on the couch while Theo and Paul cleared the dishes. Rena started the dishwasher.

After seeing to drink refills, Rena pulled a folder out of her briefcase. "The interview with Mr. Logan was fruitless." She handed Jadz a copy of the report. "He was very open, answered all our questions, his alibis are in order, and he seems genuinely puzzled that his work is connected to the murders."

"Neighbors are uniformly positive and supportive, even the couple across the street who don't approve of 'their kind,'" Paul said. "His mother lives in Sylvania, has for thirty years, widowed for twenty. No other family."

Rena read from her notes. "His co-workers at the Botanical Garden say he is prompt, courteous, and accommodating. The students love him. Only one complaint on file since he started teaching six years ago, and that was from a gentleman who thought Mr. Logan was hitting on his wife."

They shared at laugh at the incongruity.

"Too good to be true, maybe?" Jadz tossed the report on the coffee table and sank back into the sofa cushions, suppressing a groan at her sore muscles. "But no more bodies since we talked to him three days ago. What are we missing?"

"Three days is not that long," Rena said. "The deaths are separated by more than a month in the first two cases."

"But the last three have come closer together." Jadz shuffled through the papers. "They've shifted from two months apart to four weeks to just six days."

"Closer, yes," Rena said, "but still nothing in three days. And his alibis are in order. He is a very orderly, scheduled man who appears to thrive on routine."

Jadz's headache returned. She stood and stretched. "I'm not letting Logan off the hook. Not yet." She motioned Theo back to his seat as he rose to help with the empties. Jadz brought back the last two beers and a handful of fortune cookies, tossing a cellophane-wrapped treat to each of them. "Who has dibs on the beer? I probably shouldn't while my head mends."

"I am fine with water," Rena said.

"Guess that means I have to wrestle Theo for them." Paul feigned a fighting stance before surrendering one of the bottles. "Okay, you win."

Paul broke open his fortune cookie. "'The greatest danger could be your stupidity,'" he read.

"Got you pegged, don't they?" Theo ducked Paul's swat at his head.

Rena shared next. "'He who throws mud is losing ground.'" Derisive hoots mixed with laughter.

"'A closed mouth gathers no feet,'" Jadz said. "Not much better. Theo?"

"Help, I'm being held prisoner in a fortune cookie factory."

They all laughed again.

Theo shoved the slip of paper into his pocket. "It's a duplicate."

Jadz nestled into the sofa. "How did you get mixed up with these two anyway?" she asked Theo.

"I'm here about your accident. I invited myself for dinner when I heard what they were up to."

"Has Ricky turned up yet?" Paul asked.

"Nope, so the patrol car stays out front until morning," Theo said.

"There's a patrol car out front?" Jadz jumped up to check, wincing at the pain caused by sudden movement.

"Some detective. You've been under guard since you got home," Paul said.

She threw a pillow at him and sat down. "Speaking of morning, can I get a ride from one of you fine upstanding officers? I'll get a rental tomorrow."

"I'll be here," Theo offered before the others could respond. "It's on my way."

"I thought you lived in Point Place—ouch!" A sharp kick from Rena cut off Paul's comment.

As if the scuffle under the coffee table hadn't happened, Theo continued. "Welch said to tell you Ricky's family swears he had nothing to do with the accident, that he was at home at the time … yada, yada. But two more defendants are set for plea hearings, so we'll keep an eye on your building until Ricky turns up."

"I hate being watched. And I really don't think Ricky had anything to do with it. It's not his style."

"Would you rather he shot you?" Theo's voice was sharp.

"No, I mean any kind of confrontation." She sat up and met his gaze. "I've had a lot of time to think today. When I was undercover, it was pretty obvious he didn't want anything to do with drug running. He stood up to his brother when he tried to recruit him to deal. That took guts. I think Ricky's basically a good kid."

"The task force isn't so sure. Until they find him, you'll have protection, like it or not." Theo drained his beer and thumped the empty down on the coffee table.

After an awkward silence, Rena gathered the files back into her briefcase. "It is getting late. You should rest, or Lieutenant Forester will have all our heads in the morning. I believe he misses you."

"That'll be the day." Jadz followed her to the door. "I forgot we were supposed to have dinner tonight, too" she said.

"We just did," Rena said. "We will talk more another time."

Paul made a show of rubbing his shin before he followed her out, leaving Theo behind.

"I probably should go, too," Theo said.

Jadz touched his arm. "Stay for a minute. We should talk."

He closed the door and followed her back to the sofa. "Like I tried to say Saturday, if I'm out of line, you have to let me know."

Jadz considered his words. "Not out of line, maybe premature? Because of the accident, my divorce won't be final until Friday, and I'll need time to adjust to the idea of being single again. The separation was like being in limbo. Nathan wouldn't accept the marriage was over, so he's been here more than he should have." Jadz perched on the edge of the chair facing Theo. "It's my own fault. I was afraid to let go, even though I knew it had to happen. But I'm ready to admit my failures and I think Nathan finally accepts that."

"It's not a failure, at least not yours. Nathan always had an eye for a skirt."

"But I bear some of the blame. It's not like I made it easy for him, especially when I joined the task force."

"He's been a cop longer than you have. He knew what he was getting into."

Jadz wandered to the patio door to put some distance between them. "No more excuses. It's over, and I'm ready to move on."

"Could you not stand in front of the window like that?" Theo pulled the blinds and steered her back toward the center of the room. "Ricky's still out there, and whether you think he's capable of violence or not, I don't want you taking any chances."

"You don't have to protect me." Jadz stepped away. "I'm a cop, too, remember?"

"We all need to be protected once in a while, and right now it's my job to protect you as a possible victim, whether you're an officer or not."

"This is ridiculous." Jadz carried the remaining glasses to the sink. Theo's closeness unnerved her. His musky scent was wreaking havoc on her strained nerves. Nathan, Forester, the murders. *Is someone really trying to kill me?* "I'm too tired to argue. Let's change the subject."

"You haven't answered my question. Am I out of line?"

She frowned. "I said—"

"You said I was premature, as if any guy wants to hear that." Theo ambled around the small living room scanning the titles on the crowded bookshelf and almost tripping over Ford, who scurried under the armchair. "We've been friends a long time. I waited until Nathan was out of the picture, even though you never told me you were married."

"I explained that."

"I know, but where does that leave me now? And you? Is there a timetable? A formula I should know about? Or are we 'just friends'? I'd rather hear it now than later."

"Just friends is not a bad thing." Jadz moved closer and squeezed his arm gently. "But more is not out of the question. I don't want a rebound relationship. That's a recipe for disaster. If we can take things a little slower—"

He cut off her words with a soft kiss. "Not too slow, okay? I've waited a long time." Jadz didn't move. Another quick kiss and Theo said, "I'll pick you up at seven. Sleep well."

She didn't hear the door close behind him as she read the slip of paper he'd pressed into her hand. It was from his fortune cookie. "'Dare to dream.'" Jadz stood rooted to the spot long after he let himself out.

Chapter 11

Thursday morning's sun had warmed the night air by the time Jadz met Theo at the curb. As they started for downtown, she said, "The surveillance crew is gone. Does that mean they found Ricky?"

"I sent them off since their shift was about up. Ricky surfaced about an hour ago at his mother's. He called to turn himself in. Actually his lawyer did, and we picked Ricky up there. The task force has him now for questioning."

"Can we swing by?"

"Welch said you are not to be involved. Not yet, anyway. Let them do their job. You're the victim in this, remember?"

"Damn it, if he's trying to kill me, I am involved." The calmness Jadz had found in her morning meditation clashed with the inevitable tension of the day. Now she stared out at passing traffic and grumbled. "I don't like being shut out."

"They're not shutting you out. If they find anything to connect him to your accident, they'll call. Now relax." Theo sped up to make a yellow light. "If anyone is being shut out, it's me. My accident investigation and I can't interview the suspect till they're done."

"I forgot that part. We can be pissed at the task force together."

"For all the good that'll do." Theo dropped Jadz in front of the police station. "I'll check with you later to be sure you have a car."

After a slow trip up the stairs, Jadz emerged in the hallway outside the detective bureau just as Rena exited the elevator.

"Good timing," Jadz said. "Ready for another fun day?"

"I am glad you are feeling better." Rena opened the door into the bureau and followed Jadz through.

Forester met them at the desk as Jadz sorted through her accumulated mail.

"How's the head?" he asked. He didn't wait for an answer. "Welch called to say DeMarco has an alibi for your hit-skip."

"Good morning to you, too," Jadz said with a grin. "My head's fine and the alibi doesn't surprise me. I said all along it's not Ricky's style."

"That means someone else is still out to get you," Forester said. "Want to joke about that while you're at it?"

Jadz sobered. "I'm not laughing, really. But why are you so sure it was intentional? I never saw the car coming."

"Two separate witnesses say the guy was tailing you for at least six blocks. It sounds like he followed you from downtown onto the Trail waiting for an opportunity."

"Mr. Logan was working," Rena said. "I already checked."

"Until we find this guy, you two stick together, got it? And a marked unit stays outside your apartment when you're off duty." Forester was adamant. "Jadz, no showboating. This is serious." He strode into his office and slammed the door.

"Wonderful." Jadz turned to Rena. "You thought Logan was involved?"

She shrugged. "It was a possibility. We have to consider all options when your life is being threatened."

"I still think it could have been an accident."

"We will see. Now we have work to do." Rena handed Jadz a pink phone message slip. "Dispatch took this call late last night and sent it up for you."

"Samantha Gilbert," Jadz read. "Can't place the name," she said as she dialed the number. "Ms. Gilbert? Detective Jadzinski, returning your call. I'm sorry? No, we're not investigating the Adams death, that's Swanton's case. What makes you think it's related? Sure, we can meet." Jadz grabbed for a pen. "Give me your address. Okay, then where? Forty-five minutes." Jadz disconnected and cupped her chin in her hand, frowning.

Rena waited half a beat. "Well?"

"She's a friend of Felicia Adams, says she would never commit suicide and that Stanley's a lying SOB."

"Then she needs to call Detective Spiner."

"Spiner blew her off." Jadz fingered the area around her stitches. "Damn, that hurts."

"Stop playing with it or it will never heal." Rena threw a wad of paper at her. "And?"

Jadz grabbed her briefcase and headed for the door. "And we're meeting her to find out why. Let's go."

The breakfast crowd left only a few stragglers by the time Jadz and Rena reached the Bob Evans Restaurant on Reynolds Road just off exit fifty-nine of the Ohio Turnpike. Two sedans filled the handicap spaces near the front door, with a vintage Indian motorcycle parked next to them. Red and blue flames on the helmet looped over the backrest matched the customized "Sam" on the gas tank. They found Gilbert in the far corner surrounded by vacant tables. She was a short muscular woman with a mass of black curly hair, assorted piercings, and tattoos covering most of the skin visible around her sleeveless black leather vest. Faded jeans topped a pair of scuffed boots.

After short introductions, Gilbert asked, "You guys are trying to find who killed all those women, right?"

"Ms. Gilbert, you should talk to Detective Spiner about the Adams case, not us," Rena said.

"Call me Sam. Hate that 'Ms.' crap. He won't talk to me."

Jadz waited until the server poured coffee and left the alcove. "Why is that?"

"'Cause that prick Stanley told him I had an axe to grind." Gilbert shredded a napkin into a pile of confetti while she talked. "As if that matters with Lizzy dead."

"You mean Felicia Adams," Rena said.

Gilbert squinted past an eyebrow stud that nearly caught her lashes. "Of course I mean Felicia Adams. You're not a moron like Spiner, are you?"

"We're not morons." Jadz took over. "I can't speak for Spiner." Her look told Rena, *My turn*.

"Yeah, well, trust me. He's a moron." Gilbert sucked down the last of a watered-down soda, slurping noisily. "Like I said on the phone, Lizzy wouldn't kill herself. Stanley, maybe."

"Stanley would kill Lizzy?" Jadz asked. Her question earned the same disgusted look given to Rena.

"No, Lizzy wanted to kill him, lots of times." Gilbert swirled the ice in her glass. "And he hasn't got the balls to get his hands dirty. So it has to be whoever killed all those other women, right?" She waved her empty at the server across the room.

"Why would she want to kill him?"

"'Cause he wouldn't marry her, the selfish bastard."

Jadz straightened. "He said he planned to propose the night she died."

Gilbert's eyes widened. "He said that? Lying son of a bitch."

"Why do you think he was lying?"

Gilbert took the filled glass off the server's tray and shooed her away. "They had a big blow-up the day before Lizzy's birthday. She insisted, for like the twelfth time, that they should get married."

"So maybe he changed his mind and agreed," Jadz said.

"Yeah, right. Always whining about his alimony payments, child support, like it was her fault he was divorced and had a kid. I don't think so."

Neither Spiner nor Stanley had mentioned an ex-wife. Jadz looked to Rena as she asked Gilbert, "Was this ex jealous?"

"No way, she was glad to be rid of him, moved all the way to Chicago. But she wanted her money, that's for sure."

Jadz rotated her coffee cup slowly as she pondered this new information. "What's your beef with Stanley?

Gilbert snorted. "Besides the way he treated Lizzy? Nothing. He thinks I've got the hots for him. Figures all women who can't have him are jealous or something. What a joke."

"When did Lizzy tell you about the fight?"

A long silence stretched before Gilbert answered. "We had lunch on her birthday, always do—did. She was still mad, said she'd make him pay for stringing her along."

Rena asked the question Jadz avoided. "So she wasn't depressed enough at being left alone to kill herself?"

"Hell, no! Lizzy wouldn't do that." Gilbert shoved back from the table, and turned away, propping one foot on the chair next to her. She spoke to the traffic streaming down Reynolds Road, not to Jadz or Rena. "I always told her when she was done playing games with that jerk, I'd be waiting."

Jadz let the comment pass. "What did she mean she'd make him pay?"

Gilbert shrugged and drained her glass. "That's the only thing I know of that she wouldn't tell me. She had something on him though, way she talked."

Rena stepped in to ask the routine questions. "How long did you know Lizzy?"

"Fourteen years, give or take. Since her divorce, anyway." Gilbert laughed shortly. "Always talked about her 'first ex-husband,' like she had a whole string of them or something. Bet Stanley would've been her second ex, if the bastard would've ever married her."

"Where were you the night she died?"

"At work. I'm on the Delta baggage crew at the airport. I started pulling double shifts on Lizzy's birthday a few years back so I didn't have to sit home while she was out with him. She called me, about seven I guess, when he dumped her for the night. She was pretty drunk, and pissed. I tried to get off early, but we were already shorthanded." She stared into her empty glass. "That's the last time … if I'd been there, maybe she'd still be alive."

When the questions ran out, Jadz paid for the drinks and they followed Gilbert to the parking lot.

She climbed onto the motorcycle and started the engine. "Anyway, thanks for hearing me out. Will you let me know if you catch whoever killed her?"

"Sure," Jadz said.

"Wish I knew what Lizzy had on him. I'd take care of it for her." Gilbert roared away, the unused helmet bouncing behind her on the back of the bike.

"A jealous girlfriend who admits she wants revenge is not a good witness," Rena insisted during the drive back to the station.

"Maybe not, but we need to talk to Stanley again." Jadz skipped the stairs this time took the elevator with the Rena to continue the debate. By the time they reached the detective bureau, Rena gave in.

"I will call Swanton," she said when they were at the desks.

"No." Jadz stopped her. "Call Stanley's attorney. We need to talk to him again."

"But it is Detective Spiner's case."

"Spiner already had a shot at Gilbert. His loss. If we find anything he needs to know, we'll call him," Jadz said. "Right now, this is our case."

"I want to run this by Lieutenant Forester."

Jadz clenched her jaw, caught herself, and took a deep breath. "Fine. I'm going to lunch." She strode out of the office without waiting for a response.

Jadz called Paul while waiting for Coney dogs at George's. She was annoyed to find he agreed with Rena's opinion.

"But Paul, Spiner's a pain. Yes, I know he's a good cop, but he likes women even less than Forester does. I don't care if it's his suspect." Jadz propped her elbows on the table and rested her head on her free hand. The headache was back. So much for taking it easy. "Yeah, I'd be pissed if somebody pulled that on me. All right, you made your point. Forester always sides with Rena, so I guess I'm outnumbered. We'll ask him to come along. Maybe he'll say no."

With a promise to update Paul after the interview with Stanley, Jadz called Rena. Voice mail rang in. Feeling mildly guilty at the flood of relief, Jadz left a short message and hung up. She gulped down her lunch, adding heartburn to the growing headache. At the counter, she paid her bill and bought a pack of antacids.

"Is this yours?" The cashier indicated a brown carry-out bag next to the register.

"Nope."

"Guess somebody forgot it."

Jadz stopped her from tossing it in the trash. "I'll take it."

The cashier shrugged. "Already paid for, I don't care."

Back on the street, Jadz took a roundabout route to the office, circling the Lucas County Courthouse and checking the sidewalk outside the library. The steamy August afternoon was cooled by a slight breeze that almost made the humidity bearable. Clutches of office workers on break gathered under the trees and awnings to shelter from the sun's glare. Busy lunchtime traffic reflected the heavy laziness in the air as well, moving slower and with less honking than usual. Jadz walked slowly, easing the ache from her still-sore muscles as she took in the bustling street scenes. One last turn and she found Catherine on the steps outside the county jail on Spielbusch.

"Hey." Jadz sat down next to her. "You hungry?" She handed Catherine the carry-out. "I don't know what it is, but it's from George's."

Catherine tore into the bag. "Good to see you on your feet," she said around a mouthful of hot dog. "Any mustard in there?"

"Thanks again for the hospital visit." Jadz rooted through the wrappers. She found a handful of condiment packs that Catherine squeezed onto the remaining sandwich.

"S'okay. I was worried," she said.

Jadz studied Catherine's disheveled appearance. "Didn't you go back to the shelter?"

Catherine shook her head as she downed the last bite. "Good weather, don't need to."

"Your call," Jadz said. She stood and stretched. "I need to get back to work."

"I ain't seen no more murders. Catch the guy?"

"Not yet, maybe we scared him off." She handed Catherine a five-dollar bill that disappeared into a hidden pocket. "Take care of yourself."

"You, too. Thanks for the food."

As Paul predicted, Spiner wanted nothing to do with another interview of Stanley.

"He is even more unhappy with us for insisting on it, if that is possible," Rena said. "But we have Lieutenant Forester's okay to go ahead."

"How soon?" Jadz asked.

"Bulger is in court today. She is willing to meet tomorrow at ten-thirty, if we go to her office again. Since he is not officially a suspect, I agreed."

"My divorce hearing's at ten, so that should work. Let's get some background on him, so we're ready."

"Already started." Rena passed a legal pad across the desk. "He has no criminal record that I could find."

"Damn, you're good." Jadz rubbed her forehead as she skimmed the notes. "I need to start pulling my weight."

"Headache still? Have you taken your medication?"

"Yes, and no, but that's no excuse." She laid the pad aside and leaned back. "Something about this case just sets me off. All these women trusted someone enough to let them into their homes late at night. Logan seemed like our guy, but his alibis are tight. Now Adams and Stanley, but that doesn't fit either. It just makes things worse. What are we missing?" Jadz closed her eyes. "I can't even think straight."

"There is not much else we can do before the interview, other than a few background calls. I can handle those. Get some rest. Recovery from an accident like yours is not easy." Rena gathered the files. "Tomorrow is another day."

Jadz chuckled. "Been watching old movies again?" She sat up and took a deep breath. "You've been right all day, guess I should learn to listen. I'll see you in the morning."

Chapter 12

Jadz and Rena spent early Friday morning reviewing the Adams case, trying unsuccessfully to make it mesh with the other deaths.

"Even if they are not connected, Stanley has some explaining to do," Rena said. She glanced at the clock. "When is your hearing?"

The reminder brought Jadz to her feet. "Excuse me, I have to get divorced. I'll meet you at Bulger's office." She left the bureau at a trot, grabbed the elevator because of the time, and arrived in the courtroom across the street just as the bailiff called her case. Her attorney frowned as they approached the bench.

"Nothing like waiting till the last minute," he said.

The routine procedure went smoothly. Jadz answered the judge's questions in a low, measured voice. He made a finding of cause and the divorce was granted. Ten minutes later, she was in the hall with her attorney.

"Just like that, six years of my life are over."

He rested a hand on her shoulder. "I have to go. Are you okay?"

She shook off the gloom. "Sure. I have a murderer to catch."

Jadz pushed through the revolving doors at the Spitzer Building less than half an hour after leaving the detective bureau. As she entered the elevator, the realization that Nathan skipped the hearing caused an unexpected pang. *Better get used to not having him around.* The thought disturbed her more than she cared to admit.

Rena was in Bulger's empty reception area when Jadz arrived. The interior office door was closed. Raised voices seeped through.

"Eavesdropping on attorney-client consultation?" she whispered, startling Rena from her position near the door.

Rena grinned and shifted away. "Not that you know of. Mr. Stanley seems distressed at our visit."

"Any idea why?"

Bulger opened the door and deflected Rena's answer. "Detectives. I hope this is brief. Mr. Stanley's been inconvenienced enough."

Jadz followed her into the office. "A little inconvenience should be doable. Five women are dead."

"Only one of which concerns my client directly. Please keep that in mind."

Stanley watched the exchange from his seat at the far corner of Bulger's desk. The overhead fluorescent glare cast a sickly pall on his ashen features.

Rena began the interview while Jadz took notes. "Mr. Stanley, can you tell us where you were on the nights when the other women died?" She handed a list of dates to Bulger who scanned it and scrawled on a legal pad before passing it along to him.

"Other women? How should I know?" Stanley hardly glanced at the sheet. "If this serial murderer killed Felicia, what difference does it make where I was? Wait … you don't think it's me?" He choked on the question.

Bulger took over. "Just answer the question if you can. For the moment, we'll assume the detectives are simply being diligent."

He scrolled through his Blackberry calendar. "I don't know. I was at a Mud Hens game on the fourteenth with guys from work. We were out pretty late. Other than that, I was probably home with Felicia." Stanley pocketed the phone and stared at Rena defiantly. "Besides, the paper said you had a suspect. Why ask me?"

"You know quite a bit about the other deaths, do you?" Rena asked.

"I watch the news," he said. "It kind of bothered Felicia, the whole forty-year-old thing, so I made sure I could stop her from worrying she was next."

"But now you think you were wrong." Rena let the statement hang while Stanley fidgeted.

"Well, I mean, it makes sense, doesn't it? It was her birthday." He avoided the glare Jadz fixed on him, focusing instead on the pattern in the carpet.

"How do you suppose the killer knew it was her birthday?" Rena asked.

Stanley shrugged. "I don't know. You're the cop."

"You're fishing," Bulger said. "If you have a reason to think my client is involved in those deaths, say so."

Rena moved on. "We would like to clear up a discrepancy from our earlier meeting. Did you argue with Ms. Adams about marriage the day before she died?"

"No." He looked to Bulger, who frowned. "I mean, we talked. But it wasn't an argument. I realized she was right. It was time we got married."

"So the proposal was not your idea?"

"Sure it was, I mean, we agreed." Stanley squirmed. "But I've been there, and my ex-wife cleaned me out. I didn't ever want to go through that again."

"Yet this discussion convinced you that after several years and numerous arguments it was time to propose." Rena's statement stilled him.

"Who said that?" Stanley gripped the arms of the chair. "You've been talking to that bitch Gilbert, haven't you?"

Bulger sat forward. "Gilbert who? Brad, do we need to talk?"

"Samantha Gilbert, Felicia's butch friend. She's tried to break us up forever, jealous dyke." He slammed a fist onto the desk. "What else did she say about me?"

"Mr. Stanley." Bulger's tone stopped his outburst. "Excuse us, detectives." She led Stanley into the outer office and closed the door.

For several minutes, indistinguishable murmurs from the attorney-client conversation were the only sound in the room. Jadz raised her eyebrows at Rena, who simply shrugged.

When they returned, Stanley slumped into his chair. Bugler resumed her seat behind the desk and picked up her pen. "It appears Ms. Gilbert is a distinctly hostile third-party. You'll need more than her version of things to implicate my client."

"Of course," Rena said. "Mr. Stanley, this discussion about marriage took place late in the evening the night before Ms. Adams died, correct? And you worked your regular hours on her birthday, before you were called in for an emergency?"

He nodded, his eyes darting from Rena to Jadz.

"When did you buy the ring?"

Stanley looked to his attorney and stammered, "I, uh, right after I, I mean—"

"How's that relevant?" Bulger asked. "Obviously he found time."

"What did Ms. Adams say that night that caused you to change your mind?" Rena's voice was level but unrelenting.

"I told you, she just said … it was time."

Jadz noted the fists balled in Stanley's lap. At Rena's slight nod, she took over. "What information was she using to blackmail you?"

"That's enough." Bulger stood up. "If my client is a suspect, file charges so we can start discovery. I can't defend him properly if you're going to play games."

Jadz remained seated, eyes fixed on Stanley. "We have a witness who believes Adams had some kind of hold over you. If she was forcing you into marriage, we have a motive for murder. Maybe you killed all the others to hide your tracks."

"That's not what happened!" Stanley's voice shook.

"Not another word, Brad." Bulger stepped around her desk, shielding him from Jadz's accusatory glare. "This conversation is over."

"Fine." Jadz joined Rena at the door. "Understand, we'll be checking your story very carefully, Mr. Stanley. You may want to reconsider your answers."

For the next two days, Jadz and Rena tracked down every bit of information Stanley had provided. Co-workers verified the emergency shift the night Adams died, and while the victim's mother shared much of Gilbert's opinion of Stanley, she stopped short of accusing him of murder.

"She fretted over all those women who were killed," Adams' mother had said. "Being forty bothered her no end, so that just made it worse. All he had to do was marry her like she wanted and none of this would've happened."

"So now what?" Jadz spun circles in her office chair while Rena sorted through the reports.

"Unless we can tie him to any of the other victims, we need to move on," Rena said. She studied the victim spreadsheet again. "And that is not looking promising. There are no common threads."

"What if instead of killing the others to hide Adams' death, he just used the MO to dispose of her and hide his tracks?" Paul asked. He had stopped in during recess from a trial in federal court to catch up. "We know there were discrepancies at the scene."

"We tried that," Rena said. "His alibi is solid."

"According to Spiner, there weren't any unmatched fingerprints in the apartment, right?" Jadz asked. "And nothing was wiped clean."

"Right." Rena set the Swanton file aside. "Maybe it really is a suicide."

"I still want to know what she had on him." Jadz went back to her notes from the interview with Gilbert and quoted, "'She'd make him pay for stringing her along.' Somebody has to know what it was."

"Maybe not," Paul said. "And even if she had something, it still doesn't tie him to the others, so it's Spiner's problem."

"Paul is right." Rena shuffled the folders like a huge deck of cards before pulling out the file on Stanley. "As much as we would like to take Stanley down, we need to focus on our case. I will fax Detective Spiner our summary and let him deal with it."

Jadz wrinkled her nose in disgust. "Okay, fine. But if Spiner doesn't buy it, I hate thinking Stanley's getting away with murder. What's next?"

"The registrar can't be coincidence," Paul said. "It's too much. Who else has access to that data? Maybe somebody is trying to frame Logan."

"Anyone in the office could find the information, I suppose," Rena said. She retrieved the files on the agency's employees. "They have six full-time staff, two part-time, and the manager. We have spoken to them all and learned nothing."

"But what did we ask?" Jadz leaned in. "Just how Logan got along with the public, right? Not so much about personal relationships."

"Any problems in the office, that sort of thing," Paul said. "We could go back and try again from a different angle, see what turns up."

"We should talk to Mr. Logan's partner again, too." As usual, Rena was making notes. "Mr. Proust has retained Gordon Evans for himself, so we will need to go through his office to set up an interview."

Paul stood. "I have to get back for closing arguments. With any luck, we'll have a quick verdict and I'll be back this afternoon."

Rena passed the latest list to Jadz. "These are the registrar employees for follow-up. Shall we start with those who are not working today, and finish up at the agency?"

They split the names and called the off-duty staff members to schedule interviews. Jadz dug out a map of metro Toledo and plotted a course to cover all the locations as quickly as possible.

While Rena drove, Jadz called the body shop to check on her car. "Two weeks? Damn, I only want the front end and door fixed, not a whole new car." She finished the call as they reached the first address. "I just realized something," Jadz said to Rena as they walked up the front sidewalk. "If the insurance company decides the accident was work-related, they won't cover damages."

"That is why the department prefers we not use our own vehicles. You do not carry the professional rider on your policy?"

"Nathan always handled the insurance. I'm not even sure what type of coverage we had. Guess that's one more thing I need to take care of now that we're divorced. I'd better start a list."

The interviews were fast and fruitless. Jadz and Rena arrived at the registrar just before three to find Paul waiting in the parking lot.

"Jury's still out, so I'll have to leave if they come back. Any luck?" he asked.

"Nobody has a problem with Logan. No grudge, no jealousy, at least not that they're sharing," Jadz said.

"Figures our suspect had to be citizen of the year." Paul gestured toward the registrar's door. "Do they know we're coming?"

"I thought we'd surprise them." Jadz grinned. "Never know what a little upset might shake loose."

"We do not need all three of us for this," Rena said. "I will check the adjacent stores to see if anyone knows him."

"Sounds good. We can handle the employees," Jadz said.

Kim met them at the counter. Logan turned his back.

"I can't have you harassing my employees," Kim said. "Greg told me all about what you've put him through. You're not coming in here again without a warrant."

"We need to talk to your staff, Ms. Angelo, and if you insist on a warrant, we'll get one." Paul said. "I'm sure you don't want to protect a murderer."

"He's not a murderer." Kim flushed as her words drew from customers in the lobby. "You'd better come into my office."

When the door was closed, Jadz took over. "Ma'am, we're not here to cause trouble for Mr. Logan. But we need to find out who's responsible for five deaths, and there is a common link to this office. What would you have us do?"

Kim dropped into her chair. "This is horrible. Everyone's so tense." She nibbled at a fingernail, then clenched her hands on the desk. "What do you need this time?"

"We'd like to talk to each of the employees separately, for just a few minutes," Jadz said. "Someone is using information from this office to identify victims, and maybe to frame Mr. Logan."

Her knuckles turned white. "Someone else is a suspect? Oh, my goodness." She scanned the agents at the counter area as if looking for a sign. "I thought I knew all these people."

"May we use your office, please?" Jadz's impatience sharpened her voice. "I'm sure you prefer we don't disrupt your routine for any longer than necessary."

"Of course, certainly." Kim gathered a handful of papers off the desk. "Who do you want to talk to first?"

"We'll leave that to you," Paul said. "Maybe alphabetical?"

Kim's nerves erupted in a high-pitched giggle. "Alphabetical. So ordinary." She slipped through the door, relieving the first clerk and sending him to the office.

One by one, Logan's co-workers repeated their stories of kindness, courtesy, and geniality. The crew was like family, they insisted, with no resentments. Dolly came in last. Her nervousness was gone, replaced by a sad resignation.

"I almost lost my job," she said. "Now I'll probably never make manager."

"I'm sorry about that," Jadz said. "Investigations often turn up unrelated issues." She leafed through her notes for a clue on how best to proceed, knowing this was her last shot. "How long have you worked with Mr. Logan?"

"Eight years, last month."

"And he's been here fifteen, is that right?"

"I think so."

"So how come you were up for Saturday manager instead of him?"

"He didn't put in for it."

"Do you know why not?"

"I think he wanted to stay at the counter," Dolly said. "Something about hating bureaucracy."

"The whole place is bureaucracy," Paul said.

"I know, but more like the politics behind the scenes," Dolly said. "When they hired Kim, I think he wanted that job. But somebody at the county office made a big deal about his being gay and all and he didn't get it. I think that made him decide not to try again. He doesn't like confrontation."

"So Logan was angry with the agency?"

"Not the agency, somebody higher up. I never knew who it was that nixed his promotion. And he didn't stay angry, that's not like Greg. He just moved on. He's very Zen," Dolly said. "Not like Marc."

"His partner?" Jadz perked up.

"Uh-huh. I don't know what they see in each other. I mean, I guess gay men still go for looks, but they're really different, personality-wise. Greg is so nice and laid-back, just goes with the flow. And Marc, sheesh! I remember one time he was in here on Saturday and somebody made a rude comment about homosexuals. I thought he was going to take the guy's head off."

"Does Proust come in on Saturdays very often?" Paul asked.

She nodded. "Just about every week. He works out at the gym down the street and meets Greg here when we close at noon."

Adrenaline rushed Jadz's next question over Dolly's response. "Does Proust hang around in the lobby, or wait in the car?"

"He always comes in, usually a little after eleven, and flirts with the ladies. Funny how gay men get along so good with women, huh?" Dolly shifted at the sudden tension in the room. "I don't mean to be prejudiced or anything. I don't have anything against gay people."

"I'm sure you don't," Jadz said. "I think that's all for now, and I hope you get that promotion someday." She ushered Dolly out and turned to Paul.

"Proust," he said.

Jadz called Proust's attorney on the way back to the station. "We'd like to meet with him as soon as possible. When will he be back? Fine. I'll call tomorrow."

"Mr. Proust or Attorney Evans?" Rena asked as she maneuvered through traffic. Congestion was building and she hit every stop light.

"Proust. He's in New York meeting with his publisher. Damn it!" She crushed her empty coffee cup into a ball and flung it into the backseat, ignoring Rena's frown.

"So we begin with his background until he returns," Rena said, logical as always. "We will be better prepared for his interview."

"Will Logan talk to us again?"

"I doubt it. He was cooperative, but impatient. We can ask." She found Keyser's number on her cell phone and hit send. "Do not tell my mother I used the phone while driving."

"You've never said much about your mother," Jadz said. "Does she live alone?"

"We share a home near Swan Creek. Yes, Mr. Keyser, please. Detective Castillo."

An image of living with Mavis flashed through Jadz's mind, and she shuddered.

Rena tucked the phone into her pocket. "Tomorrow, one-thirty, but he is not happy. He thinks we are still trying to implicate Mr. Logan."

"He'll live."

They arrived back at the station as Forester was leaving for the day. "My bowling league starts in forty-five minutes," he said. "Talk fast."

Jadz relayed the information from the interviews. "We can't talk to Proust until he comes back from New York," she finished, "but we're meeting Logan again tomorrow afternoon and starting on background."

"Check the Internet. If he's a writer like he says, he should have a website or something." Forester said as he left. "Call me if anything turns up, and don't work all night. Tomorrow will be important."

They found Paul seated at Jadz's desk, surfing the Web. "Way ahead of you guys," he said.

"How did you get here so fast?" Jadz asked. "Never mind. I know how you drive."

"Have you found anything?" Rena pulled her chair around so she could see the computer screen. Jadz stood over Paul's shoulder.

"Georges Marcel Proust, forty-one, writes science fiction for a New York publishing house under the name Josh McDaniel. Eight books in the past twelve years. Looks like a movie deal is in the works." Paul read from the screen: "'McDaniel offers a unique perspective on the potential future of our planet and ourselves. Combining philosophy, science and religion, he weaves an unsettling vision of a world gone berserk, where the mind is god and god is king and those who dissent are eliminated in the name of the common good.' Sounds like a fun guy."

"Let's see what the local database says." Rena entered his name in the department computer system. "Valid license, three speeding tickets, an accident two years ago, no citation. No warrants, no criminal record." She tapped a few more keys. "Nothing in the state system, either."

"Try Josh McDaniel," Jadz said.

Rena entered several combinations of the names with Proust's date of birth and Social Security number before finding a match. "Here we are. New York license under McDaniel, same DOB, different SSN. Two priors, both for simple assault, six years ago and eight months. Fine and court costs, no probation. No alias noted to connect the names."

"Do we know where he went to school?" Jadz asked.

Paul checked Proust's website. "Nope, no personal history, but they call him a New Yorker."

"He has an address in Manhattan." Rena handed Jadz a scribbled note.

"I worked with a New York cop on a case last year," Paul said as he took the paper from Jadz. "Let me call him." He leafed through his notebook for the number, picked up her desk phone, and started dialing.

Jadz grumbled. "Well, if I can do anything to help you two, just let me know. You have my computer, my phone."

"I could use some coffee," Paul said while he waited for someone to answer.

She punched at his arm.

He ducked out of her reach, laughing. "Sorry, Brian? Paul Wiley, Northwood, Ohio. We worked on that tri-state forgery case last year. Right. Listen, can you check on a guy for me? He has an alias of Josh McDaniel, and a Manhattan address." Paul gave him an overview of the case, adding, "He's in your area right now, meeting with a publisher. Don't know where. We'll talk to him as soon as he gets back to Toledo. You have my number."

"So he'll check?" Jadz asked.

"No, he's going to toss it the trash."

"It is nearly five-thirty," Rena said. "Unless you have anything useful we can do now, I suggest we call it a day. I should get home."

"I have to get back to court. Pachecki said if there's no verdict, she's sending the jury home at six." Paul frowned. "Really thought they'd be back by now."

"I need to exchange this rental before the dealer closes," Jadz said. "I refuse to drive a monster SUV for two weeks. Want to get some dinner?"

"Sure, after I'm done next door," Paul said. "You owe me a drink anyway."

"I do not."

Rena begged off and they went their separate ways.

After a quick stop at the dealership, Jadz jockeyed the new Pontiac G6 into the last empty spot at a nearby Mexican restaurant. *It's still a bus compared to my Miata, but I could get used to the luxury.* She detoured to the ladies' room and returned to find Paul talking to Theo in a booth near the bar.

"Is this a set-up?" she asked as she slid into the seat next to Theo.

"You owe him a drink, too," Paul said.

"What makes you think I owe anyone?"

"I called him after we left the registrar. He has friends who did some checking on Proust. I didn't want to talk about it in front of Rena yet, not knowing her like I do you two."

Jadz was intrigued. "What did you find?"

"The gay community in Toledo is pretty small, compared to New York," Theo said. "I talked to some people who know all the gossip, who goes where with who, stuff like that. Proust is known as a hot-head, an activist for gay causes, and definitely not one to hide his sexual orientation to keep from being noticed." He waited while the server delivered chips and salsa and took their drink orders before continuing. "He has a girlfriend."

"You mean boyfriend," Jadz said.

"Girlfriend," Theo repeated. "As of three days ago. They met at a local hang-out and went dancing last night."

"Wow." Jadz let the news sink in. "Do we know who she is? I don't want another victim."

Theo crumbled a chip onto a napkin, delaying his response. "I think it's your sister."

"What?" Paul and Jadz said together.

"I wanted Jadz to hear it first," he said. "There's more."

"What, Mavis, too?" Jadz tried to laugh, but it died in her throat.

"I think might be the one who ran you off the road. Until Tuesday, he drove a charcoal Mercedes. Wednesday night, he showed up at Bretz Dance Club in a white Lexus convertible. We can't find the Mercedes."

"So he bought a new car. That doesn't mean he's the hit-skip." Even Jadz was unconvinced.

Drinks arrived and they ordered dinner. "You have to eat," Theo told Jadz when she tried to pass.

"Bring a carry-out box," she told the server.

Conversation lapsed as they nursed their drinks and absorbed Theo's information.

"He's out of town until at least tomorrow, so Betty is safe," Jadz said. "But we'll need to talk to her."

"Rena and I will talk to her," Paul said. "You need to stay out of that conversation."

"He's right," Theo agreed. "I saw you two at the hospital. I don't think she'll cooperate if you question her."

Jadz emptied her wine glass and shoved it across the table. "How do I explain this to Mom?"

"You don't," Theo said. "At least, not yet. Betty's a big girl. We'll keep an eye on her until this is over."

"Mom always hated that I went into law enforcement. She tried to talk me into quitting when Dad died, said she couldn't take it if—" Jadz swallowed her emotions. "If anything happens to Betty, it'll be my fault."

Jadz's cell phone rang and they all reached for their pockets.

"Relax, you two." She forced a grin. "Hi, Rena, what's up? Slow down. He what? How do you know? Give me your address. Why? We need to talk. No, I don't think it can wait till morning. Can you meet us somewhere else? I'm with Paul and Theo." Jadz closed her eyes and listened. "Okay, first thing tomorrow. I'll call Forester now. Are you sure? All right. Be safe."

She ignored Theo and Paul's concern and made a call. "Lieutenant? Sorry to disturb you. Seems Proust is more of a problem than we thought." After Jadz summarized Theo's story, she signaled the men to pay attention. "Right. Well, there's more. I just talked to Rena. Did you know her mother's an invalid? Anyway, a guy stopped by her house yesterday, claimed he wanted to interview them for a book he's writing. Mrs. Castillo's caregiver doesn't remember his name. She sent him away, but she just told Rena about it tonight. I don't know what to think." She listened for several seconds. "Right, I agree. Okay, see you in the morning."

Theo's face darkened. "What the hell's Proust up to?"

"Hang on, one more call." Jadz hit speed dial. "Mom? Yes, I'm fine, much better. Listen, you said something at the hospital about Betty having a new boyfriend. Have you met him? I see. Is she home tonight? Good. No, nothing to worry about. I'll talk to you tomorrow." She disconnected quickly, shutting down her mother's questions. Jadz propped her elbows on the table, head in her hands. "Damn."

A raucous birthday party across the dining room drowned out their silence.

After a minute, Jadz sat up. "Theo, do you still have a number for airport security?" As he nodded and pulled out his phone, she said, "We need to verify Proust really is out of town, and when he's coming back. He told Betty he was leaving on the first USAir flight this morning."

Theo made the call.

"We can't just sit here and do nothing." Paul glared around the room as if Proust were lurking in a corner, waiting for them.

"While he does what? Goes out on a date? Visits an old woman?" Jadz asked. "We're not even positive it's him. And if it is, as long as he's out of town, he can't do any harm."

"He left on the six-fifteen this morning to New York, scheduled to return tomorrow night, seven-thirty-five," Theo said, tossing his phone onto the table. "Security will let us know if he does."

Jadz helped up a hand and ticked off the problem areas. "Rena's with her mother. Mom and Betty are home together, and there's a cruiser outside each residence until we find Proust, on orders from Forester. So we're set until morning. We're meeting Logan at one-thirty, and we should hear from New York before that. When Proust gets back, we'll be ready for him." She moved back so the server could deliver the steaming plates, surprised to find her appetite returned with her renewed determination. "Let's eat."

Conversation turned to anything but Proust. Paul's jokes failed to earn more than tepid smiles as they worked their way through another round of drinks after dinner. They lingered over coffee and the tense silence returned.

Jadz pushed her empty glass aside and rose. "I'm going home. I have a feeling it'll be a long night."

"I'll follow you." Theo slid across the bench to stand.

"Not necessary. I won't let anyone tail me tonight. And there's a crew standing guard, remember?" Jadz patted his shoulder. "Go home."

The short drive to her apartment was uneventful. She gave the officers on watch an update on Proust before going in to greet Ford.

"Hey, old man. Miss me?" He purred loudly, winding around her ankles as she went into the kitchen to fill his dishes. As he nibbled at his food, Jadz checked the window locks and set the deadbolt. "No fresh air tonight," she told Ford, resigning herself to the hated air conditioning.

Jadz rummaged in the cupboard for chamomile tea, changed her mind, and brewed a full pot of coffee. She poured a mug and settled in on the couch, Ford at her feet. Nothing caught her interest on television. She sipped her coffee in silence, running through the last few days in her mind. *How do I protect Betty and Mom and still do my job? Is this what Dad went through all those years?*

She dislodged Ford, ignoring his meow of protest, and knelt in front of the bookcase to dig a thick scrapbook off the bottom shelf. Curled back on the sofa, Jadz browsed through the pages. Pictures of her parents, young, smiling and in love. Betty as a baby, before Jadz was born. *She looked grumpy even then*. The four of them on a rare vacation day at Cedar Point Amusement Park, dripping into their shoes after the Thunder Canyon water ride. Her dad in his deputy sheriff's uniform, first as a recruit, then proudly accepting his sergeant's stripes and, later, lieutenant's bars. High school swim meets, graduation, her wedding. A scrap of newsprint fell out as she turned the last full page. It was her father's obituary.

> JADZINSKI, Archibald, 62, devoted husband of Mavis (Beck) and father of Betty and Veronica, thirty-four-year veteran of the Lucas County Sheriff's Office

> and the federal Alcohol, Tobacco, and Firearms Office,
> killed in the line of duty September 26, 2006.

Tears obscured her vision. She didn't need to read the words she knew by heart. Jadz buried her face in the cushions as her bravado fled, and she sobbed, for her father, for her mother, and for Betty. And for herself.

Chapter 13

Jadz basked in the sun rising over the trees behind her building and finished the last cup of coffee in the pot. Remembering Theo's admonition, she was careful to stand at an angle to the window. Proust was out of town, but he could have friends. She hoped the beautiful weather was a good omen. Thirty minutes of meditation erased some of the ravages of the sleepless night. She rinsed the empty mug and stowed it in the dishwasher before grabbing her briefcase. "No wild parties today, old man." Jadz gave Ford a last ear scratch and locked the door behind her. *My turn, Proust.*

On her way downtown, Jadz phoned her mother. "Sorry to call so early. Why don't you and Betty meet me for lunch today, my treat? I want to thank you for taking care of me after the accident. I know I don't have to. Eleven-thirty's fine. Meet me at the station and we'll walk over to that new deli you've been wanting to try. Just come up to my office. Tell Betty there's a new detective I want her to meet. Yes, very cute. See you then." She brushed aside the guilt that welled in her chest. *Easier than trying to explain it all over the phone.*

Jadz stopped at Sufficient Grounds for three large coffees, adding a fourth at the last minute. *In case Theo comes in.*

Rena caught the door as Jadz juggled the coffee and her briefcase while trying to enter the detective bureau.

"Thanks," Jadz said. "The stairs were hard enough." She made it to the desks without incident. "Regular black," Jadz handed Rena a cup. "Cream and sugar in the bag. I wasn't up to sorting out all the flavor blends."

"This is wonderful, thank you." Rena doctored her coffee. "I am already over my limit for the day, but—"

"If your night was anything like mine, you'll need it," Jadz said. She squinted over the rim of her cup, studying Rena's face. "And it looks like it was."

"Sleep was elusive." Rena braced one hip against the desk. "Last night you said there was more. I apologize for not letting you finish, but Mother was a priority."

"No problem. You found somebody to stay with her today?"

"Her regular caregiver will stay until I get home instead of leaving after lunch as she usually does, and there is a marked unit outside."

"I sent a squad to my mother's last night, too. I doubt if she even noticed."

"Why your mother's?"

Jadz explained, ending with, "Mom and Betty will be here at eleven-thirty. Paul says it's better if I stay out of the interview."

"Taking my name in vain, are you?" Paul appeared behind Jadz, startling her.

"Damn, can't you wear a bell or something?"

"Rena saw me coming. Blame her." Paul shoved a chair up to the desk and sat down. "Is that coffee for me, please?"

"I'm regretting it, but yes." Jadz passed him a cup. She repeated the update on Betty's arrival. "You'll have your hands full. And she'll probably try to get your phone number."

"Maybe I'll give it to her." He sniggered at Jadz's expression. "Just kidding. I'm already spoken for."

"Who would have you?"

Paul ignored her and asked Rena, "How's your mother? I hope she wasn't scared."

"She was not aware of the visitor. But thank you for asking."

Forester joined them. "That coffee spoken for?" he asked, indicating the lone cup in the carrying tray.

Jadz handed it over. *Sorry, Theo.*

"Unless you have something new, I'll be with the captain. He needs an update on all this." He paused next to Rena and spoke to her quietly, his hand on her shoulder. She nodded as she met his gaze, flushed as he left.

Jadz followed the exchange with interest. *What else have I been missing?*

Paul pulled out a legal pad and slapped it on the desk, bringing everyone's attention back to the moment. He pointed a pen at Jadz and asked, "So what do I need to know about your sister?"

Jadz tried to be objective when describing Betty. "She's always been sort of lost, I guess. Dropped out of college after two quarters, divorced three times, never held a job for more than a year. She started drinking about five years ago with her last husband, got into pills, and ended up doing ninety days plus rehab for forgery when she tried to write her own prescriptions. Mom makes excuses for her, which doesn't help. And for some reason, Betty blames me for her screwed up life."

"So you're not close?" Paul asked, earning a scolding glance from Rena.

Jadz let the lame humor slide. "Hardly." She hated revealing family troubles to co-workers.

"How do you want to approach Mr. Logan this afternoon?" Rena changed the discussion to a safer topic.

"I've been thinking about that," Jadz said with a grateful smile. "What if they're in it together?"

"It is possible, I suppose, but not likely. Their personalities are very different. I have been trying to recall anything specific about Mr. Proust from the neighbors, and they had very little to say about him."

"He'll be tough to pin down," Paul said. "My contact in Manhattan says Proust has a pretty good rap sheet, mostly minor stuff—simple assault, harassment—and a good attorney who usually got him off. But there's a juvie record we're trying to get unsealed. And this." He tossed a fax page onto the desk. "An outstanding warrant for stalking a woman he met last fall at a bar where she was celebrating her fortieth birthday."

"Now we can get our warrant," Jadz said as she absorbed the details.

"Maybe, maybe not." Rena remained cautious. "And if we frighten him, he may just relocate and keep killing."

"She's right." Paul pushed his notes toward Jadz. "He has three other aliases that we know of, all pen names for different types of writing he does. And they have mug shots of him you wouldn't recognize as the same person, according to Manhattan."

"Can New York connect him to any suspicious suicides?" Rena asked.

"They don't have anything that matches our MO so far. When my contact gets the juvenile record, he'll let us know. And he's running a statewide check, just to be sure."

Jadz checked the time, ten forty, and tried to read Paul's scribbles. The words blurred. She blinked hard. "I need a break." She disappeared through the bureau doors leaving Rena and Paul staring after her.

"It has been a difficult case," Rena said. "I know she did not sleep well last night, and caffeine only goes so far."

"I could use a break, too." Paul stood and stretched. "Think I'll find some more coffee. Need any?" At her negative response, he followed Jadz out the door.

Rena reached for the phone. "Emi? How is mother? Good. No more visitors today? Thank you. I will be home as soon as I can. Please call if you need me." Her hand rested on the receiver for a long minute after hanging up.

After two sets of stair climbing, Jadz returned to her desk calm and in control. Paul trailed in soon after with another round of coffee. They finished prepping for the interview as Betty and Mavis arrived. Jadz met them at the door to the bureau and led them to her desk.

"Mom, Betty, this is my partner, Rena Castillo, and Detective Paul Wiley from Northwood."

Betty zeroed in on Paul. "My baby sister certainly has a wonderfully attractive work environment. What brings you to the big city from little old Northwood?"

Paul extracted his handshake from her clinging grasp. "Just offering advice on a case."

"Let me show you our new conference room." Jadz took Mavis and Betty to the prearranged meeting area and shut the door. "Have a seat, will you?"

"But I thought we were going to lunch," Mavis said.

"Can that cute detective join us?" Betty kept her eyes on Paul across the room.

"Sit down please, both of you. This is important."

Mavis complied, pulling Betty down into the chair beside her. "What's up, sweetie? Why the frown? You'll end up with wrinkles if you keep that up. I have a wonderful night cream—"

"Mom, stop." Jadz sat on the other side of Mavis and took a deep breath. "I need to apologize for bringing you here under false pretenses."

"You mean he's not available?" Betty asked, jerking her gaze away from Paul.

"There's a case I've been working on," Jadz tried again.

Mavis shuddered. "Those poor women? I know all about it. I saw it on the news."

"Rena and Paul need to talk to you about it, both of you." Jadz tapped Betty's hand to get her attention.

Betty pulled away. "Me? What for?"

"I'll let them explain." Jadz left the room as Rena and Paul entered.

For twenty minutes, Jadz paced around the office trying not to stare at the conference room, failing, and trying again. At one point, Betty stood up and shoved her chair against the wall. Raised voices filtered through the door. Mavis put an arm around Betty's shoulders, but she shoved it off and sat down as far away from the detectives as she could get in the small room. Jadz noticed the few officers still at their desks during lunch hour avoiding her gaze.

"Jadz, do you have a minute?" Forester called from his office. "Have a seat," he said, closing the door behind her. "You're wearing a path in the floor out there. Relax. They can handle your sister."

"I'm not so sure about that."

"Tough as it is, you need to stop thinking of her as family and start thinking of her as Betty Jadzinski, possible witness in a serial murder case."

"Simmons," she said, one eye still on the conference room.

"I beg your pardon?"

"Betty Simmons. She's divorced, three times, actually, and didn't take her maiden name back."

"Don't be difficult." Forester fixed her with a steady gaze. "You're deliberately misunderstanding me."

Jadz slumped in the chair. "You're right. I'm sorry. It's just that I've always felt the need to protect them, especially since." She stopped.

"Since your dad died, I know." Forester's voice carried an uncommon gentleness. "Your mom took it pretty hard, didn't she?"

Jadz swallowed the lump that rose in her throat. "She hardly ate or slept for six weeks, didn't leave the house for another month. Then she went off on a tear. We had to fight to keep her from selling the house, but she sold just about everything else. Bought all new furniture, new clothes, dyed her hair, like she wanted to forget what her life was like before he died. When Betty went to jail a few months later, I thought Mom would never recover." Jadz faced Forester. "I'm all they have. They can't survive in the real world. I have to protect them."

"And who's going to protect you?"

The conference room door slammed, drowning out Forester's quiet comment and drawing her attention back to the scene outside.

"Excuse me." Jadz met her mother halfway across the room. "Mom?"

Mavis' eyes were bright with tears. "They asked me to leave, can you believe it? They want to talk to Betty alone. I'm her mother! She needs me." She fumbled through her purse for a tissue.

Jadz guided her mother to the desk and eased her into a chair. "Stay here, I'll get you some water."

When she returned, Mavis' teary concern had shifted to flushed outrage. "Your partner is nice enough, but that young man could use some manners. He acted like Betty was hiding something."

"Paul's just doing his job. I'm sure Betty wouldn't deliberately interfere with the investigation."

"Of course she wouldn't. Don't you start on her, too." Mavis picked at the paper cup Jadz handed her, eyes fixed on Betty still arguing with Paul.

"I'm not." Jadz pulled a chair up close and sat down. She took her mother's hand and forced her attention away from the scene. "Mom, this is serious. Betty's in the middle of something she can't begin to understand. What if the killer decides she's the next victim?"

Mavis started, sloshing most of the water onto the floor. "But I thought the killer only attacked forty-year-olds."

"So far. We can't predict what someone like that will do next. We never expected him to hook up with Betty."

"This is all your fault." Mavis pulled free and unwadded her tissue as the tears started again. "I told you police work was dangerous. Your father would be so disappointed. He never brought his work home."

"I'm sorry," Jadz whispered. *But how do I protect Betty, and you?*

Her pained apology penetrated Mavis' anger. "Oh, sweetie, I didn't mean that. You didn't do it on purpose." She patted Jadz's hand. "I'm just worried about Betty."

"Excuse me." Rena appeared over Jadz's shoulder. "Jadz, could I speak with you for a moment?"

They stepped out of earshot. Rena said, "I am afraid your … Ms. Simmons is not being very cooperative."

"Figures." Jadz took a deep breath. "Has she said anything useful?"

"No. She insists she met Josh McDaniel, not Mr. Proust, at a bar she does not remember, through a mutual friend whose name she cannot recall, and that she has only seen him on two other occasions." Rena hesitated. "And she is very angry with you."

"That's nothing new."

The conference room door slammed open again as Betty exited. "Mom, I'm leaving," she called across the room without stopping.

Mavis scurried after her. Jadz let them go.

"Well, I don't think she wants my phone number anymore." Paul met them back at the desk. At Rena's look, he said, "What? She doesn't."

"It's all right." Jadz ran a hand through her hair, wincing when a few strands caught in the tape over her sutures. "Did you learn anything?"

Paul flipped through his notes. "They met Monday night at a bar. Says she doesn't remember which one. He was attentive, charming, and told her he wanted to use her in a book he was writing. Betty was flattered and spilled her life story. She didn't know he was gay. I think that's partly why she's so mad. They had dinner Tuesday at Navy Bistro and went dancing Wednesday. She remembers talking about your accident, but doesn't know if he brought it up or someone else in the club did. He told her he'd be out of town for a few days and would call when he got back. And she insists on calling him Josh McDaniel, not Proust." He tossed the legal pad on the desk.

"How do you suppose he found her?" Rena asked. "We only visited mid-day Monday."

"She said they met at a bar," Paul said. "And there's always Google."

Jadz shook her head. "We'll ask Theo for details from his friend later. Now we need to get ready for Logan. He'll be here any minute."

While Jadz and Rena reviewed their question for Logan, Paul made a lunch run. Logan and his attorney arrived at the door to the bureau a few minutes later. As planned, the interview was Rena's show. She led them to an interview room as Jadz trailed behind.

"Understand my client is here under protest," Keyser said when they were seated around the scarred wooden table. "You have nothing substantial to tie him to the murders and this repeated contact borders on harassment."

"We appreciate your willingness to cooperate." Rena directed her comments to Logan. "I realize how difficult this must be for you, but we have five dead women who deserve our best efforts."

"Of course, Detective Castillo." Logan returned her smile. "What can I help you with?"

Rena held an open, almost warm conversation with Logan about his work, his teaching and his home. It wasn't until she asked about Proust that tension rose.

"What does Marc have to do with this? He doesn't work at the registrar and that was your reason for suspecting me." Logan's voice was tight.

"Can you verify his whereabouts on these dates?" Jadz handed him a list which he tossed aside.

"No, I can't. I told you I was teaching or in class."

Rena tried again. "Does Mr. Proust visit you at work?"

Logan's eyes narrowed. "He meets me there on Saturdays after his session at the gym. We usually have lunch at the Farmer's Market on Erie."

"I think that's enough for today," Keyser said. "If my client's partner is a suspect, there's a confidentiality privilege that I'll not allow him to breach without discussing the matter with Mr. Proust." He stood and gathered his notes. "If you have no objections, Detectives."

"When will Mr. Proust be back from New York?" Jadz asked.

"How did you know—" Logan broke off his question. "Later tonight."

"We would like to talk to him when he gets home." Rena held the door for them. "Thank you for your time."

Jadz and Rena met Paul in the department break room for lunch. They shared the meager results from Logan's interview while they ate.

"He got very uptight when you asked about Proust," Jadz said. "Wonder what he's trying to hide?"

"He could just be protecting his partner." Rena reached for a second napkin to catch the mayo overflow from her club sandwich.

"Nothing to protect if there's nothing to hide," Paul said. "So do we wait for Proust to come in, or meet him at the airport?"

"Airport," Jadz decided. "There's too much at stake to risk losing him."

"What if he does not return from New York?" At Jadz's startled look, Rena said, "It is a possibility. I would guarantee Mr. Logan told him about our meeting."

Jadz threw herself back in the chair. "I hadn't even considered it. That head bump must have knocked my brains loose."

"Already covered," Paul said. "A PI in New York owed me a favor from that forgery case I told you about. He's been tailing Proust since yesterday. If he doesn't get on the plane tonight, we'll know, and we'll know where he is."

"I suppose I owe you another drink." Jadz crumpled her sandwich wrapper into a ball and tossed it at him. He deflected it into the trashcan as they went back to the office.

"You are efficient, Detective-Wiley-sir," Rena said. "And a step ahead of me." She pulled up the airport schedule on her computer. "Mr. Proust should be on the plane by five-thirty, but he has a layover in Detroit. That could be a problem. The flight will land in Toledo at seven-thirty-five."

"I'll call Detroit Metro and have security watch for him." Jadz found the number and picked up the phone.

Rena said, "If we will be working late, I need to stop home to make arrangements. Could we meet at the airport at seven?"

Paul got to his feet. "I'll swing by and let the chief know what's up, then head for Toledo Express to alert the Port Authority. See you there."

"We should let Forester know," Jadz said.

"I will do that before I leave." Rena took her bag and went in search of the lieutenant.

Jadz finished the Detroit call and left the office. She trotted down the stairs to street level, emerging into the late-afternoon sunshine feeling more optimistic about the case than she had last night.

"So, Detective, I hear you think you've got the right guy this time." Jim Dixon straightened from his slouch against the entryway and matched Jadz's stride as she left the building.

"You never cease to amaze me, Dix. What makes you think I'll talk to you?"

He shrugged. "Just doing my job. You have to talk eventually. And now that your sister's involved—"

She spun on him. "What do you know about my sister?"

"Easy!" He backed off, hands raised. "I hear things."

"What things? And from whom?"

"Tsk, tsk, you know better than that." Dixon shook his finger at her. "I can't reveal my sources any more than you can." He fell in step beside her again as she hurried away. "How come he kisses them?"

Jadz remained expressionless only with effort. "Where'd you get that? I know, you can't say." She swallowed her frustration. "Use your head for once and don't print it. We need something as leverage."

"Not much of a secret. Even your bag lady friend knows. Not that I believe much she's got to say."

"Leave Catherine out of this, and my sister, too."

"I talked to Betty about an hour ago. She doesn't like you very much."

"What?" Jadz stopped again. "She shouldn't be talking to you."

"It's a free country." Dixon looked smug. "Didn't take much to get her talking."

Jadz backed him up against a building, careful to avoid contact he could exaggerate into assault. "Stay away from my sister." Her words were barely audible over the street sounds. "And if you blow this case, you'll never cover anything bigger than traffic court again. I'll see to it."

"Sounds like you're blowing it all by yourself, you and the Miser."

"Don't call her that." Jadz shoved away from him. "This is not a game, Dix. Women are dying. If you think you know more about this than I do, remember withholding evidence is a crime. I'll lock your ass up so fast your pencil won't be able to keep up."

"Don't get testy." Dixon smoothed his jacket. "Like I said, just doing my job. If you guys were a little more friendly, I wouldn't have to pull an end run."

"You'll get the story when it's ready. Don't screw this up or I swear I'll take you down." She turned away, dismissing him.

"Sure thing, Detective. Hope your head feels better," he called to her back.

Jadz resisted the urge to haul him in for questioning out of spite. As she got into her rental car, the bell tower at St. Paul's

Lutheran Church tolled five. Jadz calculated travel time before turning east across the Maumee River instead of heading home. A few short minutes of fighting rush hour traffic and she pulled into her mother's driveway next to Betty's Jeep. Jadz steeled herself for an unpleasant scene and entered the house.

"Sweetie, I didn't know you were coming for dinner." Mavis hugged her. She flitted around the kitchen adding a place setting to the table. "I made minestrone tonight, must have known you were coming."

"I'm not staying." She caught her mother's disappointed look. "I have to work late. I need to talk to Betty for a minute."

"She's not very happy with you right now." Mavis followed Jadz down the hall to the bedrooms. "I'm not sure this is a good time."

"Doesn't matter." Jadz tapped on Betty's door and entered without waiting for answer, closing the door against her mother's anxious gaze.

Floor-length drapes were drawn against the evening sun, leaving the room bathed in shadows. Betty was curled in an armchair beside the bed.

"We need to talk," Jadz said.

"Go away."

Jadz turned the desk chair to face Betty and sat down. "You need to stop talking to reporters. Proust is dangerous."

"I don't know anybody named Proust." Betty buried her face in a fluffy animal-print pillow.

"You're being difficult. Paul explained it to you."

"You lied to me! You said Paul wanted to meet me." Betty threw the pillow at Jadz, catching her off-guard.

Jadz clutched it to her chest. "I didn't think you'd come otherwise."

"You and your *detectives* are trying to turn me against Josh, saying he's a ... a murderer." Betty broke on a sob. "You never wanted me to be happy. Always interfering. Miss High-and-Mighty know-it-all." She scrabbled to her feet and shoved Jadz off the chair. "Get out of my face." Her voice rose. "Get out of my room." She pushed Jadz again. "Get out of my life!"

Jadz didn't resist as Betty herded her out of the room and slammed the door.

Jadz slumped against the wall in the hallway for a moment before returning to the kitchen. Her face was pale.

"I knew this wasn't a good time," Mavis said as Jadz crossed to the front door.

"Why does she hate me? We used to be best friends." Jadz dropped onto the sofa and cradled her head in her hands.

Mavis paced for a minute. "This is so awkward. Your father never wanted you to know, said you'd blame yourself. It wasn't your fault."

"What wasn't my fault?" Mavis' words pulled Jadz out of her daze.

Twin girls from down the block chased their escaped St. Bernard past the house, distracting Mavis.

"Mom?"

"Do you remember how happy Betty was when you came home from college for winter break your junior year?"

"Sure, she and Don still had that honeymoon glow."

"It was the first time you'd met Don, wasn't it?"

"First and only time. I never expected Betty to elope while I was at school. They knew each other, what, three weeks?" She shifted, trying to see her mother's face. "What does that have to do with me?"

Mavis turned to meet her gaze. "You made quite an impression on him. He didn't stop talking about you for days after you left. Betty was furious, said you deliberately tried to get his attention, running around in short-shorts and a tank top in the winter."

"I was on the swim team. That was our uniform. I usually wore sweats over it and I never tried to flirt with him."

"I know you didn't, but Betty wouldn't listen to reason. They had an awful fight, and then she lost the baby a few weeks later."

Vaguely remembered words danced with snapshot memories as Jadz fought to keep up. "What baby?" was all she could manage.

"After her miscarriage, and an emergency hysterectomy, Don left her." Mavis stroked Jadz's hair. "I'm afraid Betty blamed you, still does, for some reason."

"Why didn't you tell me?"

"Like I said, your father didn't want you to feel responsible. You were having a rough time yourself. Your roommate had just committed suicide, and you took that so hard. Dad wanted you to concentrate on school, not on Betty's problems. By the time you came home for the summer, Betty had moved out again and wouldn't talk about Don or the baby at all."

Disparate scenes from her college years coalesced. Betty had stopped attending Jadz's swim meets or sibling visits. She avoided the house when Jadz was home. Letters, once a lifeline between them, went unanswered. At the time, Jadz chalked it up to different ages and lifestyles and mourned their separation as inevitable. The growing acrimony over the years had confused her further, but now she understood.

The mantel clock chimed the quarter-hour and Jadz started. Six fifteen. She patted her mother's knee and moved away.

"I have to go." She hesitated, a hand on the doorknob. "Thanks for telling me, I think."

"I love you, sweetie." Mavis kissed her cheek. "Are you sure you don't want some soup?"

"Save me some," Jadz said as she left.

When Jadz arrived at Toledo Express Airport thirty minutes later, the concourse was crowded. A young couple with a toddler juggled a stroller, a car seat, and several large suitcases decorated with fluorescent Disney stickers. Haggard-looking business travelers skirted the luggage carousels, hauling little more than an overnight bag on wheels and a briefcase. Excited families greeted a contingent of Army soldiers coming home from deployment in Iraq while television cameras recorded the tearful reunions.

Jadz spotted Logan in the receiving area and merged into the crowd to avoid him. Paul beckoned her into the Port Authority office off the lobby, and the heavy glass door cut off the noisy confusion as they closed behind her.

"Lightning storm in Detroit delayed the flight," he said. "They just took off. And Rena called. She's on her way. Detroit security called, too. Proust never got off the plane."

"That's one break." Jadz prowled around the small room.

"At least we know he's been screened for weapons." Paul's lame reassurance annoyed Jadz, and at her dark look, he said, "I'll just go see if Rena's here yet." He left the office.

Jadz flopped into a chair in the corner of the room and closed her eyes. Mavis' revelations about Betty threw her off balance when she needed all her faculties to deal with Proust. Silence descended as Jadz focused on her breathing and she brought herself back to the moment. The door swung open again and Jadz turned, expecting Paul and Rena. It was Sam Gilbert, hair stuffed under a Delta Airlines ball cap, ear protection goggles dangling around her neck.

"You found him?" she demanded. "You found the bastard who killed Lizzy?"

"No, slow down." Jadz was on her feet. She held out her hands to ward off Gilbert's fury. "We don't know who killed Lizzy."

"Security said you were here to take a guy off a plane." Gilbert stood akimbo and glared. "Is he the one or not?"

"We don't know if Lizzy was killed by the same guy," Jadz said. "Have you talked to Spiner?"

"Yeah, he called, finally, after you guys told him what I said." She pulled off the cap and ran a hand through her tangled hair. "Still not sure he believes me. What do you mean not the same guy?" Gilbert's anger faded enough for her to pick up on Jadz's comment. "You think Stanley killed Lizzy?"

Rena and Paul entered the office in time to hear her question. "Detective Spiner is considering it," Rena said. At Jadz's questioning look, she continued. "He called on my way here. Were you aware of Stanley's casino trips?" she asked Gilbert.

Gilbert frowned. "Yeah, they used to take those buses to Detroit couple times a month. So?"

"Apparently Mr. Stanley hit the slots jackpot a few months ago. Adams threatened to tell his ex, who would more than likely want a good chunk of his winnings. Detective Spiner just found out," Rena said.

"Stanley killed her over money?" Gilbert staggered into a chair. "What a bastard," she said, choking on the tears tightening her throat.

"He hasn't been charged with murder yet, but Detective Spiner is working on it. It appears he may have caused the emergency at work to give himself an alibi." Rena crouched next to Gilbert. "You need to let Detective Spiner handle this, okay?"

Gilbert swiped at the tears with the back of her hand. "Yeah, sure." She shoved her hair back under her hat and stood up.

"Long as Spiner does his job. I won't let Lizzy be dumped in a cold case file somewhere." Gilbert pushed through the heavy door, shoulders bowed, and shuffled off.

Gilbert's palpable sorrow left an awkward silence in the office, interrupted only by occasional muted sounds from the terminal outside. Paul slouched in a chair near the door. Rena leaned on the counter and rested her head in her hands. Jadz paced around the table, stumbling over Paul's feet on each circuit until he shifted out of the way.

After several laps, Jadz shook off her gloom to ask, "Why did he call?"

"Detective Spiner? He wanted to let us know we should no longer consider Stanley as our suspect," Rena said. "He and Adams were in the casinos during at least two of our murders."

"Stanley figured killing Adams the same way as the other deaths was an easy out." Paul put the pieces together. "What a guy."

"I'll give Spiner credit for letting us know," Jadz said. She summarized her talk with the reporter and with Betty, leaving out the personal details. "Dixon knows a whole lot more than I'd like, but I think he'll back off and let us wrap this thing up. And Betty won't talk to him again." *I hope.*

"Assuming Mr. Proust is the killer," Rena said. "We still have nothing linking him to the crime scenes, or the victims. He may simply be trying to protect Mr. Logan."

An announcement of the flight's arrival on the security screen in the office brought them to their feet. Paul opened the glass door with a flourish. "Show time!"

Port Authority security joined them on the way to the gate. The uniformed officers took up positions on either side of the door. Paul stood by the counter where he could see the approaching passengers while Jadz and Rena stayed out of sight of the entryway. They didn't have long to wait.

"You don't give up, do you?" Logan asked when he saw Jadz.

"No, I don't. This is a multiple homicide, remember?"

Paul whistled sharply to signal Proust's approach. "Marc Proust?" Paul flashed his badge. "Would you come with us, please?"

Proust's amused smirk rankled, but Jadz held her tongue. She followed Paul and Rena, with Proust now flanked by the uniformed security team, back to the Port Authority office. Logan trailed close behind. When he tried to follow the group through the door, Paul barred his way.

"Let him in," Jadz said. "He's part of this, too." She directed Proust to a seat in the corner of the office and sat down opposite. Security left to resume their normal duties while Rena and Paul stationed themselves near the door. "Mr. Proust, I think you know why we're here. I'm going to read your Miranda rights before I ask you some questions."

"Don't bother," he said. "I know my rights, and I have nothing to say to you until my attorney is present."

"We could simply take you into custody," Jadz said.

"If you have a warrant, arrest me. Otherwise, you're wasting your time, and mine." Proust sat back, arms crossed over his chest.

"Marc," Logan said behind him.

"It's okay, Greg." Proust waved him off without a glance. "I called my attorney during the layover in Detroit after you told me what they were up to. He said to tell these fine officers we'd be happy to talk to them tomorrow morning. Until then, I have nothing to say."

"It's your dime," Paul said. "We can wait."

Proust stood over Jadz for a long moment, his smirk even more pronounced. "Good night, Detective." He brushed past Rena and opened the door.

"Stay away from my sister," Jadz called after him. He faltered but kept walking. Logan followed, letting the door swing shut behind them.

"So much for a quick confession," Paul said. "We'll get him tomorrow."

Chapter 14

"What was that all about?" Logan asked when they were seated in the car. He had remained quiet during baggage claim, letting Proust ramble about his meeting in New York and the upcoming movie shoot. Now he waited for an answer.

"Could we at least start the car and get some air going before you give me the third degree?" Proust made exaggerated fanning motions. "I'm suffocating in this humidity."

Logan cranked the fan on high, repeating his question as he drove towards the parking turnstile. "What was that about the detective's sister?"

Proust avoided his gaze. "I ran into her at the Bier Stube the other night. I mentioned to Steve, just in passing, that we had a visit from a Detective Jadzinski. His brother's a cop, you know, and he pointed out her sister on the dance floor. So I introduced myself."

"The detective's *sister*?" Logan was bewildered. "Why didn't you tell me?"

"No big deal, really. We chatted for a bit, danced a couple times."

"And?"

"And what?"

"Why would Detective Jadzinski warn you to stay away?"

Proust shifted on the leather seat. "We had dinner while you were at the Garden on Tuesday."

"Oh, really?"

"She was interested in my work. Like everyone else, she thinks she can write a book and she wanted some pointers. I filled her in on the insane world of publishing."

"Do you think that was such a good idea?" Logan was worried now. "You see what they've put me through this week and now they're after you. Don't make things any worse."

Proust took Logan's right hand from the steering wheel and sandwiched it between his own. "I would never do anything to make trouble for you. You know that."

Logan pressed his cheek against Proust's hand. "This isn't one of your twisted fiction plots. They mean business."

"I'm sorry if I upset you." Proust leaned back with a satisfied smile on his face. "This'll all be over tomorrow. You'll see. Then I was thinking, how do you feel about Los Angeles?"

Chapter 15

The morning interview with Proust was another dead-end. With no physical evidence or witnesses tying him to the murder scenes, the registrar connection was weak and Proust's confidence seemed warranted. He dismissed his encounter with Betty as chance, on her instigation, and denied visiting Rena's mother.

"He's too damn smug," Jadz said as Proust left with his attorney. "Can't we find a way to get a search warrant?"

"Not without something more definite. The judge isn't satisfied with the New York situation." Rena rubbed her eyes. Caffeine was wearing off after another long night. "Mr. Proust managed to explain the meeting with Betty, and we cannot prove he was at my home."

"Is Betty still interested in him?" Paul asked. "Maybe she could—"

"No." Jadz cut him off.

"But if she has an inside track?"

"I said no."

Rena intervened. "I need a break. Coffee, Paul?" She pulled him away.

Jadz spun her chair around to face the window. She closed her eyes and tried a few minutes of meditation while waiting for the coffee run. When Rena and Paul returned, she faced them with a smile. "Sorry, Paul. Let's look for other options."

"I suggest we take a photo spread to the neighborhoods and knock on doors," Rena said. "The patrol questions focused on Mr. Logan, not Mr. Proust, so that may turn up something."

"Did we get any more from New York?" Jadz asked Paul.

"I'll try again." He punched in the number and waited.

"You said the neighbors didn't mention Proust much, right?" Jadz reviewed her notes.

"Very few comments about him at all," Rena said. "He does not appear to be as well liked as Mr. Logan, but nothing specific."

Paul finished his call. "Finally got the juvenile record, but it's not much. Couple of petty thefts, shoplifting. Worst was a domestic, a fight with his father when his parents were divorcing. Dad moved out of state. Mom died a few years later, when Proust was nineteen. He's been on his own ever since, as far as his file shows. No other family mentioned."

"Do we have contact information for his father?" Rena asked.

"Trevor Thompson, Denver, is all I got." Paul sipped his neglected coffee and made a face. "Cold already."

Jadz checked the computer and found a phone number. She paused in the act of dialing. "What time is it in Denver?"

"Two-hour time difference, so just after eight-thirty," Paul said. "Not too early."

She continued the call. "Trevor Thompson? Detective Sergeant Veronica Jadzinski, Toledo Police. Yes, Ohio. I'm sorry to call so early, but I'd like to ask you a few questions about your son, Marc. How long … I see. No, he didn't give us your number. No, I won't tell him where you live." Jadz raised her voice slightly to make sure Rena and Paul were listening. It was several minutes before she could get another word in. "No sir, I understand. So you haven't … of course. Yes. Thank you, sir." She hung up.

"Not ready for a family reunion, I take it," Paul said.

"Hardly," Jadz said. "He is *not* happy to hear from Proust, even second-hand. They haven't spoken since Proust broke his dad's jaw in that fight over the divorce. Claims Proust threatened to kill him if he came near his mother again, so Thompson left town."

"What caused the divorce?" Rena asked.

"That's the weird thing." Jadz was jotting down as much of the phone conversation verbatim as she could while she spoke. "Thompson said he felt like a third-wheel in his own home from the time Proust was born. His wife kicked Thompson out of the bedroom when they brought Proust home from the hospital, gave the baby her maiden name instead of his father's, and the marriage was basically over at that point. Thompson said he only stayed out of obligation."

"Obligation to what?" Paul asked.

"He's a strict Catholic. Divorce was not an option, he said. But when Proust told them he was gay, everything fell apart." Jadz tossed her pen on the desk and threw herself back in the chair, forearm covering her face. Her voice was muffled. "Thompson blamed it on his wife and moved out. She accused him of desertion, can you imagine? Last time he saw her, Thompson said he lost it and taunted her, said she'd be a lonely old woman when the boy left her for his 'queer' friends. Proust hit him with a textbook."

"Touching family scene," Paul said.

"Anyway, he hasn't spoken to either of them since. Lawyers handled the divorce long-distance. He only found out last year that she was dead."

Rena was unimpressed. "Useless information from a jealous, and apparently bigoted, ex-husband. We already knew from his record and from the clerks at the registrar that Mr. Proust has a violent streak. None of the victims had physical injuries, so this proves nothing."

"But it's an odd relationship with his mother, don't you think?" Jadz persisted.

"No, I do not. He was only defending her." Rena rose. "I am going to get copies of Mr. Proust's mug shot for the array." She left the room.

"Well, okay, then." Jadz's brow wrinkled. "Let's plot out the neighborhoods, split up the photo search."

"I'll take the Northwood scene first, since it was mine to begin with." Paul took Jadz's lead and ignored Rena's sudden departure. "And the third murder is east side, so that's close to me, too."

"I'll take Summers' neighborhood again, and the first victim, and Rena can handle the last scene, since it's near her house. Maybe she can get home early tonight."

Rena hurried back into the office. "Turn up the television."

"What?"

Rena found the remote for the television which ran local news non-stop on mute in the corner of the room. Jadz swiveled around to see the screen.

"... obviously the police have no real leads, so they persist in harassing us. Since my partner and I are gay, they assume we must be guilty of something." Proust stood in front of the Lucas County Courthouse surrounded by a half-dozen people bearing placards that read "Gays are People Too, Protect and Serve Us" and "Guilty Until Proven Innocent? Only If You're Gay." Logan stood over his shoulder, looking uncomfortable. Camera crews jostled for position.

Proust answered an inaudible question from one of the reporters. "No, they have no evidence whatsoever. Just the fact that my partner is a hard-working civil servant and may have come in contact with some of the victims in the course of his duties is apparently enough to warrant this relentless harassment. When they couldn't pin these terrible murders on him, they focused their attention on me for some reason they have yet to explain. I had to leave town for a meeting on my upcoming movie project, *Moonrise Over Mars,* and they pounced on me at the airport when I returned."

"Oh, good plug," Paul said, applauding. "Get all the free publicity you can."

The screen went dark. Forester stood behind them, remote in hand. "I've heard enough," he said. "Let's get to work."

They scrambled for their things and left the office to canvas the neighborhoods.

Jadz found her rental car and drove north while Paul headed east, Rena west. Jadz's phone rang as she pulled onto the Greenbelt Parkway. "Hey, Theo. Yeah, I saw it, too. What a joke. It'll be a pleasure on so many levels to nail that bastard. Proust reported the Mercedes stolen? The day of the accident, of course." She swore silently, dodging a youngster on a bike. "Hang on, I need to pull over." Jadz turned onto a side street. "So what's next? Tonight? I don't know when I'll be done. We're hitting the neighborhoods with Proust's mug shot. I'll call you later." She pocketed the phone and pondered the wisdom of making a date so soon after her divorce was finalized. Her phone buzzed signaling a voice mail message as she pulled back into traffic. She listened to the recording as she drove.

"Jadz, this is Rena. I talked to Lieutenant Forester. He agreed it would not be necessary to continue patrols at our homes. I suggested a tail on Mr. Proust, but he wants to clear it with the captain first, considering the television interview. He is also trying to get approval for a search warrant. I will let you know if he succeeds."

"Second message," the automated system continued.

"Veronica? It's your mother. We just saw those people on television. Call me as soon as you can."

Jadz coasted to a stop in front of Summers' apartment building as she made the call. "Mom? What's up?"

"Betty wants to talk to you." A raised voice in the background said otherwise. Mavis was muffled, but audible. "Talk to your sister, now. This is more important than your feud."

Jadz could hear the phone being shuffled back and forth, Betty arguing with Mavis, who for once stood her ground.

"All right. I'll talk to her." Betty spoke into the phone. "That guy on TV? It wasn't Josh, I mean Proust, whatever you call him. I mean, it kind of looked like him, but Josh has red hair like me, and kinda long." She didn't wait for a response. "There, are you satisfied?" Her voice faded and a slamming door echoed through the receiver as Mavis returned to the conversation.

"Did you get all that?" she asked.

"I did, thanks."

"I really wish you had become a teacher," Mavis said. "I have to go calm her down. Be careful."

Jadz dropped the phone on the seat and dug out the mug shots. Proust was definitely not a redhead. She called Rena.

"We may have a problem, sort of. Let me try to conference Paul in on this." She punched a few buttons, muttering at the pitfalls of technology. "Paul? Hang on, I've got Rena on the line too, I think." Another button and the three were connected. Jadz repeated Betty's information.

"Well, that's a perp of a different color," Paul said.

"You are *not* funny," Jadz said. "This is serious. Do we try to edit this mug shot and risk getting any ID thrown out, or do we go with it as is?"

Rena spoke up. "I say as is, for now. Editing is too risky. We can always ask follow-up questions if no one recognizes the photo."

"Sounds like a plan," Paul said. "And Jadz, some people think I'm very funny." He dropped out of the call.

"I believe you hurt his feelings," Rena said with a chuckle. "I did not think that was possible."

"He'll get over it. Look, while I have you on the line, are you okay?"

"I am fine." She hesitated. "Mr. Proust's relationship with his mother is … We will talk about this another time. I am fine." She disconnected before Jadz could respond.

Jadz started her interviews in Summers' building with Mrs. Parsons, who had reported the murder.

"That's the guy on TV," she said as soon as Jadz handed her the photo array. "Why're you picking on him if he didn't do it? Shouldn't you be looking for the real killer? I'm afraid to sleep at night."

Jadz made a vague apology and crossed the hall to the next apartment. *Damn it, Proust. Already tainted the witnesses.* After canvassing the entire area, she checked her list of no-answers, counting eight that needed call-backs, and returned to her car. No one remembered seeing Proust in the area. She had the same results in Peterson's neighborhood.

"I saw those fags on TV. Lock 'em all up."

"That nice young man doesn't look like a murderer. Shame on you for harassing homosexuals."

"I didn't see nothin'."

By six o'clock, Jadz started for home, discouraged. She called Theo as promised, and after grousing about her lack of success during the interviews, agreed to meet him for PAL movie night at Fifth Third Field.

"I need to change clothes and feed the cat before he chews up the furniture. See you in an hour." She pocketed the phone and sped up just a bit.

At home, Jadz ran through a quick shower and checked in with Rena and Paul while she took care of Ford. They came up empty as well.

"I will call Lieutenant Forester," Rena said. "Unless he feels we missed something and need to be in the office tomorrow, I will see you Monday."

When Theo arrived, Jadz grabbed a sweatshirt and tucked her cell phone in the pocket of her jeans.

"No shop talk tonight," she said as she settled into his pickup. "I need a break." Her stomach grumbled. "And a hot dog."

He laughed. "Can do, ma'am."

They arrived at Fifth Third Field just as the PAL kids spilled out of the buses pulled up to the curb on Jefferson Street. Jadz and Theo found their respective groups and herded them toward the seats.

"I wonder who the marketing genius was who came up with the idea of using the stadium for movies when the team's on the road," Theo said as the stands filled with families ready for a night of entertainment under the stars. "Bet they got a helluva bonus."

When the youngsters were occupied with hot dogs, drinks, and popcorn, Jadz dropped into a seat next to Theo. "What are we watching tonight? I didn't see an announcement."

"Something called *The Princess Bride,*" he said. "Sounds like a little girl's story."

"Inconceivable!" She laughed at his confused expression. "You'll see. It's a great show. I can quote most of it, but I promise not to be a spoiler."

The JumboTron in center field lit up as night fell across the stadium and for the next two hours the audience was spellbound with Wesley's sword-fighting exploits as he rescued Princess Buttercup from the dastardly Prince Humperdinck. When "Grandpa" Peter Falk tucked his grandson into bed at the end of the story, Jadz repeated the closing words, "As you wish," with him and brushed back a tear. She caught Theo's grin. "What? I always cry at sappy endings."

His response was cut off by the chaos of the youngsters' departure. It wasn't until the buses pulled away and Jadz and Theo were standing at the curb in the dim moonlight that he could reply.

"Rodents of Unusual Size, huh?" he asked, quoting the script. "Must have been in Toledo in July."

Jadz smiled. "It's one of my favorite movies. I'm glad you liked it."

They strolled down Monroe Street towards the parking lot along the Maumee River. Theo grabbed her hand, interlacing their fingers.

"Hey, Packo's at the Park is open." Lively jazz music blared through the front doors of the restaurant bar when a group exited. "They did such a great job renovating this place. I love the statue of the ballplayers."

Theo caught the door before it closed. "Let's check it out." They found two empty stools at the end of the shiny wood bar. He ordered a beer, then turned to Jadz.

"I'll have the same," Jadz told the server. They tapped their glasses in toast before drinking and then relaxed into the contagious energy of spirited patrons packing the tiny dance floor. "Good crowd." She had to raise her voice to be heard over the band. "Do you dance?" Her heart sank when she saw Theo grope for his cell phone.

"Be right back." He moved outside to take the call.

The light-hearted mood of the evening evaporated. Jadz refused a refill from an attentive server. She pushed the empty mug away and waited.

Theo returned. "We need to go. I'll explain on the way." He drained his glass before leading Jadz outside. "That was my brother."

"I didn't know you had a brother." She stopped at the curb, waiting for more.

"Three, actually, and a sister. Steve's the youngest."

"I can get a cab if you need to get to your family."

He steered her towards the pickup. "When I told you about Betty and Proust, I didn't tell you the friend Paul mentioned was my brother."

Jadz tensed. "What did Betty do now?"

Theo followed Summit Street north, beating the lights at Monroe and at Jefferson. "She's at Bretz dance club, asking questions about Proust, or McDaniel, as she still calls him."

"Damn it." Jadz stared out at the darkened buildings, trying to quell her anger. "Do we know where he is?"

He turned left onto Adams before answering. "Home, as far as we know. The patrol says he hasn't left all evening."

"That's a relief."

Intermittent headlights flashed through the cab of the truck, breaking the darkness enough to make Theo's tense features visible.

"Thing is, she's making people nervous. Steve's afraid someone will call Proust to tell him what's going on," he said.

"They know him that well?"

"The gay community is pretty tight-knit in Toledo. They tend to look out for each other."

Jadz made the connection. "And Steve?"

"Yeah, he's gay."

"Okay."

"Does that bother you?"

"Of course not. I'm just surprised you never mentioned it." She studied his profile as he drove. "I guess there's a lot we have to learn about each other."

He shrugged. "It's Steve's life, not mine. I'm sure he doesn't talk about my sexual preferences with his friends either."

Theo circled the block around the dance club looking for an empty parking spot. He found one the next street over.

"There's Betty's car," Jadz pointed to a Jeep at the corner. "Wait, Steve—my mechanic?"

He grinned. "Oh, yeah, forgot to mention he's your mechanic, too."

At the flashing neon entrance to the bar, they showed their ID to the bouncer.

"No cover for Toledo's finest," the stocky man said, waving them in.

It took a few seconds for Jadz's eyes to adjust to the dimly lit interior. Pulsing lights on the dance floor and overhead added to the confusion. She spotted Betty near the DJ and nudged Theo. They pushed their way through the crowd.

"Thanks, Steve," Theo greeted his brother, who hovered nearby.

"Betty." Jadz tapped her on the shoulder.

Betty spun around, her face darkening. "What the hell are you doing here? Why can't you leave me alone?"

"We need to talk." Jadz tried to take her arm, but Betty jerked free.

"No, we don't. Go away. You've caused enough trouble." Her eyes lit up when she noticed Theo. "So there is something going on with you two. Poor Nathan."

"Nathan has nothing to do with this." Jadz caught herself. "This is serious. You're interfering with a murder investigation."

Theo stepped in. "Please, Betty, let's go outside for a minute."

"Only because you asked nicely," she said. "I don't want to talk to her."

On the patio, Jadz kept her distance while Theo tried to reason with Betty. "Proust is dangerous," he said. "We ... I'm afraid he'll feel threatened by your questions. You might be next on his list."

"Josh isn't dangerous. He's nice. Besides, I'm not forty," Betty said. She dug out a cigarette and when he didn't offer to light it, a matchbook. She cupped the flame and inhaled deeply, blowing smoke over her shoulder towards Jadz.

"You know he's gay," Theo said.

She stopped mid-puff. "That Proust guy is, not Josh."

Theo forced her to meet his gaze. "You know they're the same man. He's using you to get information on the case, to see how close we are to nailing him."

"You're making that up. She's making that up!" Betty threw her cigarette butt across the cement where it landed at Jadz's feet. "She always tries to scare off my men. Or steal them."

"He tried to kill your sister."

Betty's hands shook as she shredded the matchbook cover. "What's that supposed to mean?"

"We're pretty sure Proust caused her accident. We just can't find the car."

"He said his car was stolen. Josh did, I mean." She was crying now. "Why do these things always happen to me?"

Jadz edged in to put her arm around Betty's heaving shoulders. "I'm sorry, Sis."

Theo went back into the bar and returned with his brother in tow. "Steve can drive you home, if that's okay."

Betty mopped her face with a tissue before latching onto Steve's arm. "You're cute. I suppose you're gay, too?" At his nod, she gave a short, humorless laugh. "All the good ones are gay or taken. I give up." Her words trailed off into the night as they moved down the street.

When Betty's Jeep passed them, Theo said, "Let's go. I told Steve we'd bring him back."

The ride to the east side was quiet. When Steve climbed into the cab of the pickup in front of Mavis' house, Jadz looked from Theo to his brother. "I don't see the resemblance."

"We're half-brothers. Mom remarried a few years after my dad died, when I was four. Steve takes after his father."

"Explains the different last names," Jadz said.

Steve laughed. "I never realized you didn't make the connection. He's the one who gave you my number."

"I know, but I thought he was sharing his mechanic, not his brother."

"I didn't want you to feel obligated to use him if his work sucked," Theo said.

"Thanks for the vote of confidence." Steve's arm reached far enough along the top of the seat behind Jadz to thump the back of Theo's head.

Jadz shifted to give Steve more room on the bench seat. "I hope Betty wasn't too much trouble."

"She's a nice lady, just down on herself," he said. "Glad I was there to run interference."

They dropped Steve at his car near the dance club. It was nearly midnight when Theo pulled up to Jadz's apartment. She put a hand over his to keep him from turning off the engine. "It's been a long day. Thanks for everything." Jadz planted a quick kiss on his cheek before scooting out of the truck. "Good night."

Chapter 16

Across town, Proust sat in the moon-lit shadows of the sun porch tossing his cell phone from one hand to the other. Things were getting out of control. The detectives were smarter than he'd anticipated, and persistent. Now this. He considered and discarded several options, his anxiety rising.

Logan walked onto the sun porch. "Who called so late?" he asked, handing Proust a glass of deep red merlot.

He pocketed his phone and gulped half the wine before responding. "Tyrone."

"What did he want?" Logan sat down on the glider, feet propped on the ottoman. "Not more reaction to the interview, I hope. I'm still not sure that was such a good idea."

"Someone was asking about me at Bretz." Proust peered outside, trying to see down the drive. "Is that patrol car still out front?"

"It's probably going to stay there until they find someone else to annoy." Logan scowled. "The neighbors aren't very happy with us right now."

"Whatever." He finished his wine. "I need to go out."

"Why? What did Tyrone say?" Logan followed Proust through the kitchen into the bedroom.

Proust shed his shorts and polo shirt. He pulled khakis and a button-down Oxford out of his walk-in closet, dressing quickly without answering.

"Marc, what did Tyrone say?" Logan repeated. "What's going on?"

He slipped on a pair of loafers, checked his hair in the mirror over the dresser, and brushed past Logan on his way out the door.

"Can I use your car?" Proust asked.

"Not unless you tell me what's wrong."

"Nothing. Trust me on this, okay? Let me have the keys." Proust stared down Logan's frown until he relented and dropped a key ring into Proust's outstretched hand.

"I'll be back as soon as I can. Don't wait up."

In the garage, Proust transferred a small duffle bag from the trunk of his Lexus to the front seat of Logan's midnight blue Grand Prix. As he backed the out of the drive, he activated his Bluetooth connection.

"Call Betty."

Chapter 17

Jadz was home just long enough to finish a last cup of coffee and change for bed before her cell phone rang.

Not again.

"Mom? You're up late. She what? Mom, slow down. I can't understand you. Who called? When did she leave? Where? Okay, I'll find her. No, stay home in case she comes back. Mom, I mean it. Stay put. I'll call you as soon I can."

Jadz called Rena, phone tucked under her chin while she changed back into street clothes. "I need your perspective on this," she said after relaying Mavis' frantic summons. "Will Forester go for an APB on both vehicles?"

"Have Dispatch check with the surveillance car to see when Mr. Proust left the house. I will call Lieutenant Forester on my way to the station," Rena said. "Meet me there and we will decide what to do next."

Jadz pushed the rental car to its limit in her race to the police department, coasting through red lights and passing anyone in her path. When a cruiser made a U-turn at Cherry and Bancroft to follow her, she called Dispatch to ward them off. Another quick phone call when she had to stop for traffic at the Greenbelt Parkway intersection. "Aunt Trudy? Sorry to call so late. Can you go sit with Mom? Betty … Mom needs company. She can explain. Thanks." Jadz slipped into a parking spot across from the station and took the stairs two at a time.

Rena and Forester came into the bureau as Jadz pulled her shirt back on over her Kevlar vest.

"What the hell do you think you're doing?" Forester asked.

"I don't know yet," she said, not looking at him.

"I should pull you off this case right now," he said.

"Lieutenant," Rena stepped between him and Jadz. "You said—"

"I know what I said. And I'd feel the same way if it were my sister." Forester kept an eye on Jadz as he asked Rena, "You really think you can keep her in line?"

"She is a professional," Rena said. "And my partner. We will see this through together."

Forester relented. "Put out a general APB for both of them for now. We don't know what Proust is up to. Could be he just wants to see what we know."

"He's not in the Lexus," Jadz said. "Patrol said Logan's Grand Prix left thirty-five minutes ago. They thought it was him, not Proust, so they didn't call it in." She tightened her shoulder holster, adding another clip to her belt. A navy blazer hid her gear.

"All right, give Dispatch what you know and hit the streets." Forester started for his office. "I'll let the captain know." He stopped at the door. "And Jadz, keep your head in the game."

While Jadz relayed the APB, Rena repeated the same uniform switch as Jadz, adding her bullet-proof vest and extra ammo. They checked out an unmarked cruiser from the fleet garage and started their search. Rena drove while Jadz scrutinized every vehicle they passed.

"Start with Bretz," Jadz said. "And then the Docks, where they had dinner."

Rena drove up Jackson Street slowly enough for Jadz to study the cars they passed but fast enough to temper her impatience. As they made the turn onto Adams Street, a gaggle of bar-hoppers crossing over to Manos Greek Restaurant scattered. Rena slowed to let them trip over the curb onto Eighteenth Street.

"Damn fools," Jadz muttered.

Rena sped up to pass a taxi dislodging another band of rowdies. "At least this group is not driving."

"I wasn't talking about them."

"Then who would be the fool, besides Betty?" Rena asked.

"Any of the women who fell for Proust's line." Jadz squirmed in her seat, anxiety growing. "Somehow he talked his way into their homes, drugged them, and ..." She swallowed hard. "Mom said Betty believed everything he told her, that she was going to see him so he could show her proof instead of my lies."

"You blame the victims?" Rena asked.

"Not really." Jadz floundered. "I blame Proust for preying on their vulnerability."

"You called them fools." Rena's voice was clipped, angry.

"Bad choice of words. I'm afraid Betty is going to be next, because of me." They passed into a stretch of dark street broken by an occasional lighted, and gated, storefront. Jadz's face was lost in the shadows. "Maybe I'm the fool for thinking I can protect her."

The desperation in Jadz's voice seemed to temper Rena's annoyance. She laid a hand on Jadz's knee. "We will find her."

Rena circled the streets surrounding Bretz as they searched for Betty's Jeep or Logan's Grand Prix. When they reached a three-block circumference without finding either one, Jadz called a halt. "Head for the Docks," she said.

Rena turned east on Woodruff to pick up southbound Cherry Street across the Maumee River. She veered onto the access road to the Docks, which housed a string of upscale restaurants situated to take advantage of the view of the Toledo skyline over the sluggish water. A parking lot stretching the length of the development was nearly empty. Rena cruised each row of remaining cars.

"There." Jadz pointed to a Grand Prix parked under a street light near the sand volleyball courts at the edge of the strip. "That's Logan's. Call it in. I'm going inside." She scrabbled for the handle, almost out the door before Rena stopped her.

Rena cut off Jadz's protest. "You call it in. I will check the car, and the closest bar. Betty will offer less resistance if she sees me." Left unspoken was the possibility of what Rena would find in the car.

Jadz let her go.

Rena checked the Grand Prix. It was empty, and locked. She shook her head at Jadz and started toward the first restaurant. As soon as Rena entered Elaine's Martini Bar, Jadz bolted out of the car. Back-up was on the way, but she was done waiting. She prowled the exterior of Logan's car, peering through the tinted windows. Jadz considered jimmying the locks, but thought better of it. For now. She shined her Maglite flashlight at the pavement, checking for footprints. The dry concrete was unmarked. A shadowy park to the west surrounded the restaurant parking area. No one was in sight. The night air was so still Jadz heard the muddy river lapping the shoreline twenty yards away. She stepped over the curb onto the sandy walkway of the volleyball courts, heading for park benches near the river.

"Jadz!" Rena called.

They met back at the Grand Prix as two marked units pulled into the lot next to their vehicle. "Betty is not inside," Rena said. She waited until the patrolmen joined them to continue. "The busboy at Elaine's said a man matching Mr. Proust's description—the red-haired one—came in about an hour ago, alone. He downed several shots in a hurry and got belligerent when they cut him off. They called a taxi for him."

"Damn." Jadz considered their options. "Any idea where he went?"

"No one paid any attention," Rena said.

"Open the Grand Prix." Jadz dug through the trunk of the unmarked unit for a slim jim lock pick.

"We do not have a warrant," Rena said, blocking her path to the vehicle.

Jadz stood her ground. "We have a missing person under suspicious circumstances, and a serial killer on the loose. I'm willing to take a chance on getting any evidence thrown out. Are you willing to chance another death?"

Their eyes locked. "Please," Jadz said.

Rena stepped aside.

With practiced ease, Jadz popped the lock on the driver's door. The car was empty. She found a trunk release button on the dash. As the lid lifted, Rena shined her flashlight over the interior. Nothing. Jadz sagged against the car in disappointment. And relief.

"Now what?" Rena asked.

Jadz pulled a city map out of her briefcase and laid out a search grid. Paul arrived as they finished dividing up the east side. Rena brought him up to date while Jadz gave the patrolmen final instructions.

"I want to check down by the Boyer before we hit the streets," Jadz said. Paul and the patrolmen left to resume the search. Jadz and Rena, both armed with Maglites, walked down to the riverfront.

The 1911 Willis B. Boyer Museum Ship loomed over the docks at International Park. Its moorings glistened darkly in the dim light cast across the river from downtown Toledo. A few scattered street lights were too distant to dispel the shadows along the ship's concourse. The park was deserted. Jadz and Rena searched the bank fore and aft of the ship. Nothing.

Another cruiser was parked next to Rena's car when they got back.

"Nathan, what are you doing here?" Jadz asked.

"I heard the APB and came to help," he said. "My shift just ended, but I'm available. Where do you want me?"

She smiled her thanks as Rena sketched out another grid on the map for him. They parted ways at the end of the lot. Nathan cruised along the stretch of river north of Cherry Street following the glare of his searchlight.

Back in the car, Jadz brooded in silence.

"He may not have seen Betty tonight," Rena said.

"Then where is she? Betty told Mom she was going to meet 'Josh.'" Jadz lowered the passenger window and inhaled deeply, hoping the fresh air would chill her anxiety. "To prove me wrong." She slammed her fist into the door panel.

They followed the Boyer-Boers access that paralleled the river until it intersected with Miami Street to circle back into the neighborhoods. Rena aimed the cruiser's spotlight along the banks while Jadz fixed on the beam as it bounced off the dark water. A shadowy lump rocked gently in the water, bumping along the boulders lining the bank. Jadz caught her breath and focused the light. A tree limb enmeshed in litter. She sank back into the seat, her heart pounding.

The radio crackled to life, shaking Jadz out of her mental anguish. "David-12, meet Paul-42 at East Side Auto, 214 First Street."

"David-12, en route."

Rena flipped on the dash bubble light. She sped north on Miami, slowing only for the slight jog where it became First Street. Flashing cruiser lights reflected off the front of the salvage yard office. Paul pulled in behind them as Jadz bailed out of the car.

"Over here."

Jadz followed the patrolman's voice to the northeast end of the building. Betty's Jeep was parked at the gate to the storage lot.

"Nobody around," he said. "Car's empty."

They spread out to canvas the area. The chirp of summer cicadas droned through the still night. Jadz strained to listen over the interstate traffic a few blocks away. "Do you hear a car running?" she called to the scattered team.

Paul found an opening in the fence near the back corner of the lot and shoved through. Jadz and Rena followed. The front two rows were reserved for towed vehicles waiting to be claimed. In back sat the rusting hulks left from collisions, cars no one would drive away. The uniformed officers stood guard at the gate while Jadz, Rena and Paul walked the rows of wrecks, keeping each other in sight as they scoured the twisted remains. They moved cautiously through the shadows, focusing on the now-distinct sound of an engine at the far end of the back row.

Jadz made it to the car first. It was Proust's Mercedes. The rear quarter panel was crumpled. Her light picked out red paint embedded in the deep scratches. A dryer vent hose stretched from the tailpipe to the vent window on the driver's side. She bent down to shine her Maglite into the interior and caught her breath. Betty was slumped over on the front seat.

Jadz yanked out the hose. "Call a squad, now!" When she found the door locked, she battered the window in with the stub end of the Maglite, spraying tempered glass over Betty's still body.

Rena helped Jadz pull Betty out of the car. She wasn't breathing. Even in the dim light, her ashen face clashed with her red hair. Paul ran back to guide the medics in while Jadz and Rena started CPR.

"Don't leave me, Sis," Jadz said between breaths. "Mom'll kick my butt."

Chapter 18

Proust waited until the taxi turned off Elmer Drive back onto Reynolds Road to open the side door of the garage. He disengaged the security alarm before it could chime inside the house. A lamp over the workbench offered enough light for him to empty his duffel bag. Leather gloves back on the shelf. Duct tape in the supply cupboard. He rinsed out the wine bottle in the utility sink before dropping it into the recycle bin. The clatter of glass on glass stilled his movements and he held his breath, listening for sound from the residence. The house was still. Proust exhaled in a snort of amusement at his belated nerves.

As he popped the trunk on the Lexus to replace the duffel bag, the overhead fluorescent flickered on, flooding the two-car garage with light.

"What are you doing?" Logan stood in the doorway leading to the kitchen.

Proust stashed his bag in the corner of the trunk and closed the lid. "I told you not to wait up."

Logan stepped aside to let him pass into the house. "Where's my car?"

"I went to the gym, needed to work out some of this stress. It's been a tough few days, you know," Proust said. He scrubbed his hands at the kitchen sink.

"You left my car at the gym?"

"I went to Elaine's for a drink after. The bartender was particularly parental tonight and insisted on calling me a cab. We'll get your car tomorrow." He reached for the china tea pot on the chopping block island. "Any left?"

Logan stared at him for a long moment. "Why don't you go change? I'll bring your tea."

Proust went to the bedroom. Logan hung his head, bracing himself on the counter.

They met back on the sun porch a few minutes later. Logan handed Proust a full cup of tea from the tray on the side table. He poured a cup for himself and sat down opposite.

Proust took a sip and grimaced at the taste.

"You said you needed a drink," Logan said. "Too much Jameson?"

"No, it's fine." He shuddered slightly. "I wasn't expecting it, I guess."

For several minutes, the only sound on the porch was the echo of crickets and cicadas. Fireflies glittered in the yard, flitting from bush to tree to shrub. A colony of bats swooped through the still air, feasting on the mosquitoes that buzzed overhead.

"Why did you agree to live in Toledo?" Logan's low words broke the silence.

Proust took another sip of tea. "Like I told you five years ago, and repeat every time you get nervous, it's less distracting for my work." His smile didn't reach his eyes.

Logan set his cup back on the tray. "They don't know about your mother, do they?"

"Who?"

"The police."

"No, they don't," Proust said, his jaw tight.

"Are you going to tell them?"

"What are you insinuating?" Proust's eyes narrowed.

"I don't know." Logan studied him. "You've been lying to me for months, going out alone late at night, missing our theater dates. I thought there was someone else."

"There is no one else." Proust's voice shifted from angry to coaxing. "If this is about the commitment ceremony, we can go ahead with it. On our anniversary next month, if you like. How would that be?"

"It's not about that." Logan moved slowly around the porch straightening a pillow, adjusting the blinds. "Why haven't you told the police your mother committed suicide on her birthday?"

Proust's laugh was short, hard. "Wouldn't they have a field day with that? They'd turn my personal tragedy into evidence against me for a crime I didn't commit."

"Didn't you? I found the sleeping pills."

"What?" Proust nearly snapped the handle off the fragile china. Tea leaf sediment quivered in the bottom as he sat the cup down next to the coaster. "Why were you going through my desk? I thought we trusted each other."

"I thought we did, too. Why did you have two prescriptions, one under McDaniel?"

"It's not what you think." Proust's breathing grew shallow. "I filled one in New York when I was on that publicity tour last year. You know it almost killed me. I couldn't take a chance on some reporter finding out. When Dr. Talbert wrote one for me here in January, I tossed it in the drawer and forgot about it."

"You're out of refills."

"You *checked*?" Proust sprang to his feet. He caught himself as the room spun. "Why am I so dizzy?"

"I thought you might have trouble sleeping tonight after our chat."

"You put something in my drink?" Proust staggered towards him, stumbling over the ottoman.

"Just a little." Logan eased Proust onto the wicker sofa. "I had a call tonight, too. You're not the only one with informants. The detectives are coming in the morning with a search warrant, I believe. And I need time to think."

Chapter 19

Storm clouds blanketed the early morning sun as police cruisers pulled into Elmer Drive. Slats of light shone onto the damp grass outside the screen porch at the back of the house.

"Early risers, for a Sunday," Paul said. He and Rena headed for the front door while Nathan and his partner covered the back.

Rena nodded at Paul, hand resting on her sidearm. He reached for the doorbell.

The door flew open before he could ring. "Good morning, Detective Wiley, Detective Castillo." Logan was pale but composed. Shadowy stubble covered his chin. His eyes were haggard. "Won't you come in?"

He led them through the house. When they stepped onto the porch, Rena froze. Proust lay face down on the sofa.

"Don't worry, he's only sleeping. I'm afraid he had too much last night." Logan opened the blinds, revealing the uniformed officers near the back door. He pushed open the sliding glass panel and asked, "Care to join us?"

At Rena's nod, the officers stepped inside, standing guard on either side of the door.

She checked Proust for a pulse. "He seems to be fine."

"Why don't we sit down?" Logan motioned to the various chairs. "Can I offer anyone coffee?"

"What happened?" Rena asked, perching on the edge of the nearest seat. Paul sat across from Logan.

"It's been a long night, facing down my personal demon," Logan said. He stared at Proust, his face sad. "Marc and I met almost six years ago, in New York. I was there on a theatre tour sponsored by the Valentine. He gave a reading of his latest book at a little coffee shop off Broadway. I was captivated." Logan shifted his gaze to the park behind the house, seeing not the trees, but the past. "I don't suppose you think of gay men as romantics, but he swept me off my feet. Witty, attentive, so cosmopolitan. I'd never been outside Ohio, so New York took my breath away." He gave a hollow laugh and dropped his eyes. "So did Marc."

Silence stretched.

"Mr. Logan." Rena broke in.

He roused himself and squared his shoulders. His voice grew hard. "Last night I realized I'd fallen in love with a monster." Logan gestured towards a pair of medicine bottles on the side table. "You'll find my prints on those too, unfortunately. They were in his desk. I'd imagine the drug matches what was used on your victims."

Rena and Paul exchanged startled looks. She collected the bottles using an evidence bag from her briefcase as both protection and container, reading the labels before dropping them inside. "Lorazepam," she said. "It is the same."

Logan's shoulders sagged. "I was hoping, even now." He straightened resolutely. "Marc's been lying to me. He'd go out at night when I was teaching or in class and come home late. He started missing our theatre dates, always had some excuse about work, but he was never home when I got here. I thought he was seeing someone else."

"But he was not," Rena said.

"No."

Proust's gentle snore was the only sound in the room.

Logan cleared his throat and continued, his words low and raspy. "I started noting when he stood me up, planned to confront him when I had a better idea what was happening." He reached into his pocket. Paul stiffened. "Relax." Logan handed Rena a piece of folded stationery. "I recognized the dates when you asked me about the nights of the murders."

Rena studied the list. Of the two dozen or so dates from the past four months, five were circled in red. She bagged the paper as well.

"I heard him talking to one of the victims at the registrar, Summers I think it was. It didn't hit me until I saw her picture from the police press conference after I was brought in for questioning. I don't watch the news." He grimaced. "Too much violence."

"Why do you think he killed them?" Rena asked.

A long moment elapsed before Logan answered. "His mother committed suicide on her fortieth birthday. I guess he never forgave her."

"That's where you're wrong," Proust said.

Rena jumped to her feet, hand on her sidearm, as Proust sat up. Paul and the uniformed officers drew their weapons.

"I thought you'd sleep at least another hour," Logan said.

Proust glared at the detectives. "Put those things down. I'm not armed."

Paul holstered his gun and moved in. "Stand up and raise your arms."

Proust complied, but directed his anger toward Logan. "I trusted you," he said while Paul checked him and the sofa for weapons.

"And I trusted you," Logan shot back. "Deal with it."

"What are we wrong about, Mr. Proust?" Rena sat down slowly, eyes locked on Proust as he resumed his seat. Paul remained standing. Nathan and his partner took a step back towards the door.

"I didn't have to forgive my mother. She died because of that bastard Trevor." Proust rubbed his face and tried to straighten his hair. "God, I'm a mess."

"Your father left New York years before she died," Rena said.

Proust stopped fussing and dropped back against the cushions. "You know about him? Detective Castillo, I am surprised. You're better at this than I thought." He looked around the room. "No coffee for our guests, Greg? The perfect little host is slipping."

"Stop it." Logan's face was flushed. "Be angry with me if you like, but don't inflict your petty tirades on them."

"And where is Detective Jadzinski? I can't believe she'd miss out on another chance to humiliate us," Proust said.

"Where were you last night?" Rena asked.

"I'm pretty sure Mr. Evans would tell me not to answer any more of your questions." Proust scowled at Logan. "I could really use that coffee."

"He was gone nearly three hours," Logan told Rena. "Was there another murder?"

"Shut up, Greg." Proust made a move towards him, but Paul stepped in between.

"Another staged suicide," Paul said. "We found your car."

"Marc said he left it at Elaine's."

"Not yours," Rena corrected Logan. "His."

"But the Lexus is in the garage," Logan said.

"Very good, officers. I reported the Mercedes stolen a week ago. Better late than never, I suppose." The tension on Proust's face belied the sarcasm in his voice.

"The Mercedes? I don't understand," Logan said.

"I'll bet he does," Paul said, watching Proust.

"As much as I hate to bother my attorney on a Sunday, I think it's time I called him." Proust tried to stand again but fell back, still dizzy from the drugs.

"We have a search warrant," Rena said. "Mr. Evans can wait until we are finished."

"What are you looking for?" Logan asked. "You have the drugs, and the dates."

"Shut up, Greg."

"Mr. Logan, we will talk in the kitchen. Mr. Proust will stay here with the officers." Rena motioned to the patrolmen who took Paul's place next to Proust.

"What are you looking for?" Logan asked again when they were in the kitchen.

Paul handed him a copy of the search warrant. "Any material items that may have been used in the commission of the murders in question, including drugs, clothing, gloves, disguises, duct tape, paperwork relating to the dates, people and places in question," he read off the list.

"Duct tape and gloves?" Logan frowned. "Common stuff. We have both out here." He led them to the garage and stood next to the Lexus. "What kind of clothing? He keeps a gym bag in his trunk. I don't know what's in it."

"Do you have the keys?" Rena asked.

Logan opened the car door and pushed the trunk release. "Help yourself. If Marc's really involved in this, I'm through cleaning up his messes. Duct tape's in that cabinet."

Paul placed the roll of tape into an evidence bag while Rena examined the duffle. Inside she found gym shorts, a sweaty t-shirt, athletic shoes and a towel. A blue nylon jacket lined the bottom of the bag.

"I've never seen that before," Logan said. "It's certainly not his style."

Rena unzipped a side pocket and pulled out a red wig wrapped around a pair of surgical gloves.

"I think I need to sit down." Logan disappeared into the kitchen.

Paul photographed the items where they were found while Rena tagged and bagged them.

"I'd say we got what we came for." Paul's satisfied comment was interrupted by an angry shout from the porch.

They ran back through the kitchen, tossing the evidence bags onto the counter and shoving Logan aside as a shot echoed through the house. Rena and Paul dropped to their knees on either side of the porch entry, guns drawn.

"Put those down," Proust shouted at them, his voice hoarse. "I'm not very good with these things. I wouldn't want anybody else to get hurt."

Rena edged around the corner to get a better view. Proust stood near the back of the room. He held Nathan in a headlock with one arm, the other pressing the officer's Sig Sauer service weapon against Nathan's neck. The second patrolman lay motionless on the floor near the ottoman. Blood seeped from widening stain over his left shoulder.

"David-12, officer down, hostage situation," Rena said into her portable radio. "10-33, radio silence."

Paul shifted from the door to signal Rena his intent to leave through the garage and come up behind the porch. Rena shook her head and motioned palm down, behind her hip out of Proust's line of sight. *Wait for back-up.* She met Paul's eyes and nodded in Proust's direction. Another hand signal. *Talk to him.*

"You're not getting out of here," Paul called to Proust. He peered around the frame.

"I said put down your guns." Growing anxiety echoed in Proust's voice. Rena and Paul laid their weapons on the floor, eyes never leaving his agitated face.

"Marc, what are you doing?" Logan pushed past Rena and onto the porch before she could stop him.

"Stop right there," Proust said. "I don't want to hurt you."

"You've already hurt me." He took another step.

"Then stop or I'll hurt him." Proust tightened his grip on Nathan's neck.

Logan obeyed. "Now what?"

"Tell them, Greg. Tell them I never hurt those women."

"Did you?"

"I made them feel special. I gave them love and attention on their birthday. How could that hurt them? I rescued them!" In his agitation, Proust clamped down on Nathan further and his eyes bulged. "They went to sleep feeling loved for a change, and never had to wake up alone again." Proust's voice cracked.

"What are you going to do now?" Paul and Rena had to strain to hear Logan's question.

"This nice officer and I are going to take a ride." Proust took a step backwards toward the outside door.

"And then what?" Logan asked. "Leave me to fix things, as usual?"

"You'll never get out of the garage," Paul broke in. Sirens sounded outside, growing closer.

"Shut up!" Panic showed in Proust's face. "We'll take the patrol car." He edged towards the door.

"My partner has the keys." Nathan forced the words past the stranglehold on his throat.

A large key ring splayed across the floor from a clip on the unconscious officer's belt. Proust looked from Logan to the keys and back again. The sirens faded away in front of the residence. "Greg, hand me the keys."

When Logan didn't respond, Proust said, "Listen to me. If you don't give me the keys, they'll lock me up. Do you know what happens to people like us in prison? Is that what you want?"

Logan backed towards Rena and Paul. "No."

Proust's eyes held Logan's gaze, pleading. "I thought you loved me!"

The silent emotional struggle distracted Proust from Jadz's stealthy approach to the back door. Rena and Paul waited as she eased into the room. When she was in place, Rena met Nathan's eyes and nodded.

Nathan sagged against Proust to throw him off balance and then dropped to his knees, wrenching free. Jadz hit Proust with 1,500 volts from her Taser. He crumpled to the floor, twitching.

"I told you to stay away from my sister," she said.

Rena and Paul restrained Logan's instinctive rush to Proust's side while Jadz recovered the service weapon from where it had fallen. She called off the special response team as Paul led the medics through to the porch. They stabilized the wounded patrolman before transporting both officers to the hospital while a second squad took custody of the dazed Proust, handcuffing him and strapping him down. Jadz halted the gurney before he was wheeled out.

"Georges Marcel Proust, you're under arrest for the murders of five women, and the attempted murder of Betty Simmons. You apparently don't know much about cars or it would be six counts. I'm guessing you'll want your attorney now." She turned her back as they took him away.

"What was that about the car?" Rena asked as she followed Jadz into the kitchen.

"It seems the catalytic converter keeps the exhaust from building up or something, even with a hose connection like Proust used, so Betty survived. She had a lot of drugs in her, though." Jadz swallowed. "She's recovering."

Rena directed the forensics team while Paul turned over the evidence bags discarded on the counter.

"Mr. Logan, we'll need a statement from you," Jadz said. "It can wait until tomorrow. Will you call his attorney?"

Logan nodded, choking back tears. "Take care of him, will you? He's ... broken."

After the hospital examined and released Proust, Jadz booked him into the Lucas County Jail. She met Rena and Paul in the detective bureau where Forester joined them, coffee pot in hand.

"Don't get used to this, but you've earned it today," he said, topping off each cup. "How's Nathan? And Betty?"

"Nathan's pretty shook up. He blames himself for letting Proust get his sidearm," Jadz said. An image of Nathan's haunted face flashed through her mind. *I'll need to check on him later.* She turned back to Forester. "Betty's conscious finally, but it'll take a few days to be sure there's no permanent damage. She's mad as hell, which is a good sign. Mom's with her."

"The phony suicide note Proust left with Betty made it sound like she stole his car to run you off the road." Paul looked to Jadz for answers. "Then killed herself because she felt guilty about it? I know she doesn't like you much, but damn."

Jadz flushed. "Ancient history. It doesn't matter."

"Mr. Proust is with his attorney now," Rena said. "We can get a statement this afternoon."

"Do we know why he did it?" Jadz asked. "Targeting the women he did?"

"I called Manhattan on our way back to let them know about the arrest," Paul said. "They found the report on Proust's mother. Like Logan said, she committed suicide on her fortieth birthday, pills and gas."

"Wow." Jadz let his words sink in. "Are they sure it was suicide?"

"It is too late to check now, but her death may have just pushed him over the edge," Rena said. "Thompson said they were very close."

"What about Logan?" Paul looked uncomfortable. "He was really broken up when we left."

"They were together almost seven years," Jadz said. "Imagine losing your wife like that."

Paul drained his paper cup, tossing the empty into the trash as he stood up. "I don't have a wife anymore. I'm not sure she cried that much when she left me, though." He turned away. "I'll be back this afternoon for the interview."

Forester followed him out.

"Stuck my foot in my mouth on that one, didn't I?" Jadz said. "What's next?"

"Paperwork." Rena tossed a stack of case files across the desk. "We have reports to fill out, inventories to process, affidavits to complete."

"I get the picture. Sheesh! When did you become my mother?"

"I am not your mother," Rena said with a smile. "I am your partner."

Chapter 20

After six weeks of follow-up interviews, reports, and preliminary hearings, Proust's commitment hearing was brief. His attorney did most of the talking, arguing his motion for psychiatric evaluation prior to entering a final plea. Proust spoke only when addressed directly by the judge. From her seat next to Rena in the back row of the courtroom, Jadz could barely hear his vague, disjointed answers.

The court psychiatrist offered a chilling portrait of a devoted son permanently scarred by his mother's suicide at age forty, twenty years earlier. As Proust neared the same milestone, his tortured psyche sought relief in a perverse justification of rescuing his victims from the loneliness, a fate he saw as worse than death. The thin line between right and wrong blurred. Whether or not the initial evaluation would be enough to show Proust was certifiably insane at the time of the murders would be up to the doctors.

The Lucas County prosecutor handled the high-profile case herself, but she offered no objection to the two-month evaluation period. With five deaths to his credit, and cold case officers from Toledo and New York City scouring old files, Proust would never walk free again. After a finding of cause to grant the motion, he was led away in shackles. Logan stood in the front row behind the defense table alone, head bowed.

In the hall outside the courtroom, Jadz checked her messages while Rena had a quiet word with Proust's attorney.

"I suppose I should thank you for stopping him," Logan said, walking up next to Jadz. His eyes were fixed on a spot just over her shoulder. In the time since Proust's arrest, grey flecks appeared at Logan's temples. His face was damp and splotchy.

Jadz pocketed her phone. "Just doing my job." She groped for words to ease the tension. "I hope Proust appreciates your being here. It's generous of you."

"Marc won't talk to me. His attorney asked me to stay around until this was decided."

"Now it's over, you can move on."

He laughed a sad, hollow sound. "Move on to what? The news has been relentless. You know Dolly and I were fired from the BMV? Administrative reasons, they said. I can live with it, but she's got two kids to support. The neighbors avoid me. Even the Garden won't return my calls."

Rena joined them as Jadz said, "Murder tends to create more victims than people realize. It's not just the dead. I'm sorry you were caught in the middle."

An awkward silence stretched, but Logan didn't move away. Jadz waited, giving him a chance to have his say. When he didn't speak, Rena stepped in.

"The public will find another news item to occupy them soon," she said. "What are your plans, if I may ask?"

"Still investigating?" His voice was sharp. "Never mind, I know. Just doing your job. My mother spends winters with a cousin outside Pensacola. She's always asking me to go with her. I doubt this is headlines in Florida, and the change of scenery might be a good thing." He took a deep breath. "As for victims,

I'll always wonder if I could have stopped him. Maybe if I'd been more aware, something."

Rena laid a gentle hand on his arm. "We do the best we can at the time. Do not blame yourself in hindsight."

Logan gave her a wan smile, nodded to Jadz, and left the building, Proust's attorney running interference for him with the media who converged at the door.

Jadz and Rena took the rest of the afternoon and escaped from the detective bureau to enjoy the last burst of Indian summer. They bought carry-out from the deli and wandered down to Promenade Park along the Maumee River. A pair of adjacent benches in the shade offered room to spread out. Rena picked at her sandwich, tossing crumbs to the hovering seagulls.

"You're not eating," Jadz said. "You okay?"

Rena seemed engrossed in the birds' antics. It took a second query from Jadz to rouse her.

"Now that Mr. Proust has been referred for evaluation, we are done with his case for the next few months," she said.

"Yeah, so?" Jadz finished her burger and wiped her hands on a paper napkin. "I'm sure Forester has something else to keep us busy."

"I talked to him this morning. I am taking some vacation time, leaving day after tomorrow. Today is my last day in Homicide."

"You mean till after vacation."

"There is an opening in Internal Affairs," Rena said, watching the birds. "I have requested a transfer."

Jadz choked on her coffee. "What the hell, am I that bad as a partner?"

"Of course not. That is my only regret at the move."

"Then why?"

Rena lowered her eyes. "It was Adam or me. This is easier."

"Forester?" Jadz shifted to face her. "What'd he do?"

"No, nothing like that. I thought you guessed." She flushed. "When we talked about your relationship with Nathan, I realized I was putting up unnecessary barriers."

"Between you and Forester?" Jadz laughed. "Damn, that's … wow. I'm not sure what to say."

"He offered to take the transfer, but it would be a demotion. I will not allow that."

"So you're leaving me for him. Guess I can deal with it."

"Something like that." Rena smiled. "Thank you for understanding."

Jadz gathered the empty wrappers and tossed them into a nearby trashcan. They sat in companionable silence, watching the fishing boats scoot down the river. The Arawana Princess ferryboat chugged slowly across from the Docks returning downtown workers to the west side of the Maumee after lunch.

Jadz twisted around to prop her legs on the bench. She lounged against the wooden slats and squinted at Rena through the glare that found its way between the leaves. "So this vacation, where're you going? Somewhere with Forester?"

"I am taking my mother to Kyoto for a *Bon* ceremony."

"What's that?"

"A traditional Japanese festival to remember our ancestors. Mother and I attended every year when I was growing up. We have not gone since—" Rena stopped.

Jadz allowed Rena to collect herself before finishing the sentence for her. "Since the accident." She'd pieced together enough of Rena's history to learn about her father's death, even though Rena never provided details.

"Yes." Rena's voice was lost in the squawk of the gulls. "It has been seventeen years, which is a special festival time. The fact that it coincides with the twenty-third anniversary of my grandparents' deaths makes it even more auspicious in Mother's eyes." She chuckled softly. "She was so surprised when I told her we were going, she almost thanked me."

"Almost?"

"It does not matter. She is my mother."

"Things we do for family, huh?"

For a long minute, Rena didn't answer. She threw the last bit of bread to the birds and stared out over the river. A slight breeze rustled the trees and carried the faint odor of muddy fish up from the water. Rena closed her eyes and breathed deeply. "Each of us honors our parents in the way we feel is most appropriate," she said. "Even Mr. Proust. So I will go to Kyoto."

Rena's words stayed with Jadz for the rest of the day. The thought of honoring her parents nagged at her, and picturing Rena and Forester as a couple dredged up buried thoughts of Theo. During the ride home from work that evening, Jadz called her mother. "Hey, it's me. How's Betty feeling?" Traffic came to a standstill due to a fender-bender on the Trail and she was able to give Mavis her full attention. "I'm glad she's on her feet. She's going back to school? Sure, cosmetology suits her. Hey, can you two do me a favor? Would you go with me tomorrow to look at a house? Yeah, I'm thinking about getting out of the rental and I'd like your opinion. We can talk about it over dinner, if you've got enough for one more. I'll bring chocolate ice cream for dessert. It's Betty's favorite."

The accident cleared and as Jadz passed the squad car directing vehicles around the tow truck, she spotted Theo talking to the driver. At the next light, she pulled out her cell phone again and sent a quick text.

Call me. It's time.

About the Author

C. L. (Cyndi) Pauwels and her husband left the Toledo, Ohio, area in 2004 when the empty nest set in, and after bouncing around the southwest corner of the state for a bit, finally landed in quirky Yellow Springs, Ohio. They have two grown children, a young grandson, two dogs, and eight chickens. In her previous lives, Cyndi worked as a police and fire dispatcher, and as a deputy clerk for federal court in Toledo. Lots of great experiences for story fodder, and since her first published short story in 1989, Cyndi's short fiction has appeared in numerous print and online outlets. In addition to 2014's *Forty & Out* — the first in this series of crime novels, she has also published a non-fiction book, *Historic Warren County: An Illustrated History* (2008), and several anthologized personal essays. When she's not immersed in writing her next book, Cyndi is a college adjunct teaching freshman composition and creative writing, and she serves as Assistant Director for the Antioch Writers' Workshop.

CROSSROAD
PRESS

www.ingramcontent.com/pod-product-compliance
Lightning Source LLC
Chambersburg PA
CBHW030251200626
46816CB00002BA/595

* 9 7 8 1 6 3 7 8 9 0 0 2 8 *